The Billionaire's Dance

Billionaire Bachelors
Book Two

Melody Anne

Copyright © 2011 Melody Anne

ISBN: 10: 1468008862

ISBN-13: 978-1468008869

Family comes first in the continuation of

The Billionaire Bachelors Series

Join the Anderson Family

In Book Two

The Billionaire's Dance

DEDICATION

This Book is dedicated to my amazing mother, Lucille.
She's the one who gave me a love of romance books.
Without her, I wouldn't have started my very first book.
She has been a wonderful fan and has been as excited as
I have to enter the world of the Anderson Family.

The Anderson Family

Joseph Anderson – (M) – Katherine Simerly
/
Lucas   Alex   Mark

Lucas Anderson (m) Amy Harper
/
Jasmine Katherine (c) Isaiah Allen (c)

Alex Anderson (m) Jessica Sanders
/
Jacob (c)   Katie (c)

Mark Anderson (m) Emily Jackson
/
Trevor (a,c)   Tassia (c)

George Anderson (M) Amelia Grant(d)
(M) Esther Lion
/
Trenton   Max   Bree   Austin

Trenton Anderson (m) Jennifer Stellar
/
Molly (n,a) Weston (c)

Max Anderson (m) Cassie McKentire
/
Ariel (c)

Bree Anderson (m) Chad Redington
/
Mathew (c)

Austin Anderson (m) Kinsey Shelton
/
Isabelle (c)

(m) = Married   (d) = deceased   (c) = child   (n) = niece   (a) = adopted

Books by Melody Anne

BILLIONAIRE BACHELORS

*The Billionaire Wins the Game

*The Billionaire's Dance

*The Billionaire Falls

*The Billionaire's Marriage Proposal

*Blackmailing the Billionaire

*Runaway Heiress

*The Billionaire's Final Stand

The Lost Andersons – Billionaire Bachelors Continued

*Unexpected Treasure – Book One – **June 2013**

*Hidden Treasure – Book Two – **November 2013**

*Priceless Treasure – Book Three – **March 2014**

*Unrealized Treasure – Book Four – **June 2014**

*Wanted Treasure– Book Five – **August 2014**

BABY FOR THE BILLIONAIRE

+The Tycoon's Revenge

+The Tycoon's Vacation

+The Tycoon's Proposal

+The Tycoon's Secret

+The Lost Tycoon – **May 2014**

RISE OF THE DARK ANGEL

-Midnight Fire – Rise of the Dark Angel – Book One

-Midnight Moon – Rise of the Dark Angel – Book Two

-Midnight Storm – Rise of the Dark Angel – Book Three

-Midnight Rising – Rise of the Dark Angel – Book Four – **December 2013**

Surrender

=Surrender – Book One

=Submit – Book Two

=Seduced – Book Three – **September 2013**

=Scorched – Book Four – **Jan 2014**

ACKNOWLEDGMENTS

There are so many people who have helped me to make this dream come true of writing my first romance series.

First of all, I want to thank my family for their endless patience while I've been focused on the computer screen, lost in the wonderful world of the Andersons. Secondly, I want to thank Exclusive Publishing for their phenomenal job in catching all my mistakes and designing amazing, eye-catching covers, and of course, for putting up with my thousands of emails, begging for my document back just a bit faster.

Thanks, once again, to Nikki. for your many hours of trudging through my books. Your advice and help has been invaluable and I'm so lucky having you to keep such a great eye on my work, and making it better. Thank you, as well, to my friends and all those who have supported me and encouraged me to keep doing what I love.

A really huge thank you to all those amazing romance writers who have been such an inspiration to me my entire life. I'd never be here, doing what I love, if I hadn't picked up my first romance book at the age of twelve, sneaking it out of my mother's room. Nora Roberts was my first, but certainly not my last.

And, finally, thank you to all of my fans who are so supportive. Thank you for not only purchasing my books, but for your kind words. I love the emails and Facebook messages I receive from you. It's what encourages me to keep on going, through good and bad. You've helped me to be a stronger writer, and you've made it possible for all my dreams to come true. I thank you, and my family does as well.

Prologue

"That's Grandpa's sweet baby girl," Joseph whispered as he nuzzled the neck of his first and only granddaughter, Jasmine. She cooed at him while gripping his finger and tugging on his heart.

"Now that Grandpa got your daddy and mommy married, and they gave me you as an added bonus for Christmas last year, we have to start working on finding Uncle Alex a wife."

Jasmine smiled adoringly as he continued speaking.

"I love you to pieces, Princess, and I want you to have lots of cousins running around the house."

She looked up at him with her bright, intelligent blue eyes. She obviously understood every word.

"I sure didn't get any thanks from your parents for their marriage, but of course I'm not looking for praise. Having my boys find good women and giving me grandkids to spoil is thanks enough."

Jasmine giggled as if she agreed.

"Well…a *little* thank-you wouldn't be so bad," he muttered.

"I guess I'm veering off course, aren't I? I've found the perfect bride for your Uncle Alex, and I have a feeling we'll see a cousin for you in a year or so."

Joseph had known Jessica since she was a newborn. He knew that she and Alex would be a perfect match. Just get them together in the same room again and nature would take its course. Piece of cake.

Alex's playboy lifestyle had been disturbing enough when his son was younger. Where did he get it from? He'd never seen such an example set by his elders. And now he was thirty-two. It was past time that boy settled down and got married. He'd had plenty of time to court the ladies, sow his wild oats, or whatever "they" called it. Now it was time for him to bring his mother and father grandchildren. Joseph had a mansion to fill, after all.

Joseph loved his granddaughter so much, he felt as if his heart would burst whenever he cradled her in his arms. He wanted that feeling with many, *many* more grandchildren.

"Joseph, did I just hear you plotting with your granddaughter to meddle in our middle son's life?" Katherine asked from just outside the room, catching him off guard. He could hear the clear disapproval in her tone and knew he'd been busted.

"No, not at all, dear," Joseph said with as much innocence as he could muster. "Jasmine and I were simply discussing what a blessing she is in our lives."

Katherine shook her head as she reached down to pick up the baby. "Joseph, Jasmine's only three months old and isn't discussing anything with you. She's just happy to hear the sound of your voice, no matter what nonsense you're spouting." All sternness fell from her tone as she held the precious bundle close to her heart.

"Someday your interference in our children's lives will bring unhappiness on us all, Joseph," his beloved and loving wife said. "Things were certainly rough with Lucas and Amy."

"Want to turn back the clock, dear?" he responded.

Katherine was silent. She had to admit that whatever the troubles Joseph's machinations had caused, she certainly couldn't regret that Lucas and Amy got married — what a perfect pair! —and that they had brought such a delight as Jasmine into the world.

Joseph sighed at the sight of his beautiful wife holding their granddaughter. Life was certainly good.

"Lucas will be back in a few minutes, so help me get the baby changed," Katherine said as she walked from the room.

Joseph stood and looked at the picture on his wall. "Alex, my boy, you're in for a surprise," Joseph whispered. He walked out the door chuckling under his breath.

Chapter One

"Alex, good to see you at last," Joseph said, wrapping his arm around his son's shoulders and leading him into the den.

"Hi, Dad. Sorry I haven't made it home in a while. The contract in Spain took a lot longer than I thought. Of course, I'm not complaining, because those beaches were hot, and the women — even hotter."

"Now, son, there's more to life than gallivanting all over the world and picking up pretty ladies who don't have a lick of brains or an ounce of heart," Joseph admonished.

Alex gave a hearty laugh. He knew his father wanted him and his brothers in shackles — the old ball and chain. He was more than a little suspicious that Joseph had something to do with Lucas's marriage. Lucas wasn't complaining, though, and he shouldn't have been. His wife, Amy, was a true gem, and their daughter was about the cutest thing Alex had ever seen.

"Dad, you know I'm too young to tie the knot. I neither need *nor want* a woman in my life telling me what to do. I like having many different women to wine and dine. You don't want to break the hearts of all the single women in Seattle, do you?" Alex asked.

"Son…"

"What were the principles our country was founded on, Father?"

"Well…"

"It's obvious, Dad. Freedom. Life, liberty, and the pursuit of happiness."

"Are you honestly trying to suggest that the Founding Fathers meant freedom from obligations to posterity?" Joseph worked hard to sound indignant.

Alex knew his father too well to be taken in, so he continued in his joking vein. "Who was it who said, 'Why should I care about posterity? What has posterity ever done for me?'? But seriously, Dad. you keep on pushing on me the happiness that Lucas has with Amy and their little Jasmine. But I'm not Lucas." And that was true.

"Lucas was a playboy like you, Alex."

"It was always obvious that he'd fall from grace someday, give up the good life and all that for your idea of happiness, the simple pleasures of home and hearth. The two of us are brothers, yes, but not twins like you and George. We're completely different human beings." Even when they were children, Lucas had been much more connected with his friends, more of a social animal. Alex was a loner, a guy who liked new challenges and new places, with no regrets at all for his wanderlust and his way of life. "And your ideas, Dad, which seeped through to the poor boy somehow, are from the last century — the last millennium, for heaven's sake. The world has progressed; people have changed."

"For the better?" Joseph asked, suppressing an inner smile.

Alex hesitated. "Sometimes."

If Alex had known what his father had planned for him, he'd have gotten the heck out of Dodge. He'd have found an emergency in a foreign country that couldn't wait, and then have had his pilot fire up the jet. He loved women, *many* women — of all shapes and sizes. He loved the way they smelled, the look of a flawless diamond pointing right to the heart of them — their core — and especially the way they felt while lying naked in his arms.

"OK, I quite understand. You like the single life, but you should know you're breaking your mother's heart. She wants grandchildren to fill up these cold hallways, but offspring never think of their poor parents. After all, we only sacrifice everything to raise our kids, bandage their wounds and love them unconditionally. There wouldn't be any reason to want to give back to us, I suppose," Joseph said with a melodramatic sigh.

Alex had to smile at his father's antics. He and his brothers were used to the whole guilt-trip special with house whine, since Joseph had it perfected and memorized.

"You know that I appreciate everything you and Mom do for me. *Still*, it doesn't mean I'm going to let you put an emotional shotgun to my head and force me down the aisle in a tuxedo while a decked-out and unblushing bride waits with a leering grin. I'm smarter than Lucas," he said with a wink.

He watched as his father chuckled — a gleam in his eye that had Alex more than a little concerned. At that very moment his dad was thinking, *The harder they fight, the more satisfying it is when they fall.* Alex was in deep trouble — he just didn't realize it.

"All right, then. Enough marriage talk," Joseph conceded. "We have that fundraiser banquet this weekend, and I need you to attend. Neither of your brothers can, because of previous engagements, and it would look bad for the corporation if at least one of my sons didn't show up to our own fundraiser."

Alex groaned inwardly. He really hated these auctions, but still, he'd do it. The only reason he despised the events so much was because the people in attendance were boring — with a capital *B* — and the real reason people went to these "charitable" shindigs was to rub elbows with each other and be seen in the latest fashions from Paris and Milan.

So much more money could be raised if the people simply donated what they spent on clothes and jewelry to wear for those grand parties. Why go through all the motions of a fundraiser?

He was well aware, though, that millions of dollars could be raised in one night because so many of the patrons wanted to be *seen* handing over their hard-earned dollars. Good publicity and a boost to the ego.

"Let me know when and where. Of course, I'll do it." Alex knew he sounded as if he were being dragged to the guillotine instead of an evening filled with great food and dancing. On a positive note, he'd most likely not leave the event alone. And sad to say, it had been a while. As much as he liked the world to think he was a nonstop party boy, he'd slowed down in the last few years. Not that he'd let any of his family know that — his father would surely be hearing wedding bells — heck, the old man would be ringing them himself — if he had even the slightest inkling.

He was just finding the women more and more shallow, their tinkly laughter starting to annoy him, their smiles as fake as their breasts and Botox faces. But Alex shook the thought off as he smiled with confidence at his father. He was sure bringing a woman home for a night of no-holds-barred sex would cure him of his moodiness and lack of interest in beautiful socialites.

"It's being held at the Fairmont Olympic Hotel on Friday night, starting at nine," Joseph said.

"At least if I have to go out and act as if I actually care about the newest and greatest fashions, I'll be in a great place. I always enjoy myself there."

The Fairmont was spectacular, inside and out. It was listed on the National Register of Historical Places, and the owners had done a fantastic job of bringing in new designs without taking away from its history and grandeur. Alex enjoyed doing business there, and he knew the food would be top quality. He was anticipating his favorite dish, the hotel's famous Cedar Plank Smoked Salmon.

"Also, could you please keep an eye out for Jessica Sanders? I know it's been many years since the two of you have seen each other, but her father,

John Sanders, is one of my oldest business associates. She's going to be there alone, as her father's out of town on business. Do you remember little Jessica?"

"Dad, what have I told you about matchmaking? I can choose my own dates," Alex grumbled, ignoring the question while losing his normally endless patience. He didn't want to be set up, especially not with Jessica.

If he had to say it again and again, so be it: a committed relationship or marriage just wasn't in the cards for him — and in no way did he want kids. He idolized his gorgeous niece, but the family thing was for Lucas, not him. He was still young at thirty-two, and he wasn't ready to trade in the Lamborghini for a minivan. He shuddered at the thought. That was one reason for his reaction to his dad's request. Here was another: it was Jessica. They had history together — a strange sort of history — one preferably left buried in the molten depths of the earth.

"I haven't done any such thing. I know you're more than capable of finding your own dates," Joseph grumbled. "Too many, if you ask me," he added under his breath, but Alex still heard him.

"Dad…" Alex warned, but Joseph was just getting started.

"I didn't ask you to take her *to* the fundraiser. I simply asked if you'd keep a lookout for her and say hello — maybe ask for a dance. She's been away from the Seattle area for a long time and her father said she isn't used to huge events. She normally avoids them, but this fundraiser is important to her. I know you two haven't seen each other in years; here are a couple pictures so you can recognize her."

Alex reached for the photos; he didn't want to encourage the old man, but his curiosity got the better of him. *Wow*. She was pretty darned attractive now that she was all grown up. He searched his mind for his last memory of her, trying to recall how many years it had been.

It was like banging on one of those old-time televisions. The fuzzy snow and static stopped and suddenly the last time he saw her started playing in his head.

She'd been sixteen, and more the type of girl the guys had thought kinda cute. Fun to hang out with, but not a girl they asked to the prom. Her hair had always been in a tight ponytail, her clothes rumpled, and shiny braces adorned her teeth. She looked twelve instead of sixteen, and her attitude had told the rest of the world to *back off*.

Her father had been a wealthy man, so Alex hadn't understood her desire to dress herself down and try to hide. Most of the rich girls he knew were flashing diamonds and rubies by the time they were ten — when they could sneak out of the house with them, that was. But Jessica didn't even own a pair of designer jeans.

He recalled she hadn't been very social, always choosing to sit on the sidelines while everyone else was out having a good time. While he'd been splashing in the water during one of the school's outings, she'd been on the beach, covered up, and reading a book.

Still, he remembered one time when her parents had been at the house and she'd joined his brothers and him for a game of flashlight tag. After about an hour, Alex had been thrilled he hadn't been caught yet, taking pride in outwitting his brothers, but he was also impressed at the way shy little Jessica had managed to elude all three of them.

He'd heard a slight noise, and jumped from behind the tree he'd been trying to find a way to climb, when the two of them collided, flying to the ground. She'd landed right on top of him, and he'd discovered for the first time that she had curves hidden beneath her baggy clothes.

Without thought, he'd grabbed her head, pulling her mouth to his. By the time he heard Lucas calling for him, his head was in a fog, and his heart thundering. He slowly opened his eyes to gaze into her shocked ones, then he'd watched in fascination as her cheeks flooded with color.

He couldn't remember any of his past girlfriends ever kissing with so much passion and enthusiasm. He wanted to pull her back to him and try again — see whether the kiss was really that good, or if he was just imagining it to be.

Before he got the chance, she mumbled an apology, stumbled to her feet, and ran off. He remembered lying there for several moments, his teenage body on fire for a girl he'd never looked twice at before that searing moment. Lucas caught up to him, and Alex dismissed it from his mind, as teenage boys often do.

For the rest of his senior year, he'd started noticing her, finding himself stealing glances, but he'd never approached her again. She'd brushed him off, and he really didn't like the feeling. Then college had started and life got busy.

He hadn't run into her again, though he'd heard she'd become a do-gooder, and hadn't thought about it since — or he'd *thought* he hadn't thought about it — but gazing at her pictures, seeing the woman she'd grown into, suddenly had his body tightening again as it had that night so many years ago.

She was softer now, more inviting — stunning, actually. One of the pictures was of her and her father. She had her head thrown back in laughter, while her eyes were rounded, causing a sparkle to shine through the still photography.

Maybe a reunion with the girl he'd once known wouldn't be so deadly. Alex wondered whether she remembered him. It would be interesting to find out.

"I do remember Jessica. It'll be a pleasure to say hello, take her for a spin around the dance floor, and catch up on old times," Alex finally muttered, completely unaware of the knowing look in his father's eyes.

Alex's curiosity was piqued, and his father was patting himself on the back. Little did Alex know what was to come…

Chapter Two

Jessica descended the wide staircase, admiring the spectacular golden railing with its ornate Italian Renaissance design. A mixture of feelings ran through her, taking turns with her attention. She hated parties that masqueraded as fundraisers; she was delighted, however, to be home again. She'd missed the rainy freshness of the Northwest. This last trip had kept her away for an entire year, but it had been worth it.

The adventure had had helped her grow in ways she hadn't known were possible. She was stronger, more confident, refusing now to be the shy wallflower she'd been for so many years, refusing to back down and avoid conflict at all costs.

When she'd first approached her father about volunteering in Kenya, East Africa, his answer had been an emphatic *no!* Her relentlessness had paid off: he'd eventually caved in to her pleas. He was a giving man and wanted her to be happy, and he loved to help others as much as she did. But he was also a worried father.

She could have told him she was going no matter what he thought, but she had too much respect for both her parents to take off for such an extended amount of time without their blessing. Sometimes she laughed at how old-fashioned she was, what a throwback she was to an earlier age.

So off she'd gone, to live in a small village in a remote area of Africa. She'd met so many people, and she knew she'd stay in contact with quite a few of them. She'd fallen in love with the locals and befriended a few other volunteers from the States.

The experience had certainly been both humbling and eye-opening. The things she thought were wrong with her own life were from another universe when compared with the heartache of so many people around the world.

She hoped to do a lot more volunteering in the near future. She'd also be more active in fundraising, the reason she was in the beautiful Seattle hotel that evening.

It helped that she loved the hotel the Andersons had chosen for the event. It was steeped in history, with so many areas to explore. The room she'd rented had a spectacular view of the gardens and was decorated to look more like a guest room in a distinguished home than a cold and sterile room for hire.

She'd walked into the suite to the sweet fragrance of fresh-cut flowers and an overflowing bowl of colorful fruit. On the small table had been a bottle of champagne, chilling in a bucket of ice. The bed was beautifully made; a note from the staff welcoming her to the hotel and offering any assistance, should she need it, sat there on her pillow.

Jessica was used to the red-carpet treatment, and she knew it wasn't always the blessing people seemed to believe it. When your father was a multimillionaire, you never knew who liked you for you, or who liked you for what they could get out of your father — especially in her case, since she was his only heir. Every place she went people would do all they could to accommodate her, but it was usually a double-edged sword.

After her last tragic breakup, she'd decided to forgo relationships altogether. That bit of heartbreak was enough, thank you very much. Her former boyfriend had seemed like the perfect man. Oh, she so wished she could stop thinking about it all, but pain had its uses.

He'd ridden into her life like a knight in shining armor — it was a cliché from the get-go — and she'd fallen for him hard and fast. He said all the right things without the usual fawning or flattery. He'd also romanced her unlike any other man she'd known. He could be fun and playful, but he was also a master at seeming smitten but not sappy. His wealth was also a big plus. Not in itself, of course, but because she didn't think that her could be after what she had, not what she was. He and his love seemed so genuine. Yeah, right.

He courted her because his company was going under from the millions of dollars he'd gambled away. She'd found out later. If he snatched her up, he'd figured, he could go into business with her father and save himself. His plan would probably have worked, too.

She would have remained blind if she hadn't showed up at his house early one day and discovered him with the maid.

When she walked into his gazebo to pick up a plant he'd promised her and saw the two of them wrapped in each other's arms, Jessica hadn't even blinked, almost expecting the betrayal from anyone she was with. She'd just quickly shut the door and walked from the house.

This wasn't the first time a man had tried to get to her money. It was just the first time she'd truly believed he wanted her for her. With the other men, at least she'd been aware of who and what they were. Greedy. Her wealth was quite beautiful to them.

She'd imagined that her ex had respected and loved her enough to wait to have sex until their wedding night, but he'd never desired her in the first place. The waiting had fallen in perfectly with his plans, because the "maid" he'd hired was really his long-time girlfriend.

Jessica snapped back to the present and walked into the Spanish Ballroom. She wasn't easily impressed, but every time she'd been here, the room had made her breath stall. Every detail was exquisite, starting with its twenty-foot ceilings. There were several chandeliers hanging at least three feet down and almost equally as wide. The crystals dripping from them fired off prisms of light in every direction.

The linen-covered tables held only the finest dinnerware, and the candles gave off a romantic glow.

The room had the added appeal of strategically placed tall shrubs, offering privacy if a couple chose to steal a kiss.

Jessica began feeling more positive about the evening ahead. It was a beautiful night, and the organization she often donated to, the National Center for Missing & Exploited Children, was going to receive a substantial amount of money. She would enjoy herself even if it killed her.

Remember, you're not allowed to be a wallflower, she lectured herself as she joined the other guests. Breaking that habit had taken a world of concentration. But her time in the villages in Africa had shown her that it didn't matter what other people thought of you; it only mattered what you thought of yourself.

If the world wanted to judge, let it. Just turn your head the other way and walk away proudly.

Jessica sat at one of the tables, and before she knew it, dinner was over; she'd had a delightful time talking with her companions during the meal. When an older gentleman asked her to dance, she gladly accepted.

They hadn't been on the dance floor for long when they were interrupted.

"May I cut in?"

Even though the words came out as a question, Jessica had no doubt they were a command. The gentleman she was dancing with heard it as well and stepped aside without a word of protest.

Jessica wasn't fond of men who felt they deserved anything that caught their fancy, but she wouldn't cause a scene. Was being "ladylike" still considered a virtue? If not, common civility would forbid her to refuse the dance. At least the song was halfway finished, so she wouldn't have to endure being in such an arrogant man's company for long.

As she looked up at him, there was something familiar, something she couldn't quite place; intrigued, she allowed him to pull her into his arms.

As she placed one of her hands in his and the other on his shoulder, she could feel the raw power of his hold. He had the most piercing and beautiful blue eyes she'd ever seen. They were the kind of eyes that could easily penetrate straight into your soul. She'd have to be on guard with this man. Who *was* he?

Suddenly, it clicked — Alex Anderson.

Their fathers had been doing business together since she was a child, though it had been years since she'd last seen him. In fact, not since she was a teenage girl. This man, with the entrancing eyes, kissable mouth, and sexy body, was also a playboy unlike any other.

He was known to be *uncatchable*, as the single women often put it. He dated many women but made it clear he wouldn't settle down. He was serious only in business. His grin had graced a number of magazine covers, making women, both young and old, lose a bit of sleep at night.

He was also the boy who had awakened her desires at the tender age of sixteen.

He'd aged well from the boy she'd once known into the man now trying to seduce her.

Her heart was racing as they played a twist on the game of cat and mouse. He kept attempting to pull her body intimately against his, while she was concentrating on keeping the proper amount of distance between them.

If she hadn't been on a self-imposed leave from men, she could have easily considered a night of flirting with him — possibly even another electrifying kiss like the one they'd shared on one cold, dark night.

She shook her head to clear it and decided to get through the dance so she could move on as quickly as possible before her flash of memory from the past overrode her good sense in favor of the five less rational ones.

His smoldering blue eyes flashed into hers as his perfectly sculpted lips turned up in a sexy-as-sin smile. He knew he was hard to resist, and he seemed to be treating her to his full arsenal of charms without even uttering a word.

He slowly brought her fingers to his mouth and ran his lips across her knuckles. She felt a shudder ripple through her. He then flicked his tongue across the same spot, and desire pooled deep inside her core.

"I'm Alex Anderson, and you're intriguing," he whispered.

"Jessica Sanders, but you already knew that," she retorted. She had to keep her wits about her. Without her notice, the song ended, and a new began. Her escape was forgotten momentarily as she continued this dangerous game with a man she knew better than to play with.

The look in his eyes said he wasn't willing to give up on his quest — whatever it was. She didn't understand why he pretended they were meeting for the first time. What advantage did it give him?

With sudden horror, she realized he actually might *not* know who she was.

She knew the kiss they'd shared had a far greater impact on her than on him. But if she'd been completely forgotten? That would be a serious blow to her ego, especially considering the months, years even, that she'd dreamt of him, waking in a cold sweat as her body hungered for something she couldn't even describe.

As he dipped her low to the ground, then pulled her back to him, letting her body slide across his, she felt her resolve crumbling. She'd been with him for all of three minutes and she was ready to sneak behind one of those strategically placed plants and allow him to devour her.

Surely it was just the setting. The place was magical, and even though the hotel was, as always, everything she could have imagined, it dimmed in comparison with the man holding her. While she was in his arms, the rest of the people — and even the room itself — seemed to disappear.

She knew how very dangerous he was, and she also knew she was playing a game she couldn't possibly win. But for some reason, she wasn't able to pull away. She was locked to him for at least the moment.

There could be only one explanation for Alex Anderson — supernatural powers! As he spun her across the softly lit dance floor, her feet feeling as if they weren't even touching the ground, she was sinking further under his spell. She could feel his solid muscles beneath her fingertips — and his scent mesmerized her. It was the combination of his masculinity, enhanced by the barest hint of citrus, herbs and sandalwood. Probably brewed in a witch's cauldron.

"I haven't had someone cut in on a dance since I was in high school. Don't you see that as a little overzealous?" she asked, raising her eyebrow, wishing to express her displeasure. "Perhaps I didn't wish to dance with you."

"Not at all," he answered.

Jessica raised her eyebrows, questioningly — and waited for him to go on. *Not at all* wasn't an explanation.

"I don't think it was at all presumptuous to cut in. Your previous partner was so boring that you could barely keep your eyes open. *In the middle of a dance floor.* So, you see, I should be thanked for saving you from a mind-numbingly tedious evening," Alex said with a grin that left her speechless.

And he moved with dazzling grace. If he hadn't been undressing her with his eyes the entire time she was locked in his arms, she might have given up and let the seduction continue, but she simply couldn't allow him this much leverage over her. She knew he was the type of man to take ten miles when given an inch. And then another twenty, fast.

She was trying to work up the will to end their dance, but everything about him was too compelling for her to pull herself away. Besides, she argued silently, they were in a room full of people — safe, or so she thought. Really, though, what could possibly happen?

She decided to enjoy the flirtation for a moment, going with the flow of her new motto of not being a wallflower, of now following a "ladylike" assertiveness. This was the man who'd haunted the best of her teenage years, after all, and to have him so obviously want her gave her a slight sense of power.

"You're unbelievably stunning. I can barely concentrate on mere words while my body touches yours. Why don't we leave the dance now and head up to my suite?" he offered with the confidence of a man used to getting the answer he wanted.

She laughed nervously — his words were actually pretty funny — before replying. "I don't think so." Why wasn't she even thinking of slapping him?

He rubbed his hand from the center of her back, dangerously low, and then back up again, causing a rush of heat to flash through her center. He was challenging her to take a chance, from the brush of his hands — to the look in his eyes. She was surprised at how badly she wanted to take him up on his offer.

If nothing else, she was actually enjoying the sexual play — the desire swimming through her, proving to herself that she was indeed a woman, capable of feeling strong emotions.

She'd been told too often she was cold, an ice maiden, incapable of thawing long enough to warm a man's body. She closed her eyes as she fought down the pain of those thoughts. She had told herself it didn't matter, but having Alex's arms around her as he whispered sensual promises in her ear made her realize, all the more, how much she wanted a man to make her come alive.

It couldn't be Alex, though — any man but him. She feared one night in his embrace would leave her scarred and empty the rest of her life. She knew he wouldn't be someone she'd easily walk away from and forget.

"I think we have danced enough," she said breathlessly. She didn't know how much more she could take before surrendering.

"But our song hasn't ended," he said, not mentioning it was their second song, as he pushed against the small of her back, bringing her hips into contact with the hard evidence of his arousal. Before she could stop him — and she was beginning to worry that she didn't think she had the will to stop anything — he bent his head down to the exposed skin of her neck.

His tongue slipped from his parted lips as he began running kisses across her pounding pulse, stopping every few inches to lightly nip her skin, each bite making her fight the need to grind against him.

If he hadn't been holding her so closely, her knees would have buckled, and she'd have melted into a pool at his feet. No man had ever made her feel so breathless — certainly not her weasel of an ex-boyfriend... Ah! Salvation. That's why she insisted on remembering the jerk. She could call a halt right now.

"Alex, it's been very pleasant to see you again — "

Alex moved his mouth over her ear and whispered, "And quite soon it will be more than pleasant. Again and again. When you're lying beneath me, I'll have you trembling under my hands and mouth as they turn your body into liquid fire. You'll be calling out my name, begging me to finish this."

Jessica gasped as his words both horrified her and made her insides quiver uncontrollably. She'd never been seduced like this before, certainly not in a crowded room. And it was bizarre. If they had been alone, she'd have been begging him to take her right there, saying a fond but quick farewell to her self-imposed celibacy.

She tried to gather her wits, looking away from his lethal eyes at the crowded room. It helped, but only a little.

"Have you ever been told how arrogant you are?" She tried to make her voice stern, But the fact that it was choked with arousal called her a liar.

"No, just how *good* I am."

The comment brought her a little closer to reality. "You need to stop this *now*. People are beginning to stare," she whispered.

"Let them stare. They're only wishing they could trade places with me," he replied while running his lips back up her neck and across her cheek to the corner of her mouth where he gently trailed his tongue out along her bottom lip. "Or you."

She allowed herself to run her fingers through his hair and down his neck and shoulders, and then she took a step back. "Thank you for the dance, Mr. Anderson," she said politely, as if they hadn't almost been making love in front of a crowded room.

"The pleasure was all mine, Jessica, and after what we just shared, don't you think it's a little formal to be calling me by my last name?" he answered with mockery.

"*Mr. Anderson*," she emphasized, "there are plenty of women here who'd be more than willing to play a game or two with you tonight. I'm not one of them."

Jessica turned and walked away, though it took all her willpower not to glance back over her shoulder just to drink him in one last time. It had been well over ten years since she's seen him last, and heaven knew how long it might be again.

Chapter Three

Alex stayed where he was, watching her exit, enjoying the sway of her hips with each step she took. Damn, that do-gooder was hot, and he wouldn't mind an entire night with her. The way her body responded to him gave away her secret — she was eager for his touch. Not that his secret was any different from hers, or any less obvious.

He wasn't done with Jessica Sanders. She didn't realize it yet, but when he decided he wanted something, he *always* got it. Her denial was like a red flag to a bull, and he was definitely feeling bullish about her. By the end of the evening, she'd be in his bed. He needed a drink right now, or the entire room would know just what effect she'd had on him.

He walked slowly to the bar on the opposite side of the room, deciding to give her a bit of space. The game was more fun with the opportunity of circling your prey. He wondered if she ever thought about the first game they'd played together.

Under the cream-colored silk dress that clung to her curves was a body made for sin. Alex couldn't believe he'd ever been fooled by her prim exterior, for a fire was clearly raging underneath. He intended to finish what they'd started so many years earlier — and he had a feeling it would set rockets glaring and bombs bursting in air.

From her reaction to him, he knew she wanted it just as badly. Yes, he was arrogant when it came to women. How could he deny it? It was hard to stay humble when they were always throwing themselves at him.

Still, though his experience was wide — and deep — he wasn't entirely on familiar ground. The sexual tension was so strong, he could hear it crackle. And it was a nice change to have a desirable woman not fawn all over him. Jessica was making it hard for him, and that was making him hard. Knowing that she wanted him but was fighting it was about the most erotic thing he could imagine.

He wanted to be there when she exploded, holding her tightly in his arms when he pushed her over the edge. Taking her there wouldn't be difficult; she was smoldering, and he'd need only an instant to ignite the flame.

A smile began at the corner of Alex's lips even though his body ached.

"Hello, Alex. I wasn't expecting to see you here."

Alex turned to find one of his former lovers on her tiptoes and breathing heavily on his neck. Like many in her social circle, she wouldn't miss a function that brought out high society's wealthiest men. Diamonds and five-star restaurants didn't grow on Main Street trees.

The bracelet she wore was a gift from him. The reminder of their time together made him a little queasy.

He looked at the voluptuous form before him, her breasts spilling out of her extremely low-cut gown and her makeup painted on to perfection. She shifted her leg, opening a slit in the side of her gown to reveal gloriously toned thighs that he knew from experience could grip a man's back tightly.

"Hello, Kathy," he said, coolly and curtly.

She blinked in surprise at his rudeness. And she had a right to be surprised. On any other night, he might well have accepted what she was clearly offering when her long fingernail scraped inside the cuff of his jacket, rubbing over the skin of his wrist.

Alex was surprised he'd ever been turned on by her silicone breasts and her porcelain smile.

With a weary sigh, and feeling much older than his thirty-two years, Alex gave her his standard business smile.

"Sorry. I don't have time to chat. I need to start the auction," he said and then easily, and quickly, walked away.

He heard her shocked intake of breath at his dismissal. Soon, it would spread all across the room. He didn't care. Let them talk about his dance with Jessica — let them think what they wanted.

*****

Jessica ordered a glass of wine and guzzled it down, trying desperately to calm her nerves. Alex Anderson should have a danger sign attached to him. Her legs were weak with arousal, and her breathing still hadn't returned to normal. She planned to cut and run as soon as it was socially acceptable.

Suddenly, the room started feeling as if it were closing in around her, so Jessica quickly stepped through the patio doors. A strong gust of wind nearly lifted her off her feet, blowing so hard it actually took her breath away.

Lightning slashed across the sky; thunder boomed, and roared, and bellowed. She walked farther out, lifting her arms, feeling as if she could almost take flight. She loved the feel of her dress whipping around her legs, and the smell of nature cleansing the earth.

Her family had always thought she was a bit crazy, because while everyone else ran for cover whenever a strong storm blew in, she'd grab a chair to watch the show. She delighted in the smells, sights, sounds, and excitement.

When the wind picked up even more, pushing Jessica farther from the patio doors, even Jessica decided she'd better head back inside. Still, she knew she'd chosen the wrong field to study. She should have majored in meteorology rather than journalism — then she could have been a professional storm chaser, on the tail of tornadoes and hurricanes.

The cool night air was just what she needed to gather her wits and face the devil in disguise. Though she didn't intend to talk with Alex the rest of the evening, just being in the same room was going to take some willpower.

With a final longing look toward the flashing sky, and a fresh intake of night air, Jessica stepped back through the doors, unaware that Alex had watched both her exit and her return.

*****

"Come on, ladies, you can bid higher than that," Alex said with a flirtatious wink at the two women bidding against each other for a one-of-a-kind necklace donated from the Neil Lane collection.

Without them realizing that his attention had ever wandered from them, Alex breathed a sigh of relief as Jessica walked back through the outside doors. If she hadn't come in when she did, he would have stopped the auction and gone after her before a gust of high wind carried her off.

The raging storm, which was keeping most of the guests locked inside the warm confines of the hotel, hadn't harmed her in the least — quite the opposite, actually. She was breathtaking as she looked around self-consciously while trying to put herself back together.

Some of her hair had escaped the tight confines of her classic French twist, and her cheeks were flushed a becoming shade of red. She looked as if she'd just crawled from bed — after a vigorous night of lovemaking.

He tried not to think about her, or look for her, but his eyes kept seeking her out. He'd already rejected several women who had made it more than clear that they'd be willing to warm his bed that night.

He had to face it. He wanted only one woman to do that. The rest of the "ladies" in the room paled in comparison with Jessica Sanders.

"Fine. Twenty-five thousand, and it had better be worth it, Alex."

Alex twisted his eyes back to the smiling brunette who was holding up her bidding card in front of him.

Without missing a beat, Alex answered her. "Neil Lane is *always* worth it," he practically purred, a bit disgusted with himself for what he was willing to do for charity donations.

"Anything for a few extra dollars, huh, Alex?" Mark said with a laugh as he entered the room, looking extremely uncomfortable in his tux.

"If you ladies offer sufficiently high bids tonight, I might just bring my *very* eligible brother up here with me on the auction block," Alex said, sending a smirk toward Mark.

"Ooh, forget the diamonds! I want to bid on him!" one woman shouted.

"Yes, me, too," another called out.

Within seconds, there was a chant for Mark to go up onstage. Alex looked at him with a self-satisfied grin. Alex knew he'd put him on the spot, because if his brother didn't give the bidders what they were demanding, the poor fellow would hear about it for too long to make his temporary escape worthwhile.

"You owe me big time, Alex. My revenge won't be pretty," Mark growled under his breath as he jumped onto the stage. He then plastered a megawatt smile on his face and turned toward the crowd.

"I don't know what the fuss is all about, girls. This man behind me is quite the eligible bachelor, himself. I have it on good authority that he was speaking with our father the other night — hinting at the possibility of a happily-ever-after once he's found the right woman," Mark said, playing to the crowd.

Alex barely managed to catch his jaw from hitting the ground. He should have known better than to try to one-up his younger brother. Mark was far too quick on his feet. As Alex felt the panic rise up within him, he glanced over the crowd and his eyes collided with Jessica's. She was looking at him with some disbelief.

Inspiration hit.

"Sorry, ladies, but my brother is sadly mistaken. I'm spoken for at the moment," Alex said as he sent a loving look at Jessica, staring just long enough to make several heads turn in her direction, following his gaze.

Her jaw *did* drop to the floor, or at least as far in that direction as it could get.

Have fun with that, Alex thought, happy his diversion had worked.

"Now, let's get the bidding underway. Who'd like to start at ten thousand dollars for the perfect date with our very own Mark Anderson? I've been told he's quite the catch, treating the ladies to a *really* good time."

The crowd roared as bids started flying in, one right after the other. Mark smiled and winked at each woman who called out a higher bid, then sent a few seductive looks toward the ones who looked as if they wanted to jump in the battle.

"One hundred thousand."

"One twenty five."

"Two hundred thousand."

"Two fifty."

The room was finally silent.

"I've got two hundred and fifty thousand dollars, ladies. Is that the final bid?" Alex asked as he looked around. "Going once, going twice…sold to Ms. Gina Marsden for two hundred fifty thousand dollars!"

"Seriously, you're dead," Mark whispered before he leaped off the stage to lead his date to the cashier.

Alex continued the auction for another half hour, not in the least worried about what Mark had planned for him. Toward the end of his duties as auctioneer, he lost sight of Jessica and sighed, thinking she'd left when he wasn't looking.

In his mind, his night was about to take a nosedive.

Chapter Four

Jessica watched Alex work his magic on the crowd, with the women edging closer to the stage, trying their hardest to get his attention.

She was still steamed that he had dared to point her out, insinuating publicly that they were some kind of couple. She didn't need anyone thinking she was in a relationship with that arrogant, narcissistic, self-satisfied pig. She was sure half the women in the room wouldn't be above scratching her eyes out over the wretched man. Heck, they could have him with her blessing. Or he could just go...satisfy himself.

Wandering the room, Jessica was feeling a hint of exhaustion coming on. She'd had one too many glasses of wine and her feet were killing her. It was worth it, though, for her shoes were absolutely stunning, and, after all, "Pain is beauty," her friends would often say. Her lips formed a reminiscent smile at the thought.

She made small talk with several people, only half listening to what they were saying, and then finally gave up and went to the restroom to freshen up. When that still wasn't helping her head to clear, she decided to call it a night.

She made her way to the hotel lobby. It was time to sleep the evening off and then get out of the hotel and as far from Alex Anderson as she possibly could. She felt another stint of foreign volunteering coming on.

The doors of the elevator were just about to close, so she picked up her pace and called out, "Please, hold the doors."

She was relieved to see a hand reach out and prevent them from closing.

"Thank you," she said, a little short of breath as she quickly slipped inside.

To avoid tripping on her long dress, she was staring at the floor as she moved all the way to the back, where she could hold on to the bar when the car started moving. When the doors slammed shut, she finally looked up, and her eyes locked with Alex's.

Like a frightened animal, she jumped into the furthest corner of the elevator, basically hugging the wall. The ride would last only a moment, and then she'd be blessedly alone in her room. In such a confined space, it was impossible for Jessica to ignore his eyes burning into her — the sexual tension between them was practically a living, breathing entity.

As the ride up became unbearably awkward, the lights flickered and the elevator stopped abruptly, causing them both to lose their footing and grab for the support of the railing. Then, darkness and complete and utter silence. No music filtering through the speakers, no light to speak of whatsoever — not even from the buttons to each floor in the hotel. Putting her hand right up in front of her face, Jessica couldn't see even an outline of it.

Her heart thundered as a mixture of fear and desire coursed through her.

Fear was winning out, however, because she was terrified of the dark.

"Jessica, are you all right? You aren't claustrophobic, are you?"

She took several deep breaths before answering him. "I'm not afraid of small places, but I can't say that I'm a huge fan of the dark."

She was trying to stay brave, but as the seconds ticked by, the pure blackness felt as if it were closing in around her. To add to her fear was the thought of the cables snapping, plunging them to their deaths.

She wouldn't panic. The lights would return at any moment, and the elevator would continue on its upward journey, safely returning her to her floor and ridding her of the horrors of the dark. She started counting in her head. When she'd reached twenty, she heard Alex shuffling in her direction and then felt his hand on her arm.

She jumped at his touch. She was trying so hard not to be frightened, but the darkness was all-consuming.

"Everything will be OK. This will be over in a few minutes, I'm sure. Buildings have contingency plans for when this kind of thing happens," he tried to reassure her.

"I don't understand why there isn't any noise — not the slightest sound," she replied, barely above a whisper.

"We're most likely around the fourth floor, so there wouldn't be any noise from the lobby," he reasoned. "I wonder what happened."

"I went out earlier in the evening, and there was a pretty spectacular storm outside. A power line was most likely knocked over," Jessica whispered.

Some of Jessica's fear had subsided with the soothing tone of his voice and his gentle reassuring touch — a comforting reminder she wasn't alone.

"I'm going to feel around for the phone and see if I can get someone on the line. They need to know we're in here. Hopefully, I can find out what's going on," he said before releasing her.

She had to fight the response to reach out and grab him again as the feeling of panic quickly rose within her.

Sinking to the floor, she hugged her knees to her chest in quiet desperation. She was grateful now for the extra alcohol she'd had. The slight buzz she felt was the only thing keeping her from a total meltdown.

"The phone isn't picking up." Alex's voice startled her. "We're going to have to wait this out, but don't worry. Elevators are extremely secure, and it won't take them long to rescue us."

His voice drew closer, and then his foot kicked her in the ribs. She let out a whoosh of breath.

"Oh! I'm sorry, Jessica! Are you OK?" He dropped to his knees and began running his hands up her legs, then across her sides. Her lungs exploded in a gasp as heat pooled in her core.

"I'm fine, really. You barely touched me," she said huskily.

He seemed to realize what he was doing, because she felt his hands grow still almost instantly, and then they were gone. She breathed another sigh, not sure whether it was of relief or disappointment.

On the one hand, she needed him to continue talking and touching her, so she didn't feel alone in the all-consuming blackness. On the other hand, if he did keep touching her, she didn't know how long she could hold out against him.

After the dance they'd shared, her body was still throbbing, and the longer his scent drifted around her and into her brain, the more she wanted — needed — just *had* to have him.

*****

Hearing the huskiness in her voice sent a jolt right to Alex's groin. He wanted to take her right then, without giving either of them a chance to change their minds. He was trying to be rational — and he'd tried to base most of his adult life on reason — but they were alone...in the dark...for who knew how long. He was walking a very thin line, and it wasn't going to take much to push him over. Everything about her was intoxicating, and that simple touch moments ago had made him ache for her in a way that wasn't rational at all.

"How long do you think it'll take for them to get us out?" Jessica asked, thankfully distracting him for a few seconds.

"It won't take long. What did you think of the party? There was about one and a half million raised by the time I left," he said, trying to fill the otherwise silent box with sound.

She didn't speak for several moments, and Alex began to wonder whether she was having a panic attack. He really hoped not. He didn't know how to deal with hysterical women. The only sure-fire cure in his house had always been chocolate, and he didn't have any of that on him.

"You know, we really are safe, Jessica. These things don't just plunge through the shaft and explode at the bottom, like in the movies. That's just Hollywood's way of making things exciting."

When she still didn't speak, he moved close to her again and let his leg rest against hers. Her body seemed to relax, and he heard her breath escape in a sigh.

"Sorry. I just really hate the dark," she finally said. He felt her body edge closer to his, as she sought his warmth for comfort. "What do you do in your free time?" she asked.

"I like to travel. I handle most of our international business because my older brother has so much work to do here, and Mark would choose to never fly if he could get away with it. I, on the other hand, am happy to be in a different country each month. My father usually has to drag me home," he said with a chuckle.

He was noticing lately, though, that he was staying home more often. He'd started to miss his family when he was away too long. That had been the case recently. He was even finding himself enjoying the time spent on his brother's ranch, herding cattle. Sheesh.

Many things that had once excited him were starting to lose their appeal. He figured he was just getting older. Wait! What was he thinking? He was only thirty-two, and that wasn't aging; it was pretty hot and tasty. He had to stop this line of thinking now. "So, what about you? What makes Jessica happy?"

"I used to travel a lot with my father, but it became boring after a while. I'm really more of a homebody now. I do a lot of volunteer work, which keeps me plenty busy. I've been taking some courses at the college — nothing major, just some art, cooking, and photography classes. I have a master's degree in business because my father wanted me to go into the family corporation, but I can't stand sitting behind a desk all day…"

Alex was surprised she'd gone so far in school. Most of the women he knew with the same amount of money at their disposal didn't feel the need to get an advanced degree or treat college as anything other than a finishing school and a party place, a chance to spread their social wings. They just lived on their parents' money and name until they snagged a rich husband.

"If you can't stand it, then why get the degree?"

"That's a long story — one that, hopefully, we won't have time to get into. The short version is that I wanted to please my dad. I found out, though, that he loves me no matter what I choose to do. I love to write, I've done some articles for different papers throughout the world. I thought about doing it full time, but…" She trailed off again.

"What kind of writing?" he asked, his curiosity piqued.

"Nothing that's going to win me a Pulitzer or anything," she said with a chuckle. "I've done some pieces on life in primitive villages around the world. It's amazing, really. These people have no electricity, water, or any of the conveniences that we take for granted, yet they're so happy, at least when they're not starving. It just works for them. I loved some of the places I got to stay during my trips. It's amazing to wake up and smell a part of the world almost completely untouched by modern society."

"Sounds interesting," he mumbled, though he couldn't imagine what it would be like not to have at least his iPhone with him. He couldn't remember a day he'd gone without checking his email at least once.

Jessica laughed — the sound like music to his ears. "You don't *sound* very interested. You sound horrified."

"OK, I admit that the thought of no electricity terrifies me. I'm very used to walking into my kitchen and pouring a hot cup of coffee from my pot that's pre-programmed to start brewing right before I wake up. I don't think I'd function too well if I had to light a fire, then boil the water, before I had my morning caffeine," he admitted.

"That's what I thought, too…but somehow, you get used to it. Then, when you leave, you actually miss it. Really, with all the travel you do, you should stop at one of the native villages some time. You'd be amazed and humbled by how accepting they are, especially the children."

"Maybe you'll just have to take me to one of these places," he said, the sentence just popping out. And as he thought more about it, it didn't sound so bad. The idea of Jessica in a secluded village in a remote, muggy jungle, where she'd have to strip to practically nothing, had his body hardening.

"Careful what you wish for. I don't think I'd mind seeing you work up a sweat," she said with a chuckle.

Alex went from uncomfortable to downright miserable at the image her words evoked. He'd wanted her all night, and she wasn't helping his problem. Neither was their current situation. Her enticing body was pressed solidly against him, and her words making him play film strips in his head of their bodies entwined in a flurry of movement.

Everything went silent as he tried to do anything to get his mind off sex. Nothing was working. He shifted, but ended up pressed even closer to her.

His control could last only so long. If the lights didn't come back on soon...

Chapter Five

Jessica sat motionless, achingly aware, and wary, of Alex's leg pressing against hers. The silence seemed to drag on and on. She didn't know which was worse — the fear or the desire.

She was impossibly attracted to him, but it didn't matter — men like him wouldn't normally give her the time of day, except maybe for a quick trip to bed and rarely even then. His hormones must be out of whack right now, because, away from the cameras, Alexes of the world always went after blond bimbos with big bazongas and no brains, and, for public consumption, strutted around with buffed and polished socialites, trophies too rich and too thin and sometimes too horny, but with an impeccable pedigree.

If women wanted marriage, the Alexes ran like hell. Rumor had it that Alex's dad would probably force him kicking and screaming into the matrimonial noose someday, but it wouldn't change him. He'd sire his heirs with the trophy wife and her glittering genes, but with her full approval, he'd keep having his fun on the side. So if Alex did finally settle down, it certainly wouldn't be with a shy, sheltered, earnest girl who didn't know how to play the games in the upper-class universe.

Jessica wanted to be desired and loved *and* to be the only one on a man's mind. Those *to-be*s weren't meant to be.

More silence engulfed the two of them, making her wish that something, anything, would happen to fill the void. It would be so easy to lean into him and find comfort, to take a small taste of his neck — just let go for once in her life. Though the thoughts went through her mind, she knew she'd never be brave enough to do it. She just wasn't one of those women.

The elevator made a groaning sound and jerked. Jessica let out a gasp, and without a second thought, she flung her arms around Alex, her entire body shaking in fear. She was going to die in this dark, tiny box.

"It's OK, Jessica. The elevator's just settling a bit. I promise you, it won't fall. There are several backup safety features for all emergencies. Even if it did fall — which I guarantee you it won't — we'd get a little bruised and banged up in the worst-case scenario. You have nothing to worry about." He pulled her onto his lap and wrapped his arms around her trembling body.

He kept speaking in a soothing whisper and stroked her from the small of her spine up to her neck and back down again. She didn't know whether it was his words or the touch of his hands, but soon her anxiety abated.

"I really am sorry, Alex. I've just always had a fear of the dark. Believe it or not, I still keep a small light on at my place at all times. I know, logically, that nothing is going to come and get me in the dark, but I think I watched too many Stephen King movies as a child, and they stuck with me," she said with a self-deprecating laugh.

"You'd be surprised by the number of people who have the same fear. It's not so much a fear of the dark, but of the unknown. We're creatures of comfort. We want to use all our senses — to see, hear, feel…touch…taste…"

Jessica thought she heard a slight groan at the end of his sentence, and she wasn't sure which of them it came from. His words were delicious, evoking dark desire on all levels.

She didn't offer to climb from his lap. Being there was the only thing keeping her from panicking, and the feel of his hands caressing her back was soothing. He really had large hands. They splayed the whole of her back as he gently moved them up and down the skin laid bare by the low cut of her dress. *A little closer…little closer….little more….stop it!* She silently reprimanded herself as his hands came nearer and nearer to the small of her back.

Jessica forced herself to speak. "What things are *you* afraid of?" she asked, leaning her head against his shoulder. She loved how solid he felt, as if being in his arms made her invincible. He was her superhero in that moment, and she felt…safe. Well, as safe as she could feel in a pitch-black box about to plunge her to an agonizing death.

"Nothing," he answered with confidence.

"Oh, come on. You know what a big baby I am, now. The least you can do is give me something," she demanded.

He paused for a long moment as his hands continued stroking her silk dress and the bare skin of her back, causing goose bumps to break out wherever his fingers trailed. She'd given up waiting for an answer when he finally spoke.

"If you tell anyone, and I mean, *anyone*, I'll deny it…" he trailed off.

"Promise," she eagerly accepted.

"I'm absolutely terrified of monkeys."

Jessica waited for him to go on. He didn't say anything further.

"Monkeys?"

"Yes! They're hair-raising creatures. They scale trees and just look at you with their beady little eyes. I know they're plotting amongst themselves, hashing out the best method to attack the unsuspecting person on the ground below. For that matter, they're most likely scheming to take over the world."

The tone of his voice was so serious that Jessica began laughing. She couldn't help herself. She'd never heard once of anyone afraid of monkeys.

"Yes, those little creatures with the furry tails terrify me, too," she gasped in between bursts of laughter.

"There have been several reports of monkey attacks, so I wouldn't be surprised if there are many more people out there afraid of the miserable creatures," he said, but she was relieved to hear the humor in his voice.

"Yes, I know. You'd better keep a pocket full of bananas with you at all times, so when they invade Seattle, you'll be safe. Just throw the fruit in one direction, and then run like heck in the other."

"Are you taunting me about my deepest fear, Jessica?" he asked with mock consternation.

The changing quality of his voice wiped all traces of humor from Jessica. She realized that through her laughter, her shaking body had pressed her even more tightly against him, and his breathing was becoming more ragged by the second.

After a long pause, the movement of his hands caressing her skin stopped comforting her and heat started to pool inside her stomach. His hands began traveling lower with each pass he took, and his fingers spread around to her sides. She could feel him brushing against the sides of her breasts, stomach, and hips.

Her breathing quickened and she could feel her body responding, her nipples peaking, and her core growing hot and moist. She should move, put some distance between them — but she couldn't force herself to do it.

"I've been dying to do this since our dance," he whispered as his hand ran up the back of her neck and undid her hair, letting it flow free around her shoulders. He then grasped the loose strands and turned her face to him.

Alex's fingers hungrily searched the outline of her parted lips in the dark and without hesitation pressed his mouth to hers in a confident kiss, clearing any thoughts of protest from her mind. The intensity of their kiss fueled the fire, unleashing avid flames of urgency, obliterating all reason and logic from their minds.

His tongue slipped inside her mouth, with the hunger of obsession. Never before had she felt so wanton. If he made love as aggressively as he kissed, she had no doubt he'd be a fantastic lover. She knew she needed to stop him — and she would, definitely, in just a few more seconds.

When his hand slid underneath her gown and skimmed her bare hip, her body trembled with need. The only thing separating his hands from her heated core was a tiny wisp of fabric.

He moved his lips down her neck, nibbling the skin of her throat as his hand ran over her hips and gripped her backside, squeezing her sensitive flesh. She groaned as he sipped at her skin, causing her entire body to arch in response, begging for more.

"You smell so incredible, it's been driving me crazy all night," he moaned, making her shiver. He smelled pretty appetizing, himself. As if the separation of their mouths was too much for him, he quickly licked his way back up her throat, then ran his tongue along the outside of her lips, making her lean into him, demanding he kiss her fully.

As his mouth claimed hers again, he shifted their bodies, pushing her gown up around her waist so she was straddling his lap, allowing his hands more access for their explorations. She could feel his desire pressing against her aching heat, and her body yearned to experience all he was offering.

Abandoning her internal battle, she became lost in every sensation he awoke within her. He ran his tongue from her mouth to her neck again, gently biting at her pounding pulse. She pressed against his pulsing arousal while he slowly slid the thin strap of her dress down her shoulder, his lips following the strap's descent.

She felt the cool air touch her tender nipples only seconds before his mouth was washing the hardened peaks. She threw her head back and groaned as rolling waves of sensation washed through her. Thoroughly loving her tender breasts, he continued ravishing them, sucking and licking, hearing her cry out her appreciation. When she felt she could take no more, his mouth slowly rose back up her neck and fastened onto her lips once more, while he pressed his erection even harder against her body in frustration and need.

"I want to be inside you so badly," Alex growled.

"Please..." Jessica whimpered in return.

Not waiting a moment longer, she felt him swiftly shift her panties as she heard the metallic clicking of his zipper and sensed him spring free from his clothing. Excitement coursed through her at the thought that now nothing separated them, and she felt the warm, hard steel of his arousal begging for entrance at her slick folds.

Grasping her hips tightly in his large hands he used a hard thrust, enclosing himself inside her, causing her to cry out at the exquisite feeling of fullness, with just the tiniest twinge of pain.

He sat motionless, giving her body time to adjust to his thickness. She hoped he had no idea that it was her first time; she'd be humiliated if he knew of her shocking inexperience.

As the pinch of pain receded, she felt pressure and need start building again. Her body swayed against his as she gasped in need and amazement, resting her forehead against his, relishing in the unbelievable pleasure caused by their joined bodies.

In tune to her readiness, he gripped her hips, and began guiding her up and down his considerable length. With his silent tutoring, she picked up quickly on what she needed to do. She took over the motion and started moving, encouraged by his quickly accelerating breathing.

With both hands, he cradled the back of her head, and flexed his hips to meet each movement she made, increasing the pleasure for both of them. Guiding her, he pushed her onto his throbbing erection, deeper and deeper, with greater intensity. Releasing one hand, he brought it down to her swollen womanhood and delivered the most delicious sensation, causing her head to fall back and inarticulate moans to escape her mouth.

She was reaching....trying to find something she didn't even know existed until this one perfect moment in time.

"Baby, I can't hold on much longer. Your body is so incredibly sexy...I'm gonna come. Inside you. Now..." Alex's last words were strained as he fought to bring her the ultimate pleasure, not ready for it to end.

With a hard thrust upward, filling her to completion, Alex stilled as he cried out his release, the violent pulse of his orgasm sending her body spiraling out of control along with his, her muscles tightening in spasms as she reached the peak of such foreign pleasure.

She closed her eyes, lost in sweet ecstasy, never wanting the moment to end.

As she continued convulsing around him, gripping him tighter with each pulse of her body, he moaned, before holding her tight and gently pushing in and out of her in long, slow thrusts, drawing out the pleasure for each of them.

"You just completely made me lose my mind," Alex murmured in disbelief, his ragged breathing on her neck causing warmth to quickly spread through her.

With an exhausted laugh, she collapsed against the slick hardness of his chest, trying to regain control of her breathing, feeling the incredible girth of him still filling her full as their bodies remained locked together.

Jessica was so satisfied, she wanted nothing more than to close her eyes and fall asleep in his arms. She'd never even imagined sex could be so powerful — so fulfilling.

"Mmm, if you keep sighing like that, I won't be able to resist taking you again," Alex mumbled as his lips danced across her neck.

"I could do that again," she whispered shyly, shocked by the words escaping her mouth.

Surprised by her comment, she heard his sharp intake of breath and felt him tense beneath her. Much to her delight, he began moving again, doing so easily, their connection never having been broken.

Just as she started to feel her body begin heating again, there was a clanking noise.

"What —" He never got to finish his sentence.

There was another jolt of the elevator, and the lights flickered on, and then off again.

Jessica jumped off Alex in a panic, quickly fumbling with her clothes, trying to get them straightened as fast as possible. She'd be mortified if the doors opened to a roomful of people with her standing there half-dressed.

Luckily, he'd only moved her dress around, instead of removing it entirely. She backed away from him, reality quickly setting in, growing horrified as her uncharacteristic behavior sank fully into her brain. She didn't stop her retreat until she felt the wall behind her. She prayed he was putting his clothes back in place, too.

The lights turned back on — and stayed on. As her eyes adjusted from the darkness, Jessica was relieved to see him standing before her, fully clothed — with an expression of guilt and regret on his face. The elevator began moving downward.

"Look, Jessica..." he began when the door whisked open.

She didn't want to hear him make excuses about how sorry he was and about how he wouldn't be calling her. She couldn't take that kind of rejection with her heart still healing from her ex's nightmarish betrayal.

What had been amazing and wonderful for her had most likely been disappointing to him. She couldn't listen to him downplay what had happened.

She wanted to remember her one impulsive moment as magical, but she was struggling to do so. She knew he was the type to make love in all sorts of exotic places, but she wasn't. That is, if you could call an elevator exotic.

Even as she ran from the elevator, his voice receding as she left him behind, she could think of little more than the pleasure still coursing through her body. She wouldn't regret her moment with Alex Anderson — it had been too memorable. But she would try to forget the man himself.

****

Jessica jumped out of the elevator and into the crowd milling around the lobby, and then was quickly lost from Alex's sight. He'd thought about chasing her down but decided to let her go. All good things had to come to an end, and his time with her was certainly good. He'd never felt more excitement in the arms of a woman. It had been passionate and thrilling, and he wanted to do it all over again. His body wasn't nearly satisfied enough.

He couldn't believe he was unhappy about being freed from the dark elevator, but he wished the power had remained off the rest of the night.

It was obvious Jessica already regretted what had taken place, so it was better to forget all about the incident and move on. Alex cut through the crowd and headed to the stairs. He had a feeling that sleep wouldn't come easily.

He was wrong. The minute his head hit the pillow he was out, his dreams filled with one woman.

The next morning, Alex grabbed his bags and checked out, thinking that his time in the elevator with Jessica wouldn't be something he'd forget about anytime soon. He knew she'd been scared last night. Heck, he was pretty frightened by the strange feelings invading him, too. He'd been seriously considering chasing after her.

But no, that would have been illogical. He had his freedom to think about.

Chapter Six

One Year Later

Joseph was meeting his good friend John for lunch. It had been a long time since they'd seen each other — too long.

"Joseph, so good to see you," John said as he grasped his friend's hand.

"Great to see you, too. Is there anything new happening in your life?"

"Everything is great. I have a new grandson, who's the light of my world. Here, I brought pictures. Look how handsome he is," the proud grandfather said.

"Congratulations. He's a mighty fine-looking boy. Did Jessica get married?" Joseph asked, knowing he hadn't heard of any nuptials, but it could have been a private ceremony. Joseph was still upset that she and Alex hadn't hit it off. He'd been so sure they were a perfect match and Joseph had already formed wedding plans in his head...

"No, I'm afraid not. It's like this: Jessica won't even discuss the father. I've tried, on several occasions, to ask her about him, and she closes right up. She said it was a one-time deal, the father didn't know, and she was keeping it that way."

"None of that sounds at all like the Jessica I know," said Joseph gently, touching his friend on the shoulder in commiseration.

"No, it doesn't, not at all. I've done everything to find out more. I tried to bribe her, threaten her, and beg her — all to no avail. She's being tight-lipped about the whole situation," John said with frustration.

"Was she seeing anyone around the time she became pregnant — someone whom you could possibly question?" Joseph asked. If one of his sons got a young woman pregnant, he'd have expected them to do the right thing. Hell, he hoped he'd raised them well enough that they'd do the right thing because it was *right*, not because it was expected of them.

"She hasn't been in a relationship for a few years — not that I know of. She'd been hurt pretty badly. Her last serious relationship ended when she found the guy in bed with another woman. She found out he'd been like many others before him — only after money," John said with pain in his voice.

"How old is your grandson? Maybe, somehow, I can help you figure this out," Joseph offered, although he didn't have a lot of confidence in being of any use.

"Jacob is three months old and, father or no father, he's amazing. I'm so grateful he's been given to us. Jessica adores him. She loves being a mother, and it's lifted her out of the depression she was in for so long," John said, instantly brightening.

"She was in a depression?"

"It all started after that big fundraiser last year at the Fairmont Olympic. She came home for a while and was so distant. I was actually a little relieved when she announced her pregnancy, because she started taking better care of herself," John said with a sigh.

Joseph sat up, on instant alert. "Can I see those pictures again, John?"

John was more than willing. This time, when Joseph examined the photos before him, he looked closely at the features. There was a real possibility that the baby was Alex's son.

"John, has she given you any clues about the father?"

John was picking up on Joseph's changed demeanor. "Do you think it could be one of your boys?" he asked with hope. John knew that Alex or Mark would step up and do the honorable thing.

"I think there's a chance he could be Alex's. Alex was at the fundraiser, and I asked him to look after Jessica, since she was to be there alone. After the event, he came home and wasn't himself. He wasn't even going out for a while — very unusual for Alex. Then, after a couple of months, he went completely in the opposite direction. It seemed like he couldn't get far enough away, as if he was trying to outrun some demons or something."

"The only time she ever let something slip was to say it was only one night and the guy hadn't mistreated her in any way. She told me she'd made a mistake and wouldn't make him sacrifice his life because of her imprudence. I told her that the father at least had the right to know, and he certainly should own up to his responsibilities, but she closed down after that and wouldn't make any more comments on the matter."

"I think we can get our answer of whether he's Alex's or not if I can see her and the child. I think we'll be able to tell from her reaction alone," Joseph said with sparkling eyes. The possibility of having another grandchild was exhilarating.

"She's coming to dinner tonight. Why don't you and Katherine join us?" John spoke with trepidation.

"It's a plan, my friend, and, John, if Alex turns out to be the father, please don't say anything tonight. Let me tell my son first. I know he'll do the right thing, and I don't want Jessica to think you or I forced him into it," Joseph asked.

"I can respect that, and I'll honor your wishes. I have no doubt Alex will take responsibility for any child of his," John said. "Joseph, I'm really sorry if he's the father and she didn't say anything. I'm sure she believed she was doing the right thing."

"I've known Jessica since she was a little girl, John, and I know that she would have valid reasons for keeping this to herself. She most likely thought she was doing Alex a favor, since he doesn't exactly portray himself as the stay-at-home-with-babies kind of guy," Joseph acknowledged. "But I know that if he's a father, he'll make a good one. I have to admit,

I'm hoping the baby *is* his son, because that means I'll have my first grandson."

"I didn't think about it like that. Let me order a bottle of champagne for us to celebrate. We may as well do it now, just in case we're disappointed later."

"Right you are, John, right you are." John signaled the waiter and ordered the champagne, and then the two men pored over the pictures, trying to spot Alex's features in his tiny face.

The infant certainly looked as if he could be an Anderson…

The two friends finished lunch and went their separate ways, both eagerly awaiting the evening ahead.

Joseph made sure to arrive before Jessica was expected. He wanted to see her face when she noticed that he and Katherine were at her father's house.

Jessica's face gave her away instantly. When she walked into the family room and saw Katherine and him sitting there, the fingers of her free hand flew up to her parted lips, her eyes widened in shock, and her color heightened. She took only about two seconds to compose her features, but in that unguarded moment, John and Joseph both had their answer.

"Hello, darling, you're running late," John said as his daughter finally moved forward into the room.

"You know how it is with a baby, Dad. Jacob took a while to eat, and then had to be changed." Jessica laughed, and stroked her baby's head. "I need to start planning ahead and scheduling my departures at least an hour before I'm actually supposed to leave."

"I know it's been a long time, but you remember my good friends Joseph and Katherine, don't you?"

"Yes, of course. How are you both doing?" Jessica asked as she approached them.

"We're wonderful, dear, and how are you? I must say you have a beautiful son. He's three months old, right? I've been hearing all about him from your father," Katherine said as she gave Jessica a hug and then looked at Jacob with longing.

"I'm doing great. Yes, he's three months old already. Would you like to hold him?" Jessica asked, her voice choking a bit on the last word. She tried covering up her emotions with a cough, but Joseph wasn't fooled.

"Oh, yes, please. I have my darling granddaughter, Jasmine, now, but she seems so big compared with Jacob. She's already a year old, and going strong," Katherine said as she bent down to unbuckle Jacob from his car seat.

He was wide awake and looking at Katherine with big blue eyes, most certainly an Anderson feature. He was a mighty handsome boy, Joseph thought with pride, and he felt himself getting a little emotional as he watched Katherine hold their only grandson — so far — for the first time. He'd wanted to tell her as soon as he'd returned home from lunch, but he hadn't wanted to disappoint her if it turned out that Jacob wasn't Alex's.

"He's a great baby and allows me get plenty of sleep, but I still feel as if I'm a walking zombie," Jessica said.

John interrupted. "If you'd let us help you out..."

Melody Anne

"I can do this, Dad. Mom didn't have a nanny, and not only did I turn out fine, but she's radiant. I just want to be as strong as she is," Jessica said, her shoulders straightening.

"I also had sisters who were here for the first six months, and my mother-in-law, who lived for you," Jessica's mother remarked as she came up next to Katherine and clasped Jacob's little hand. "I wasn't trying to do it all alone."

"I know, Mom. If it gets too difficult, I promise to ask for some help," Jessica conceded.

"No, you won't. You're just as stubborn as your father."

"That's also an apt description for my boy, Alex. Do you remember him, Jessica?" Joseph asked, watching as her cheeks instantly flushed. *Very interesting*, Joseph thought. Things were looking up for that wedding.

"Um…yeah…vaguely…"

"Weren't the two of you at that fundraiser together last year?" Joseph pushed.

"Um…which fundraiser?" she hedged.

"You know. The one they had at the Fairmont Olympic for exploited and missing children."

"Oh, I think so. Yes, now that I think of it, he *was* there. We may have said hello," she answered, refusing to look Joseph in the eye.

"The only reason I remember that event so well was the mood Alex was in afterward…" Joseph trailed off, noticing her eyes instantly popping out as she tried to decide whether to question him or not. Her curiosity won out, it seemed.

"Oh, he was in a bad mood?" she asked with what Alex's father was sure she thought was polite indifference in her voice. Not quite.

"No, not really in a bad mood; it was more like he was upset about something. I thought that maybe he'd met someone there and he was...missing her? Well, nothing came from it, so I guess I was wrong."

"Oh, yes. I wouldn't know," she said, lowering her head.

"Of course you wouldn't, dear," Katherine said as she finally looked away from Jacob long enough to join in the conversation.

"Is the baby getting too heavy?" Jessica asked.

"Not at all. I just love cuddling these precious bundles. I wish all my children would settle down and have families. Large families. I would so love to have a bunch of grandkids to spoil," Katherine said with a longing smile.

Jessica's eyes filled with tears and she turned away.

Was it guilt? Joseph was sure she felt remorse for denying a grandmother access to her grandchild.

"I'm sure you'll have that someday," Jessica finally said.

"Oh, I have no doubt about it. But be careful, Joseph," she added. "I wasn't giving you free rein to meddle in our children's lives, Joseph."

"I wouldn't dream of it, dear," he said as he bent down and kissed her cheek.

She rolled her eyes, but smiled at him, too happy to be holding a baby in her arms to bother with scolding him. He patted himself on the back for getting out of that one. Whenever she was distracted, he could make plenty of plans for his wayward sons.

"Dinner is ready, if you'd like to follow me," John said, and Joseph watched Jessica breathe a sigh of relief.

The rest of the night went smoothly, with their conversation filled with the hot-button issues of the word — the agonies and ecstasies of being recent grandparents, the latest vacation they'd enjoyed, how real estate was faring in their area, major mergers and political scandals.

Katherine didn't know why, but she was drawn to Jacob. She held him throughout the meal, though Jessica offered to relieve her several times. Even when the evening drew to an end, Katherine was still reluctant to release the tiny boy.

Jessica had a few tears in her eyes as she collected her son and left the house. She'd made a joke at dinner about postpartum blues to cover up her emotional state. Joseph knew what it had to be — guilt, guilt, guilt for keeping the baby from his family! He also knew that if they stood back and waited, she'd come around on her own. She was simply too kind a person to keep her child away from loving grandparents.

Neither Joseph nor John was patient, though, so no waiting lay ahead. Alex was going to find out he was a father as soon as Joseph summoned him home.

Chapter Seven

When Alex didn't bring home a fiancée soon after the fundraiser, Joseph had been surprised and disappointed. He'd been sure that his son and Jessica would have an instant connection and make the perfect couple, but Alex had returned the confirmed bachelor he'd been before and hadn't said a single word about the girl.

Joseph had then gotten his hopes up, once more, as he'd watched Alex moping about and not in a hurry to travel off to his beloved faraway places. But after a month, Alex started disappearing again and his life returned to its normal schedule.

After lunch with John, Joseph had a suspicion of why his son had been so down. Alex still had that empty look about him, but all that was about to change. When Alex walked in the door, he did not look pleased that Joseph had asked him to rush home.

"You'd better sit down, Alex. I have news that's about to change your life," Joseph told him.

"Whatever it is, spit it out, Dad. I had a twenty-hour flight and didn't get any sleep. I want to have a hot meal first and then to fall face first into bed," Alex said. His drooping eyes and haggard face underscored his exhaustion.

"You're a father," Joseph said crisply.

Suddenly fully awake, Alex stared at his dad as if waiting for the punch line. Their eyes were locked together, with Alex seemingly frozen to the spot and neither of them speaking.

"Would you care to elaborate?" Alex finally asked.

"I met your child a couple of days ago. You have a three-month-old son," was the only elaboration Joseph gave.

"That's impossible…" Alex began, when he suddenly stopped. Joseph could see the wheels turning in his head.

*****

Alex started thinking back to his night in the elevator. He'd had unprotected sex only one time in his life. He began doing the math in his head, and the time line fit.

"But it was just that once…" He stopped again. He hadn't slept through all his classes. He'd taken human biology, and he knew how to spell *denial*.

Alex's legs could no longer support him, so he sank into the chair directly behind him. "Why…why wouldn't she tell me?" He managed to squeeze the words out of his constricted throat.

"I don't know the whys. All I know is that I met your son, and I just knew. Would you care to see some pictures?"

"Please."

Joseph passed the pictures over without saying another word.

Alex stared down at them, and when he finally looked at his father, there were tears in his eyes. "It must be true. He really is mine. I'm a father." He placed his head in his hands and let it all sink in.

It didn't take Alex long to go from shock to anger. How dare Jessica keep his son from him? He hadn't mistreated her in any way, and she had no right to keep something this important to herself. She *would* explain herself, and he wouldn't miss out on a second more of his son's life.

"I need to leave."

"I know," Joseph replied.

Alex looked at his father for a moment, wishing he could see into the man's mind. His father's face was solemn and serious, but he knew that gleeful twinkle in the old man's eyes — not what Alex would have expected, considering a child produced out of wedlock was involved.

Without saying anything more, Alex got up and walked out the door, almost in a trance. He stood next to his car and took several deep breaths of the cool Seattle air before allowing himself behind the wheel. He would do his son no good if he crashed on the way to meeting him.

As he began driving, wonder filled him as he realized that in only a few minutes time, he'd probably be holding his son. He hadn't thought he wanted to be a father, but the warmth he felt in his chest contradicted what he'd always told himself. The miles seemed endless as he weaved through traffic toward Jessica's apartment.

"I'm here to see Jessica Sanders," he said to the man at the security desk in the secure complex.

"Name please?"

"Alex Anderson."

"We don't have you on the list," the man said as he looked up with suspicion; then his eyes widened. "Oh…uh…sorry, Mr. Anderson…but…I…uh…don't have you listed as an approved visitor."

"Yes, that must just be an oversight. You're aware that I have access to the entire building, right? I want to surprise Ms. Sanders since it's been a while since I've seen her. So, if you'll give me her apartment number, I can be on my way," Alex said with authority. Normally, he wouldn't have been so short with an employee who was only doing his job. Luck was on Alex's side that Jessica happened to live in one of the many properties throughout the city that his family owned. Getting in to see his son might have proved far more difficult.

"I'll just…um…get my supervisor," the employee said before quickly pushing a button and mumbling something into his handless phone set.

Alex managed to hold onto his temper — but just barely.

"Mr. Anderson, I'm so sorry about the delay, but you know how your family feels about security," the supervisor said as he came through the door.

"I understand, Don, and I'll be sure to let Lucas know what a fine job you're doing here," Alex told him with a tight smile on his face.

"Thank you, Mr. Anderson. I have Ms. Sanders' information here," he said quickly.

Alex noted her apartment number, then headed straight for the staircase. He needed the exertion of climbing the stairs to stabilize his adrenaline. When he reached her floor, he paused, taking a few deep breaths to calm himself. Only then did he knock on her door and then wait as the seconds dragged on.

Finally, the door opened, and Jessica was standing in front of him, her eyes wide — filled with a mixture of shock and fear.

"Where's my son?"

There was no "Hello, it's been so long; how are you?" Alex didn't have the time or the energy for small talk. He was exhausted and angry and at the end of his patience for the day. He couldn't believe she'd dared keep his child from him. Yes, he hadn't bothered to call her, but he had his reasons for that. She'd affected him in a way that scared him to his very soul, and he hadn't trusted himself near her. Heck, even with anger coursing through him, he couldn't help but drink in the sight of her.

He noticed the soft thickness of her longer hair, which was cascading across her face and down her neck. She wasn't wearing a spot of makeup, and the dark circles under her eyes stood out, showing her lack of sleep. But it did nothing to detract from her looks.

What he noticed most about her was the new glow practically radiating from her skin. Just looking at her was messing with his head — and points south. It had been a year since that night, a full year, and yet not a single day had gone by without thoughts of her.

He had to remember what she'd done to him, the amount of time with his child she'd cost him. If he didn't, he suspected he could easily lose himself again in her eyes.

*****

Jessica stood frozen in the doorway, beyond petrified as she gazed at Alex. She'd been terrified the other night when she saw Joseph and Katherine, but they hadn't seemed to realize the baby was their grandson, so how had Alex found out about his son? She'd told absolutely no one, not even her best friends, and they'd badgered her endlessly.

He looked even better than she remembered, even with the shadows dancing beneath his eyes and his hair looking as if he'd dragged his fingers through it a dozen times. The sexy five o'clock shadow covering his chin made him appear more touchable, and his scent, with its mixture of masculinity and sensuality, drifted seductively around her, filling her nostrils, awakening her senses, bringing back erotic memories she'd tried so hard to suppress.

She realized, in that moment, how very much she'd missed him — more than she should have. She thought about him often, of course. How could she not, when she saw him in the face of her child each day? Jacob looked so much like his father, especially around the eyes.

She'd fallen for Alex when she was an awkward teenager, and then fallen even harder that night in the elevator. She didn't believe in love at first sight, but she had never been able to get Alex from her mind, even though she'd always known he was far out of her league. He always had been. Money wasn't the issue — she had plenty of her own. It was his confidence, his aura of superiority. She'd always been timid, insecure, no match for a man like him.

"Alex, what are you doing here?" she asked with slight exasperation. She wanted so much to sound neutral, though her heart was beating erratically and she felt as if she could possibly faint, her knees threatening to buckle beneath her.

Alex stood silently looking at her, a simmering rage burning through his eyes. Beyond the rage, she saw something else, though, something that was far worse than any amount of anger he could project — pain.

With a blink of his eyes, the shutters came down and the window into his soul disappeared. She was once again gazing into the eyes of a stranger — a very irate stranger.

*****

Alex chose to ignore Jessica's question. She was obviously stalling, and too much time had been wasted already. He wouldn't let her push him away, so he repeated himself. "I asked you a simple question. *Where is my son?*"

He wasn't known for having a great deal of patience on an ordinary day, and with the news of his being an instant father, the day was far from ordinary. He refused to stand in her doorway when his child was only a few short feet away.

Before she was able to say anything more, he heard a cry from inside the apartment. His eyes rounded with wonder at the first sound he heard from his son.

He was done standing on the doorstep.

Alex grabbed Jessica by the waist and physically removed her from his path.

He heard Jessica release a shocked gasp, but he was already halfway across the living room. He ignored the sound of her footsteps as she chased after him.

"Alex, I do have a son, but he isn't yours," she tried to claim. He'd reached the swing the baby was rocking in, and he was gazing down in fascination when her words slammed against him.

At Jessica's words, Alex whipped his head around, facing her with a look of contempt. She took a step back seeing his violent expression. Good! She should be afraid of what he was going to do next. Normally, Alex was about the most laid back guy around, but at the moment his blood was boiling.

No, he would never hit her, but if she dared to try and keep his child from him for a moment longer, he would have no aversion to taking her to the courts. He might have felt something for Jessica, but what she'd done, costing him the first three months of his son's life, was unacceptable, and he wanted her to pay.

"Don't you dare try to lie to me for one more second, Jessica. You've already stolen three months of my son's life from me. You won't deceive me one more minute. Do I make myself clear?"

He was beyond threats, his anger was so great. How dare she deprive him of the knowledge that he'd created a life! And yet as he turned back toward the innocent expression on his son's face, his outrage started to dissipate. How could he stay upset when he was looking at the most impressive creation he'd ever witnessed?

He couldn't.

Chapter Eight

Jessica knew trying to deny it again would only unleash more of his resentment, so she sank to the couch as her knees grew weak. She said nothing else, just watched as Alex stared at their child. Jacob eventually became tired of the staring game and let out a cry of displeasure. He wanted to be picked up.

She started to rise, but Alex was already taking care of him.

"Hey, little guy. You want your daddy?" he lovingly spoke. The adoration in Alex's voice brought tears to her eyes. He unlatched the safety belt and gently pulled Jacob from the seat.

She'd thought she was doing the right thing, but as she looked at the unadulterated love in Alex's eyes as he gazed in wonder at their son, she wasn't certain anymore. Perhaps she owed him, but she certainly didn't know how to make things right.

She suddenly felt like an intruder in her own home. She brushed the thought aside. This was her apartment, and she'd done just fine on her own with Jacob. The fact that Alex was a father didn't mean he'd be sticking around. She'd done him a favor by not telling him. He'd obviously made it clear that children weren't for him…

Even as she argued with herself, she wished she had handled things differently. Yes, he probably had the right to know. But if he expected her to sit there like a doormat while he snarled out his self-righteous wrath, he might well be quite surprised at her response. Motherhood changed a woman, and she was no longer the shy, retiring Jessica she once was.

*****

Alex held Jacob close to his chest, never taking his eyes from the tiny bundle in his arms. He was amazed at the love flowing through him. How could something so small completely claim his soul in the space of a single heartbeat? He had no doubt this was his boy. He looked like an Anderson — strong and proud.

Jessica had a lot to answer for.

He sat on the couch and softly spoke to his son. The baby looked at him and cooed for a while before his face scrunched up and he let out another full-fledged roar of displeasure. Alex turned to Jessica with a worried look. "What's wrong?"

"He's hungry. Give him to me, and I'll take care of his dinner," Jessica said, reaching her arms out.

"I'll feed him. Just grab me a bottle," Alex responded, not wanting to release Jacob.

Jessica looked uncomfortable, and then Alex noticed that the front of her shirt was damp. His groin tightened as the thin fabric suddenly hid nothing from his view. Her wet nipples were clearly showing, reminding him it had been a very long time...

Alex didn't say another word. He handed the baby to her, then got up and walked from the room, giving her privacy.

*****

Jessica let out a relieved sigh when Alex was gone. She quickly quieted Jacob, smiling as she looked into her son's relieved face. He took no time latching on, and he always let out a tiny growl that seemed to say, *"Finally, Mom. I was so hungry."* Jacob was so much like the father he was meeting for the first time. He had little patience when he wanted something. She'd have to work on that...

She enjoyed these moments together, stroking her son's head while he filled his stomach. He closed his eyes in concentration and made little gulping sounds. She leaned her head against the back of the couch and sighed out loud. She tried to convince herself she'd only imagined that look of instant lust in Alex's eyes when she answered the door, but she'd felt the same sensation, leaving little doubt that their desire for each other hadn't faded. It made no sense.

Anyway, it didn't matter how much she wanted him, or if he wanted her. That was a closed chapter in both their lives. They'd kissed once as teens, then had steamy, mind-boggling sex in a stalled elevator car, and finally walked away from each other. It wasn't as if they'd been a real couple...

But still...even in his obvious anger with her, desire had shone through those expressive eyes, reminding her of how very lonely she'd been. As much as she loved her son, it would have been nice to have an adult to share the tender moments with. She shook away from such thoughts and concentrated on Jacob instead.

*****

Alex wandered into his son's nursery. Jessica had done a beautiful job decorating it. There was a painted mural of elephants and bears, and in the corner a dancing monkey on one wall with bright, attractive colors, instantly drawing his eyes. The monkey caused a shudder to pass through him and he quickly looked away. He walked to the crib and ran his hand along the quilt his son slept under every night. He looked at the wall above the bed, and the breath rushed from his lungs.

There, on the wall, visible to his son, was a frame with several pictures of him in it. He knew the baby was too young to recognize people, but it filled his heart with joy that she'd thought to let Jacob know who he was.

Some of his animosity instantly vanished as he stood in the room his son slept each night. How could he be filled with rage when he was going to get to know his child? Even if it was three months too late — three months that he'd never get back.

As if Jacob were calling out to him, he couldn't stand to be away from his son and his son's mother any longer. He quietly walked from the nursery and stepped into the living room just in time to hear Jacob let out a loud burp, which Jessica praised. She then cradled him back into her arms, and Alex watched as Jacob latched onto her breast again.

He felt like an intruder, spying on the intimate moment between mother and son, but he couldn't turn away. It was obvious they had a strong bond. He was feeling a bit jealous he couldn't be a part of the ritual. He'd love to be able to hold her in his arms while she cradled their son.

He should want nothing to do with her, but the reality of the situation was that they were a family now. She'd given birth to his child, making her the most important woman in his life. His son and Jessica were — had to be —a package deal. Even in his anger, he knew he would never separate a loving mother from her child.

Once the baby latched on again, she leaned her head against the couch and closed her eyes. Alex finally entered the room and sat next to her. Her head quickly popped up and she stared at him with shock at his rudeness.

Jacob, seeming to feel her tension, let out a small protest and she broke their eye contact as she looked down. He watched as she took in a deep breath, and then lowered her shoulders in an obvious attempt to relax. She quickly glanced in Alex's direction. "Would you please hand me that blanket?"

He was disappointed when she used it to cover herself and he lost sight of his son. Still, there was an upside — he didn't have to look at her breasts. Not only had her curves grown in a most appealing way, but since their one and only time of having sex had been in a dark elevator, he was naturally curious to see what he'd touched and tasted on that hot night.

Jacob had apparently had enough to eat, because Jessica started fumbling underneath the blanket, and then she switched the baby to her shoulder and started patting him on the back. After a few minutes, he let out another burp and then started cooing at his mother.

"That's my big boy. Good job," she praised Jacob. He rewarded her by talking more gibberish.

"Can I hold him now?" Alex asked, though what he really wanted was to demand she hand him over. Bitterness resurfaced at the reminder he didn't have a routine with his son such as she had. She knew the boy, knew when he was hungry or tired, and knew what each cry meant.

Alex was determined to know his son just as well — starting right this moment.

Chapter Nine

Jessica reluctantly handed her son to Alex. Watching father and son together made her somehow feel as if she weren't needed in the perfect picture they made.

"Why did you place pictures of me by the crib?" Alex asked suddenly.

"I wanted him to know his father."

"He could have known his father in person, had you told me I was going to be one."

"Alex, we both know you're not the type of man to settle down. You have been in the papers with multiple women on your arm. There was no way that I was going to trap you into instant fatherhood because we had a one-night stand in a dark elevator. I would have told you about Jacob eventually, but I didn't feel it was the right time."

"I am not some irresponsible playboy who doesn't know when it is right to take responsibility for my child," he snapped.

"I wouldn't know that, Alex. I don't know you! We spent little time together when we were young, and then we had one night together. I didn't know what to do. I panicked."

"You chose wrong."

"I didn't think you'd want him. You're…" She trailed off, not knowing how to finish that sentence.

"So you're just the model of human decency? You do so much good among strangers that you don't feel you need to do right by people you actually know? And you just knew what choice I would have made without bothering to ask?"

His snide remark made her bristle. "Maybe I got my example from you."

"What the hell do you mean by that?" Alex put Jacob in his crib.

"I had no reason to believe you would care that you'd had some part in making another human being." He snorted, but Jessica continued. "You hardly showed yourself concerned about me or my future after our night together. You didn't go after me, or call me."

"You walked away, sweetheart."

"Of course I did. That's traditional for a woman after an unplanned night of…passion with a relative stranger. Doing so was especially appropriate because you were thoroughly disgusted with me."

"Disgusted? Where did you get that idea?"

"You hightailed it out so fast, you left tracks."

"I had my reasons, Jessica."

"Would you care to tell me about them?"

"I'd rather not." And Alex would most certainly rather not. Telling Jessica that he'd been afraid of being trapped by commitment wouldn't go over very well. "They're not relevant now. I'll admit I wasn't blameless. But your sin was greater than mine — you kept my son from me."

"And you showed yourself to be *so* responsible, Alex. Let's talk about tradition again. It's traditional for a man to check up on a woman's...health after a night of unprotected sex. Just in case there are consequences. And there were, but you didn't bother to ask, let alone send me a thank-you note. I don't think you wanted to know. As a matter of fact, I think you are simply trying to appease your conscience, or save face when speaking to our parents. I don't think this is about my not telling you about our son — I think this is only about your pride being wounded."

"Don't try to imply that everything was *my* fault, Jessica. You danced that tango, too. You were just as responsible as I was for what happened."

As their argument continued, Jessica grew more angry, and in her anger began to see that night very differently. What had been bright and almost magical was transformed into something dark and seedy. Such a classy guy — love in an elevator. She wanted to strike out at him, hit him where it hurt. His ego.

"Was I really responsible? Did you smell the wine on my breath? Yes, I know you kissed me, but your focus was clearly elsewhere that night."

"Wine?"

"I loathe parties, and I'd drunk a few too many glasses of wine. So your conquest was really a notch on your bedpost. Oh, on your elevator post. When our son asks how he was conceived, I can tell him that he was a miracle. I had sex for the very first time while I was drunk and in an elevator. I was with a man whom I barely knew and who definitely didn't want to know me." Gosh, that was unfair. Jessica hated herself for what she'd said as soon as the words had left her mouth. But he wasn't a prize, either.

Your first time? You were a…?"

"Yes, my first time. But really, it wasn't so bad…" *Not so great, either*, she muttered beneath her breath, knowing he would hear. It was a lie. She'd felt incredible, but on her quest to hurt his pride, she couldn't help herself.

The two of them fell into an uncomfortable silence. Jessica moved around the room, straightening items that she'd left for later during her exhausting afternoon. She regretted telling him a lie to hurt him, but didn't regret it *that* much. He'd been the one to crash through her door demanding an answer. Well, she hadn't been prepared to give him any, so he'd gotten her wrath instead.

They were both in the wrong. He could stand there in his indignant anger all night, but it wouldn't change that fact that he had been just as capable as she'd been of picking up a phone, and even in this century it was still *traditional* for men to call women and not the other way around. He knew he hadn't used protection, and he should have at least asked whether she had. He had a duty to call on her to make sure she hadn't gotten pregnant.

Besides, if he was the type of man to have sex with women unprotected, he could have given her so much more than a baby. What was he thinking? The more she thought over it all, the angrier she became. What right did he have for throwing all of this at her?

Exhaustion was overwhelming her as she picked up the last discarded blanket and took the full basket to her small washer. All she wanted to do was sleep, but she couldn't do that right now. If she let the chores go for even a single night, the next day would be too overwhelming. Maybe she should consider her mother's words, and get some help.

Jessica had no idea how much Alex was beating himself up in his own head. He'd had no clue she'd been an innocent, and he was a man of honor. The rumors about him were much more gossip than fact.

Yes, he liked to be with women, but that he took them for a night on the town didn't necessarily mean he took each of them to his bed. But he certainly wouldn't listen right now if she tried to explain that. They were just too upset with one another.

When she finally stopped moving, Alex was gazing at her, and the light in his eyes made her stomach sick. She was afraid to hear his next words.

"We'll wed as soon as the license clears. My father's already making the arrangements. I spoke to your father on the way over here, and he agrees with me. I won't miss out on any more of my son's life." He spoke the words matter-of-factly. He said them as if the deal was done and she had no say in it.

Jessica picked up one of her son's colorful bendy ball toys and smiled bitterly at its yellow smiley face. "Give me a break. I won't — yes, *won't* — marry you, Alex. My son will not be raised in a home with parents trapped into a marriage that neither one wants." She dug into the toy with her fingers, then cast it down. "I've seen too many lives destroyed by rash decisions and rash actions. If you really want to be part of Jacob's life, and I have my doubts, then we'll set up visitation arrangements."

Alex simply smiled at her. It was obvious to her that in his mind he'd already made the only decision he felt possible, and as far he was concerned, there was no need to discuss the matter. What an arrogant, insufferable jerk.

"Do you really want to have our son labeled a bastard?" he asked.

Seething with rage, she spat, "How dare you? You won't use my son to get what you want, and you certainly won't call my child names!"

"Jessica, we *will* marry. My son *will* have my name. I have the full support of *both* our families. We would both lose all of their respect if we did anything less than that. I want my son in my life, full time. I don't want to be a weekend father. You owe me for keeping him from me, and *your* parents agree that we should marry right away. You're dishonoring both our families by not doing the right thing," he finished. His voice was more frightening because he wasn't getting angry or threatening. He was talking as if he were just stating facts.

Jessica stilled, bristling for a few moments, glaring at her knotted hands, then transferring her glare to him she looked up. She finally stood and left the room, walking into her office to make a phone call to her father.

John answered on the second ring, "Hello."

"Dad, what did you and Alex talk about?" she asked, not bothering with any pleasantries.

"How are you doing?" John asked, ignoring her question.

"Dad, I asked you a question," she said, in no mood to play games.

"We talked about your upcoming nuptials, sweetie. When he found out he was a father, he told me he wanted to do the right thing. He wanted to marry you and be a full-time father to his son. You know how much I love you and how I will always stand by your side, but in this case, I support him, Jessica. I know you had your reasons for not telling him, but you don't keep a father from his child. It was wrong to keep Jacob from him," he said with disapproval in his voice.

Jessica hung her head, not liking to disappoint her father, but not ready to give up the fight. "Dad, I had my reasons, and some of them were very good. I won't get married because everyone is telling me what I should do," she said.

"Jessica, Alex wants to marry you and be with his child. He's a good man. Are you willing to bring shame on Joseph by having people think his son would get you pregnant and then walk away?" he asked.

Jessica didn't answer immediately. Her dad wasn't playing fair; he knew how much she loved her family and what deep respect she had for Joseph and Katherine. She'd never want to inflict pain or embarrassment on their family.

"I don't want to hurt them, but I don't love him, Dad. I can't live in a marriage like that," she pleaded, her emotions hanging by a thread. The crazy thing was that, despite everything, she could see herself falling for Alex, and that scared her more than almost any of it. If he left her once she was completely his, she might not recover.

"I'll support you no matter what choice you make; you know that. You also know Joseph has been a good friend to me, and it would mean a lot if you'd at least go through with the wedding. That way, Alex won't look as if he abandoned his son. If you're still miserable after a few months, you can rethink your choices, but at least Alex will keep his honor and Joseph won't be hurt," her father said.

The words he spoke made sense — in an alternate-universe sort of way. Though it went against everything she believed, it looked as if she'd be getting married, and she was, once again, with a man who wanted her only for what she could give him. At least this time it wasn't about her money.

After father and daughter talked for a few more minutes, Jessica hung up the phone, feeling as if her world had been upended. She took her time walking back out to the living room. When she entered, she felt a tear slip down her face when she saw Alex sleeping on the couch with Jacob held securely in his arms.

She picked the baby up, instantly jolting Alex awake. "I've got him…," he started to say.

"He's ready for bed," she said quietly, and then turned and walked toward the nursery.

She felt Alex behind her as she gently tucked her son underneath his blanket and waited a few moments to make sure he would stay asleep. Turning on his music box, she imagined him dreaming of swimming beneath the oceans with Nemo and friends. She wished her life were as simple as that of her son's.

She said nothing as she walked to the kitchen, with Alex following closely behind. After she prepared two cups of coffee, they sat down at the table and sipped silently from the steaming mugs.

"Jessica, we didn't get off to a great start, but I hope by now you understand what needs to be done," Alex said.

It was obvious from the expression in his eyes that he knew she would give in. At least she saw only relief in his face when she didn't contradict him — not victory or gloating.

"OK, Alex. It looks like you've won this round. I'll go ahead with this farce of a marriage, but I'm telling you, it's not a real one. I'll let you protect your family name, and when the time is appropriate, I'll file for divorce," she said with a strength coming through her voice that she didn't know she had left in her.

"There won't be a divorce," he said. "We'll make it work — for the sake of our son. I never planned on marrying, anyway, so it's not like I'm missing out on something else by being with you," he added, almost as an afterthought, as he took a sip of hot coffee.

What a gentleman! His words made her wince. He was basically telling her he could stand to be married to her because marriage meant nothing to him. She did not feel the same way. She'd always wanted to get married — she cherished the institution — but not like this. Yet maybe her situation wasn't that different from his. After all, she had given up on the idea of marriage after her last betrayal.

So she conceded that a loveless union awaited them both, and it would tear her apart. She was a mother now, however, and sacrifices were expected from her. She just hoped that this sacrifice wouldn't require her soul.

There was nothing she wouldn't do for her son. Her only regret was that their union wouldn't be real and she wouldn't be giving Jacob any siblings. She'd been an only child and had always wanted to have lots of kids when she finally settled down.

She loved her son more than she'd ever known was possible, and the thought of never having the feeling of carrying another child inside of her — of never again looking at her newborn for the first time — was almost enough to bring her to her knees with the heartache of it all.

"Alex, I'm exhausted. Can you come back tomorrow, and we'll figure out the details then? Jacob is still waking up a couple of times each night, and I wasn't able to take a nap this afternoon."

"I'll sleep in the spare room. I want to be here when Jacob wakes," he said, once again with that voice of authority she was coming to hate.

Jessica was too tired to argue any more that night. The thought of him sleeping only one wall away from her was enough to cause her stomach to tighten and her nerves to fray. She figured she'd need to get used to it, however, as they would permanently reside in the same house, and far too soon for her comfort.

She knew he wouldn't agree to her staying where she was now. He wanted them to marry only so he could be with his son and protect his family name at the same time. It defeated the purpose if they married and then lived apart.

"I'm going to bed." She said not a word more before she left the table.

Chapter Ten

Alex stayed where he was for several minutes after she left. He was barely able to stay awake himself, but the thought of her in bed, just down the hall, was playing havoc with his senses. Their one time together had been in a dark elevator and was over much too quickly. He'd be able to bring them both so much more pleasure in a comfortable bed.

His groin strained against the zipper of his jeans. He groaned aloud and then headed toward her bathroom for a cold shower. He wouldn't be taking them nightly, though, he assured himself. Once they were married, they wouldn't be sleeping in separate rooms.

Alex climbed into bed and gazed at the dark ceiling above him, wondering what his future had in store. While holding Jacob close to his heart, he'd felt an instant bond. He'd once wondered how Lucas, also a confirmed bachelor, could throw away his freedom for a wife and kids and not be miserable. Now, Alex understood a lot more.

If someone asked him to explain how he was feeling, he wouldn't know what to say. Real men didn't use the word *elated*. It was as if he'd been going through his life only halfway invested, without realizing anything was missing. Then, a steamroller passed right over him, and flattened out what he'd always believed he'd wanted and when he rose again — we all have our fantasies — he awoke to the possibilities he'd never even thought to imagine.

He marveled at how easy it was for him to instantly love a tiny human being, but he did. He loved his son with an overwhelming joy that brought a bright smile to his face even as he drifted off to sleep.

Alex was instantly jolted awake by the sound of distress coming from his son. At once fully alert, he glanced at the clock as he climbed from the bed, registering that it was three in the morning.

He walked into Jacob's room and gazed down at him in the crib. His son looked so tiny and fragile as he began kicking his legs in excitement as soon as he spotted his father.

Alex picked up his son and discovered that the child's diaper was soaked. When he babysat for his beautiful niece, he'd learned how to change her. Though he hadn't been particularly grateful at the time, the experience was coming in handy now. "You ready to get out of that dirty diaper?"

Jacob answered him with a giggle and kicked his legs more. Alex changed him, and then moved to the rocking chair and cuddled him for a while. Jacob's temperament changed after about ten minutes, and he looked on the verge of a major tantrum. Even after only a day with him, Alex knew his son wanted to be fed.

"Let's go wake your mom. *I* certainly can't feed you," Alex said with a chuckle. He walked into Jessica's room, with the light softly shining in from the hallway, and his heart skipped a beat. Her unguarded, peaceful expression almost took his breath away. In sleep, she seemed so young and innocent.

Jacob started wiggling in his arms — *time to eat!* — and Alex snapped out of his trance. He walked over to Jessica's bed and sat down.

*****

Jessica was awakened by a stirring on her bed. She jerked upright and looked around in terror and panic. "What's wrong?" she asked.

"It's OK," Alex said, placing a warm hand on her shoulder in reassurance. "Jacob woke up, and he's hungry. I already changed him, so if you feed him, I'll burp him and put him back to bed," he said.

Jessica was still disoriented, but she held her arms out for her child. "You don't need to stay up. We do this every night," she almost pleaded. She didn't want him there while her body was exposed. She had to face it — he still affected her, and she didn't want him to see how much. What if she just threw herself at him because it was the middle of the night and she wasn't quite awake?

"I want to be with him. If you get some of that bottle stuff, then I can take over the night feedings," he said, with hope in his voice. Jessica had to smile at his ignorance of the word *formula*.

"No, I like our nighttime ritual," she said simply. She figured it was dark enough that she could feed her baby without having to put him under a blanket. She liked to watch his face as he ate. She could gently caress his head and soothe him. He liked it, too, and would fall asleep quickly after he burped.

When Jacob made a little growling noise, followed by gulping sounds, Alex let out a quiet laugh, making Jacob jump. Surprisingly, he stayed latched on and slurped away.

"My son likes his food," Alex stated proudly.

Jessica smiled at Alex for the first time since he'd shown up at her door. She let down her guard for one short moment, enjoying the feeling of them sitting together like a real family.

*****

Alex couldn't help feeling he needed physical contact with Jessica and his son. He scooted a little closer on the bed, so his shoulder was pressing against hers. Reaching his hand up, he brushed the soft strands of hair away from Jacob's face.

Alex's eyes were locked together with Jessica's, and, unable to resist reaching toward her, he bent down and gently touched his lips to hers. Her taste was exquisite, and pleasure shot through his overheated body. He wanted her — badly. Only his son's presence kept him from taking her right there.

She pulled back, her breathing uneven, and looked down at Jacob's head. Alex's hand was still resting there, and the edge of his thumb was touching her breast. With another sharp intake of air, she twisted so that his hand would have to drop.

Alex felt his pulse increase. Though the light was dim, his eyes had adjusted and he had no trouble seeing the contrast of his dark thumb pressing up lightly against her light, creamy skin. He wanted to move his fingers, caress her, *feel* if she was as soft as he remembered her being.

He could remember the texture of her body as if it had been only yesterday they were together. Not being able to see her in the elevator had enhanced his other senses, and touching her silky soft skin had been pleasurable beyond imagination.

They were soon to be wed, so why shouldn't he hold her — caress her — ease both their suffering? He knew she needed time. For that matter, so did he. Yes, they'd have intimacy in their marriage — she was going to be his wife — of course, they would. *But* they needed to be able to tolerate each other as well. He wouldn't fight with her in front of his son; they'd come too close to that once. He'd been lucky enough to grow up in a healthy, positive environment, and he'd provide the same kind of atmosphere for Jacob.

Jessica pulled Jacob to her shoulder and quickly covered herself as she started to burp him. "Let me do that," he said, then gently took Jacob and placed him over his own shoulder. Jacob gave a loud burp and started rooting around Alex's shoulder, looking for more food.

The torture of having seen and touched her breast had been too great, and Alex wanted her too much to sit next to her in the bed any longer. "I'll let you finish," he muttered and left the room.

Two more nights, he told himself. He'd be lucky to get even a few minutes of sleep with the amount of sexual tension coursing through his body.

*****

Jessica breathed a sigh of relief as she watched Alex leave the room. She still had tingles zipping through her body where he'd pressed up against her, and especially where his thumb had grazed the top of her breast. She knew he was trying to be a part of everything, but she didn't think she had the willpower to have him next to her in bed. She'd been so lonely and so in need of affection for the past year. Add to that the extra hormones filling her body, and she was a ticking bomb racing toward detonation.

She'd be glad when the newness of the baby wore off and Alex backed off a bit. If he kept coming into her room in the middle of the night, she'd end up grabbing him and having a repeat performance of their night in the elevator.

How could one night with a man imprint him so deeply inside her very soul? She looked at their son and sighed. But Jessica had to be honest with herself, and she knew it was about so much more than just their son. Alex was dynamic in a way no other person even came close to being. He was intriguing and gorgeous beyond what any mere mortal should be.

And if she really wanted to be truthful with herself, she'd admit that he'd intrigued her since she was young, when she secretly watched him from the sidelines as he'd smiled that Anderson smile, flirted with all the girls, and had the boys following him around like puppy dogs.

She'd known he was far out of her league, even back then. Heck, he was still out of her league. If it weren't for Jacob, she most likely wouldn't have crossed paths with Alex Anderson ever again.

What had happened in the elevator... Well, it was unexplainable, just a freak occurrence for two people in a dangerous situation who had lost their minds for a short period of time.

As she looked at Jacob, though, she couldn't regret her impulsiveness. She loved her son too much ever to regret the moment he'd been created.

She finished feeding Jacob, placed him in bed, and fell into a much needed sleep, her thoughts turning into dreams, dreams that would leave her aching when she woke.

Chapter Eleven

"I hope you enjoy eggs, because that's the one dish I'm famous for, both near and far," Alex said as Jessica came into the kitchen.

He could see from her startled expression that she wasn't expecting him to be in such a good mood. Let her wonder...

The day was beautiful, he had a son, and he refused to dwell on things he couldn't change. He had woken up with that on his mind, and he decided to cook breakfast, then take Jessica and Jacob out for a stroll.

"Um...sure," Jessica finally answered.

"Great! Have you fed Jacob already?"

"Yes," she answered with some hesitation.

"Perfect. I brought his little bed thingamajig in here so you could set him in that and treat yourself to a nice long shower. I'll watch him while you get ready for the day. I want to take Jacob to play at the park."

"He's too young for the park, for anything other than staying in his stroller," Jessica said, her eyes rounding. Alex could see he was overwhelming her, but too bad. He figured the only way for them to get past all the awkwardness of their situation was to move full steam ahead.

"You're never too young for the park. There are baby swings. I'll have Lucas meet us there with Jasmine. You'll just adore her. She's about the sweetest little girl in the entire world. Have you met Lucas's wife, Amy?"

"Um...no. I don't think so," Jessica murmured.

"She's great, too. I never thought Lucas would get married, but once you meet Amy, you'll see why he took the plunge. She's about as perfect as a woman gets."

Alex noticed a hurt expression flash across Jessica's features, but in a blink it was gone, so he thought he might have imagined it. He was hardly trying to make the situation more hostile.

"I'll...um...take you up on the shower idea," she mumbled, then buckled Jacob into the contraption sitting on the table. She turned and practically ran from the room.

*****

Jessica shut the bathroom door as the first tear fell down her face.

"It's just your hormones, that's all," she said out loud to her reflection in the mirror. "No need to get all worked up. Who cares if he thinks his brother's wife is perfect? It doesn't matter to you. You don't love him. You don't want to get married."

After her little pep talk, she took in a deep lungful of oxygen, and then turned the shower on to as close to scalding hot as she could stand it. She hadn't had the luxury of a long shower in more than six months. At the end of her pregnancy, she'd been afraid to stay in too long, in case she'd relax so much, she'd never make it out. Then, as a new mother, she just didn't have time to shower for more than five minutes. What if Jacob needed her and she didn't hear him?

As she stood beneath the hot spray, she felt the tension in her neck and shoulders start to ease. She stayed there until the water ran cold, then climbed out, barely able to see past the heavy steam in the room. She'd forgotten to turn on the fan again.

She quickly did her best to dry off, then threw on her robe and opened the door. The cooler temperature of the rest of her apartment slapped her in the face, and she shivered as she rushed to her room and quickly bundled up.

If Alex was planning to have them walk around outside, she'd need to dress in layers. She was cold on a normal basis, but with the cool fall wind drifting over the water surrounding Seattle, it was even worse than normal.

"You ready to go?" Alex asked, making her jump as she stepped into the living room.

She looked around, noticing that Alex had found Jacob's stroller and diaper bag. The baby was sound asleep and buckled in. They weren't wasting any time.

"Go ahead and eat first," he said. "I left your food on the warming tray, so it's good to go. I'm going to throw on a few more layers of clothes. I found Jacob's blanket-coat thing."

Alex practically jogged from the room, making Jessica feel as if she was in a wind tunnel. She walked to the stove and picked up the plate he'd kept warm. *Thanks a bunch*, she said to herself. She stood at the counter, forcing down a few bites. She needed the fuel or she'd never be able to keep up with her son, let alone Alex.

As she was rinsing her plate, Alex joined her back in the kitchen, bundled up and ready to go.

"Let me grab my coat," Jessica told Alex as she began walking toward the closet. "Can you get the bottles from the fridge? I have a couple of spare ones with pumped milk for emergencies."

"You could have told me that last night and I would have gotten up with him and not bothered you," he said accusingly.

"I love my night hours with Jacob. It's our time."

"I wouldn't know when *our* time is, because I haven't gotten to be with my son. You're going to have to learn to share, Jessica," he snapped, his good mood cast aside.

"You can rebuke me all you want, Alex, but it won't change what's already been done. I'm sorry I kept the truth from you, OK? Do you want a pound of my flesh to make it all better?"

"Nothing that drastic, but you can start making me believe you're sorry by telling me the truth. I can feed him next," he demanded.

Melody Anne

Jessica decided it was best to avoid their dispute about Jacob right then. He wouldn't be rational; men rarely were. So to give vent to her feelings, she fastened on the last thing that he'd said. "Maybe you could feed me too sometime."

"What's that supposed to mean? I made your breakfast."

"Oh, that's what you called it. I am exhausted; I'm always exhausted. And yet you forced me to eat old, tired, stringy, warmed-over eggs while standing up so that you could force us to go out into the park on your schedule. I'll accept *your* apology, however."

"Where is *that* coming from?"

Unable to stop herself from guffawing, Jessica just grabbed the stroller and started moving toward the door.

"I'll push him," Alex said, his voice calmer, though with a hint of irritation.

"Fine," she said. If he wanted to be civilized, she would go along happily. She moved to the door and opened it wide so he could maneuver the large stroller though.

"It amazes me how many items are needed for one small human being," Alex said as they approached the elevator. "I would have never believed it before being around Jasmine. It's like packing for a vacation just to take her to the store. What's even more funny is that the bigger they get, the less stuff you need. The size of the stroller gets smaller, you need fewer items in the diaper bag, and even their car seat shrinks."

"I know. I was a bit shocked when I entered my first baby furniture store. Luckily, there were amazing employees there who helped me."

"Did you go to ours?" She knew he was referring to one of the Anderson department stores. She hadn't wanted to take even the smallest chance of running into Alex, so she'd gone elsewhere. She changed the subject.

"Have you already called your brother?"

He looked at her for a minute, then sighed. "Yes. Lucas will meet us in half an hour. Amy had an appointment she couldn't get out of, and she said to tell you she's very sorry she won't be there, and that she can't wait to meet you."

"That's too bad," Jessica said, and she was surprised to find that she meant it. She didn't have a lot of female friends — none at all who lived close by — and it would be nice to have another new mother to talk to. She hoped she and Amy got along.

They rode the elevator together in silence. Jessica was trying to deal with the fact that she'd have to share her child, and she was sure Alex wasn't speaking because of his irritation with her. *Well, join the club.*

They left the complex and walked the few blocks to a nearby park. As they arrived, Alex's phone rang, and Jessica tried to take the stroller so she could walk ahead and give him privacy, but he looked at her and silently mouthed the word *no*.

He spoke for a few minutes before hanging up.

"That was Lucas. Jasmine just threw up, so he won't be able to make it. He doesn't know if it was something she ate or if she's getting the flu. I'm sorry. I really wanted the kids to meet," Alex said as he glanced down at Jacob.

Jessica couldn't help but smile.

"You do realize that Jacob is only three months old and won't remember meeting anyone, right?"

"I know, but they'll start getting to know each other, and it begins with the first visit," he responded, scarily making perfect sense.

They arrived at the park and began strolling down a paved walk. Though it was cold out, the sun was shining and the Seattle residents were taking advantage of the rain-free afternoon. Several people were throwing balls for their dogs, while the playground was filled with bundled-up children squealing in delight as their parents pushed them on swings and helped them down the slides.

"Do you come here often?"

"Yes. Jacob can't play yet, but I've needed to get all the exercise I can. The first couple of months, I really struggled with the baby weight. It's been only in the last month that I've been able to get it off."

Alex gave her a long glance, taking in her body from head to toe, which made her start to squirm a bit beneath his intense gaze.

"You look as if you could actually put on a few pounds more, Jessica. I've always been fascinated with how beautiful a pregnant woman is and how her body is able to make room for this little being to grow inside her womb. Pregnancy has been good to you."

Jessica was stunned by his praise, especially when his glance rested appreciatively on her hips. She'd felt so worn out and frumpy lately that a little male attention felt good, even if she didn't want it to.

"Thank you," she finally murmured, not knowing what else to say.

Alex pushed the stroller into a small alcove with a bench, then quickly put his arms around her, stunning her as he pulled her body flush against his. Jessica's pulse quickened as she looked up into his sparkling blue eyes.

"We had a reckless night together that ended up creating an unimaginable blessing for both of us. We can either dwell on the negative of the situation or look for the good. I still want you, Jessica. Seeing you again has only added to that desire. I can feel that you want me, too. There's no point in fighting it."

With those words, he lowered his head and captured her lips, instantly sending heat rushing through her body. Forgetting her fears, her feeling of entrapment, forgetting that she was supposed to be on guard against Alex, Jessica opened up to him and enjoyed the heat of his kiss as he ravished her mouth.

A group of teenagers walking by and giggling dragged Jessica from her sexual haze, and she pushed against him to get free. She secretly felt a bit of womanly pride at the look of lust filling Alex's eyes.

"We'll be good together," he promised as he let her go and checked on Jacob, who was still sleeping contently in the stroller.

Jessica didn't know what to say, so she walked next to him in an almost trancelike state as they continued meandering through the park. Despite its inauspicious beginnings, their morning turned out to be quite pleasant. They began chatting companionably, both of them steering clear of confrontational topics, and instead enjoying the warm rays of the sun shining down on them through the crisp autumn air.

When Jacob awoke, Alex tried to feed him, but the baby found fault with his bottle and began throwing a fit. Alex handed him over with reluctance, and Jessica gladly held the baby against her chest. She was back to her beloved routine. She knew she was going to have to share, but she wasn't ready to share everything — and feeding time was hers alone.

When hunger started making her stomach growl, Alex brought her to a small café close to her apartment. Jacob rested in Alex's arms while they had a small lunch, and Jessica was careful not to mention breakfast again.

It was only early afternoon when they arrived back at her small apartment, but it felt as if they'd been gone all day and night. Thank heavens Jacob wanted another nap.

Minutes after Jacob was safe in his crib, she dropped off to sleep. Her last thoughts before blackness took over were fantasies of lying entwined in Alex's arms after a much needed session of lovemaking.

Chapter Twelve

What a day to be exhausted.

Today was the day of Jessica's wedding, and she felt as if a panic attack were plotting its ambush. She had to keep telling herself that everything would work out for the best, but her little lectures were less than convincing. She went through her morning routine with Jacob, and then she was whisked away to the wedding site.

"I'll take Jacob for you so your mother can help you finish getting ready," Joseph offered.

Jessica jumped at the sound of Joseph's voice. She hadn't heard him walk up. *The man sure moves quietly for a guy his size*, she thought.

"I'd appreciate that, Joseph. He's had his breakfast, so he should be in a good mood for a while."

"You look beautiful," Joseph told her and then bent down and planted a kiss on her cheek before heading out of the room.

Jessica's mother came in to help put on the finishing touches.

"How are you feeling, darling?"

"Terrified," Jessica answered honestly.

"I know you've been pushed into this by your father, and I just want to let you know that we can turn around and walk out the door right now if you want. I won't think any less of you," her mother said, bringing tears to Jessica's eyes.

"You don't know how much I needed to hear that, Mama. This has all been so much pressure, and Alex is just…always there. One part of me wants to run and hide," she said as her tears now fell freely. "The other part sees what an incredible father he is. If I have to serve some penance for keeping him away from Jacob, I'm willing to do it."

"Baby, you don't have to sacrifice yourself for your child. Jacob will love you and grow up healthy and happy no matter what you choose. You can't be a great mother if you're miserable," her mom told her.

Jessica thought about her words for a few minutes, while still contending with tears. Did she want to walk away? She honestly didn't know. She hadn't had time to think the last few days. Alex was just there — always there.

She had to admit he was a huge help with Jacob, though. He fed and changed him, played with him, and let her take naps without fear of not waking when Jacob needed her.

"No. I want to do this, Mom. I really didn't think I did, and the big wedding is overkill, but I think it's right for him to be with Jacob as much as I am. I can make it through this without getting my heart broken because I know it's temporary," she said. Her tears dried as she strengthened her resolve.

"Those words break my heart, Jessica. I want you to marry for love," her mom softly replied as her own tears welled up and spilled out.

"Mom, this is the real world, and sometimes we don't get it all. I'm OK, though; I promise," Jessica reassured her.

The two women held each other tightly until they couldn't delay the wedding any further. When the third knock on the door came, they finally broke apart and her mom answered, telling her father they'd be right out. Jessica didn't want to imagine what Alex was thinking at that moment.

The walk down the aisle went by in a blur, and the next thing she knew, the minister was speaking.

She was standing at the altar, next to a man she barely knew, and she was closer to having a panic attack than she'd ever been in her life. He looked so handsome and yet so aloof. She was wishing for some divine intervention to stop this absurd circus. Maybe he'd come to his senses and tell her he couldn't go through with it. If it was his choice, she could walk away free of guilt. But was that really what she wanted? Did she want him to leave? She didn't even know anymore.

No ancient god descended from the skies, and no one stood up with just cause to halt the wedding. Nor did her groom turn on his heels and walk away.

Instead, the minister pronounced them man and wife. Before she had time to blink, Alex was pulling her into his arms. The rest of the world disappeared as his mouth fastened onto hers. She'd expected a chaste kiss, but she was wrong. He coaxed her mouth open and then had her forgetting her worries in seconds.

Her knees went to jelly, and she would have slid to the floor if it hadn't been for his arms supporting her. When laughter rose from the pews, along with a lot of throat clearing, he finally pulled away, and she was left to stand beside him with one of his arms around her. She gazed blankly at the mass of people before her.

She was officially Mrs. Anderson now, and she and Jacob were no longer their own little world. A mixture of emotions flowed through her, but she wasn't miserable, just worried — worried her life would never be the same again.

Taking Alex's hand, she walked back down the aisle, even managing to smile at her parents and some of the other guests present. She would be OK, because she was determined to be.

*****

"Share that pretty bride of yours," someone called out.

"I'm claiming the first dance after my brother," another voice hollered with a chuckle.

"You can back off and find your own wife, Mark," Alex said. He sounded almost jealous.

"Doesn't feel so good to be on this side of the ribbing, huh, little brother?" Lucas goaded him while thumping him on the back.

Alex knew he deserved the teasing. He'd given Lucas hell not that long ago, when his big brother had started dating Amy. Lucas had been trying to fight his attraction toward Amy, so Mark and Alex had decided to push their brother's buttons.

Each of them had planted a kiss on her in front of Lucas and flirted shamelessly. Amy had known they were kidding around, trying to get a rise out of their brother, but now Alex regretted what he'd put Lucas through, because he sure as hell wanted to punch Mark out for even thinking about pulling Jessica into his arms.

"I guess hindsight is always better," Alex said with a sheepish grin.

"Yeah. I went a bit nuts when I was dating Amy. I can't believe how hard I fought against the happily-ever-after. When it hits, it hits, and nothing will stand in its path. That's why they say love can move mountains. It's an unstoppable force," Lucas said as his eyes sought his wife and child. "Hell, you can see I'm now a master of the romantic cliché!"

"You're one of the lucky ones, Lucas."

"Well, you've joined the ranks, little brother. Congratulations."

"Nah, Jessica and I have an understanding, that's all. She's the mother of my child," Alex countered, starting to become uncomfortable.

Lucas looked at him and laughed outright. Alex glared as Lucas took his time pulling himself together.

"Fight all you want, Alex, but you *will* fall…" Lucas trailed off before leaving Alex by himself. Alex glared after his brother.

Chapter Thirteen

A shudder ran through Jessica's body as she watched the interplay between the brothers. She couldn't hear what they were saying, but it looked intense. Both men — heck, all three brothers — were so virile and appealing.

Alex had his faults. Boy, did he. But was it a wonder that she had eyes only for him? He was the most sensual man she'd ever been around, and in any other circumstances, she surely would have exulted to be held and kissed by him.

Jessica glanced over to where her father was laughing at something Joseph said. She tried to stay mad at both men for manipulating the whole situation, but she knew they only wanted what they deemed best for her and her son. She loved them to death, but she didn't like the methods they used to get their own way.

As if the men knew she was thinking about them, they both turned and gave her a smile. She was too frazzled at the moment even to pretend to smile back, so she turned away and let her thoughts continue to run.

Things could be a lot worse, she decided. Alex was a sexy, incredible man, and it was obvious he was already in love with his son. She could have been forced into a marriage in which the man resented not only her, but her son as well. She knew, no matter how Alex felt about her, he'd always love Jacob.

"Time for photographs," she heard a voice call. She grimaced until Alex looked her way, their small son resting in his arms. For one moment, they shared a real smile. Her mask fell away and the love she had for her son and the love that was starting to grow for Alex was shining through her eyes. His breath seemed to catch and he was about to say something when the camera flash snapped them both.

He quickly walked over, no longer looking in her eyes, and bent down to speak quietly, making sure no one else could hear. "Let's get these pictures over with. We don't need to announce to everyone in the room that this is a shotgun wedding." He placed her arm through his and headed toward the rest of the family.

Jessica's eyes flashed fire and ice. "Come on, Alex. Everyone knows why we did this, so I don't see why we need to have this huge masquerade. We could just as easily have taken care of our marriage in a courthouse and not put on a big show."

"There's no way my father would ever allow one of his sons to get married that way, and I'm sure your father feels the same. Jessica, this marriage may be happening because of our son, but we *are* married now. It needed to be started this way. Something about our relationship needed to be done correctly."

Jessica gave in without any more protest and put on a happy face for the photographer as he put her in many different poses with Alex and their family members. She felt as if her cheeks were going to crack, she'd been holding the same expression so long. All she had to do, though, was look at her son and she was able to continue.

Jacob may have been an unexpected surprise, one she didn't even know she wanted, but she couldn't imagine her life without him. There was nothing she wouldn't sacrifice for him. She'd give up her entire world to make his better. She could live in a loveless marriage because that meant her son was with his father and would be loved, cherished and spoiled.

The photographer was finally happy with the shots he'd taken, and Jessica was able to step away and gain control of herself. She heard a hearty laugh and glanced up to see Alex slapping his brother on the back, his features lit up with mirth. She sucked in a breath at the beauty of the man.

Jessica kept coming back to that thought: Alex was the most handsome guy she'd ever known — from his dark, silky hair, piercing blue eyes and devastating smile, to his rock-hard stomach and sculpted arms. When you added in the confidence, which was as second nature to the man as breathing, he was every woman's dream come true.

She knew there were plenty of women who would love to be in her place. They wouldn't have even cared if Alex loved them or not. They'd just love to have him on their arm. He was a trophy, for sure. The thought caused a small giggle to bubble up inside of her. She'd heard of all the men with their trophy wives. Well, it looked like she'd snagged herself a trophy husband.

"It's time to head out back to the reception," Joseph said in his booming voice, which could be heard by everyone. The announcement made Jessica's head snap to attention. She thought this *was* the reception. Why did the wedding keep getting bigger and bigger?

She saw Alex hand their son over to his mother, and then he was at her side. "I know you're tired, but in a few more hours we can get out of here and rest," he reassured her.

They walked through the huge Anderson mansion and, as they crossed through the patio doors, she looked around in awe at the backyard, which had been transformed into a fairy tale. She'd grown up rich, but the Andersons' wealth made her family look middle class.

There was a white carpet laid out from the back door to a group of tents. Thousands of cascading lights looked like diamonds raining from the sky. Tables were set up with beautiful settings, and waiters were at the ready, loaded down with trays of champagne and hors d'oeuvres.

A small orchestra was playing in the center of the whole affair, with a beautiful dance floor waiting for people to occupy its space. As they walked out into the midst of everything, Jessica noticed that more people were at the reception than at the wedding. She knew some of them, but by no means all.

"Do you like everything?" Joseph asked, seeming to appear from nowhere.

"It's amazing, but you really didn't need to go to this much trouble. Some cake and champagne would have been fine."

Joseph let out a hearty laugh and then leaned down to kiss her cheek. "Only the best for my boys and the beautiful women they choose to marry," he said before walking away to visit with some of the guests.

"Try not to feel too overwhelmed. I got really flustered when I walked out these same doors on my wedding day, but now I'll cherish those memories forever," Amy said. Jessica was surprised to see Lucas's wife standing beside her.

Jessica knew the story of Lucas and Amy's rocky start. Amy had been working for Lucas and found herself pregnant with his child. They'd married for the sake of the unborn baby, but it was now obvious to everyone around them that they loved one another deeply and irrevocably. Alex was clearly following in his brother's footsteps, at least in one respect; Jessica hoped that Mark, if he ever got married, wasn't also led to the altar by an unplanned pregnancy.

Amy and Lucas had one daughter who was over a year old and was obviously adored. Amy was also looking very pregnant with baby number two. A perfect marriage for them. so why did Jessica experience a twinge of sadness? She just didn't see how she and Alex could end up with the happily-ever-after that Amy and Lucas had achieved.

"You startled me," Jessica finally managed to say to Amy. "This whole thing is a little overwhelming."

"I know how you feel. It doesn't seem like it right now, but you'll appreciate all of this someday. You'll have the pictures to look over and the memories of the perfect wedding to tell your children about," Amy said comfortingly.

Jessica didn't think she'd ever be appreciative of the wedding, but she wasn't going to voice that to her new sister-in-law.

She decided to change the subject. "How far along are you?" Jessica asked.

"Six months," Amy said, beaming. "I couldn't be happier. I love Lucas, Jasmine and this entire family, as well. My situation was similar to yours, not that long ago, but it worked out so much better than I could have ever imagined. This family loves big, and I've seen the way Alex looks at you. I know you're scared right now, but I want you to know I'll be there for you if ever you need a woman to talk to. Things do get better," she finished and then gave Jessica a hug before she had to take off to join her husband.

Jessica watched as the other couple embraced as if they'd been apart for months instead of mere minutes. Such obvious love radiated from them. Damn. She didn't expect ever to have Alex look at her the way Lucas was gazing at Amy. It was work, but Jessica finally shook herself out of her grumpy mood; what else could she do?

Once Jessica decided to let go of her worries, she found herself enjoying the reception. The cake was incredible, with its five tiers, and with glittering water cascading down the center in a fountain with cut crystals and polished gemstones. Tiny flowers and butterflies, created from fondant, were expertly placed on the cake's exterior. She was almost afraid to cut it and ruin such a work of art.

Alex swiped a piece of the frosting and stuck his finger in his mouth, making her stomach churn with desire. So dang sexy, and she had no idea why.

When Alex's hand fit gently over hers, they cut the cake, and her worries vanished completely. Whenever he touched her, the rest of the world could tumble down with an unceremonious crash, and she'd just tingle away, unaware. She looked into her husband's eyes and was drawn wholly within a new universe. He leaned down and kissed her intimately, to the delight of the crowd. His mouth tasted sweet from the frosting, and she could feel shivers running down her spine.

The laughter pulled Jessica from her thoughts. She fed him gently, and the look of lust in his eyes as her fingers grazed his mouth made her knees go weak. She started to tremble, praying the rest of the audience didn't notice. Then he fed her a small piece of cake, and heat shot through her body. She sucked his finger into her mouth, and the fire in his eyes created an ache within her that only he could satisfy.

When he wiped a piece of frosting from her lips and then licked the tip of his finger, she actually swooned. She thought swooning was something that happened only in the movies, but if he hadn't been there to pull her close, she would have fallen into the table.

His eyes smoldered dangerously, and he pulled her close, kissing her with far less restraint than he'd exhibited earlier. She wrapped her arms around his neck and gave into the passion she'd been feeling since he'd first walked through her door.

"Well, I guess that's some great cake." She heard the chuckling voice of her father.

Jessica's head snapped back, and she stared at her husband with horror. She couldn't believe she'd kissed him like that in front of so many people. He smiled down at her and turned toward the guests.

"We need to get this over with. I want my wife to myself."

"Hear, hear," she heard Lucas shout, as he lifted his glass in a toast.

Jessica heard the sound of Jacob letting his mom know it was time for his dinner, and she was relieved to get a few minutes of privacy as she took him into the house. She knew she was running, but she didn't care. It was time to regroup. As she rocked Jacob, she reflected on the overwhelming day.

She wasn't anxious to get back out to the reception. She knew most of the people there had to be talking about how poor Alex had had to marry Jessica to make his son legitimate. It made her very uncomfortable, even though it was obvious he wasn't averse to sealing their marriage in the bedroom if his public kisses were a preview of what was to come.

Even though no one had treated her badly, or said anything negative, they had to be thinking she'd trapped him. Although she had plenty of her own money, Alex Anderson was a real catch. He could choose any bride he wanted, but the choice had been stolen from him the minute he'd found out he was a father, because he had honor and that's how men like him operated.

As Jessica took a little longer to rock Jacob, she heard footsteps enter the softly lit den. "I'm glad to have a few moments to speak with you alone," Joseph said softly. "I know all of this has been a little much for you, and I just wanted to let you know how happy I am that you're a part of our family." He finished walking in and sat down next to her.

"I'm very pleased to join your family, Joseph. This is all just a little too much right now, though," she said with a nervous laugh.

"I understand how you feel, Jessica, but know you have a lot of people to turn to for support. Also, remember that lasting marriages have started with less going for them than what you and Alex have. I think your union is off to a great start. You have this beautiful baby boy, and it's obvious to anyone who watches that you and Alex have chemistry. I can understand if you're afraid to admit *love* yet, but I see the way you look at my boy, and it fills my heart with joy."

Jessica didn't know what to say. She didn't want to admit her growing love for Alex, but she couldn't tell his father a lie, either, so she smiled weakly and looked at the floor.

"Let me take that wonderful grandson of mine and lay him down so you can get back out to the party," Joseph offered. She was reluctant to hand Jacob over, but she knew she was being silly.

"Thank you" was her only reply, and then, empty-handed again, she had no choice but to return to the reception.

"It's time for our first dance as a married couple," Alex said the moment she returned, taking her hand and pulling her onto the dance floor. All her worries washed away again as he took her into his arms. Dancing intimately with him was little more than a prelude to sex. The way he moved his hips against hers and rubbed on her lower back had her insides burning.

When he bent down and kissed her on the neck, goose bumps appeared, and a small shiver spread through her middle. He gazed into her eyes, and neither of them needed to say a word. Her heartbeat accelerated as he whirled her around the floor, and she breathed a sigh of relief when the song came to an end.

She didn't think she would have been able to remain in his arms much longer without beginning to undress him. She'd never been such a wanton woman before she'd met Alex. One night in a dark elevator, and now she couldn't turn the heat down.

The next half hour passed slowly as she moved from one person to the next on the dance floor. A few tears fell during the father-daughter dance as the man who helped give her life told her how much he would miss having his little girl all to himself.

She laughed with both Lucas and Mark, genuinely enjoying Alex's brothers. That Mark hadn't been snatched up yet amazed her. Of course, from her understanding, all the Anderson males held onto their bachelorhood the way a rancher held on to his prize bull.

After being whisked around, she was once again in Alex's arms, and it felt like coming home. "Are you ready to get out of here?" he whispered in her ear. Before she had a chance to reply, the music stopped.

"I hope everyone is having a great time," Joseph spoke into the microphone. There was a burst of applause at his words.

"Good, good. Now I'd like to make a toast for my son and my beautiful daughter-in-law. I couldn't be happier to have you join our family, Jessica. You're a true blessing and a perfect match for our stubborn child, who, we happen to think, is just about flawless, although we were worried no woman would ever put up with him." The crowd erupted with laughter.

"All joking aside, we're grateful for this union and the blessing of our first grandson. Katherine and I both wish you the best and hope your marriage will be filled with laughter, joy and surprises. And, best of all, remember that a little fight now and again makes life exciting and gives you a chance to make up," he said with a wink.

"Katherine and I have a wedding gift for you that we couldn't quite gift wrap," he said with a chuckle. "A new family needs a real home — not some apartment in the city. We got you a place about a mile down the road from here. It's all set up for a nice honeymoon since Jessica doesn't want to hare off somewhere without the baby. We do insist on babysitting so you two can get some time alone, though. It's never too soon to start thinking about a sibling for Jacob."

Jessica gasped at his words, with embarrassment at his remark about time alone, and shock that they'd bought Alex and her a house. She couldn't believe

Joseph and Katherine had given such a generous gift.
What if this all fell apart within a week, or even a
month? So many people were already involved in
their union, and now she and Alex would have a
home, which she'd get attached to. She watched as
Alex strode over to his father and gave him a hug.
Then he did the same to his mom.

Jessica didn't realize that tears were falling down
her cheeks until Alex came back and gently wiped
them away. "If you don't like the place, we can find
something different," he said, mistaking her anxiety.

"No, it's just that we aren't in a real marriage.
This is all too much." She couldn't say anything else,
so she quickly hugged Joseph and Katherine before
excusing herself so that she could go check on the
baby.

This day had been a lot for her to take in, and she
knew she'd made the right decision. She just didn't
know how she was supposed to keep her heart out of
it. Just when she began feeling as if she were gaining
some control, something else would happen to knock
her feet out from under her.

Chapter Fourteen

Alex stood there, shocked for a few moments, and then he was angry. He led Jessica away to a bench near the house.

"So you wanted to speak to me, Alex? You've been awfully quiet."

Jessica looked up at him with those wide and oh so innocent eyes. It made him almost sick.

"Are you enjoying yourself, dear?" he asked tightly.

"Yes, I think I am. At times it's been a little stressful, but..."

Alex broke it. "I *was* enjoying both the wedding and my new bride. *Was* being the operative word."

"What's wrong now?"

"Everything was going just great, and then you had to remind me that it was a forced marriage. How considerate. I knew you were having a hard time with the whole situation, but a lot of people made a great effort to make it enjoyable for you. And what do you do? 'Not a real marriage,'" he said, in an unflattering imitation of her voice.

"I don't know why I'm surprised that you're pulling this again."

"Pulling what?" Alex rolled his eyes.

"Allow me to quote *you*. 'Let's get these pictures over with,'" she began, with an imitation quite as unflattering as his. "'We don't need to announce to everyone in the room that this is a shotgun wedding.' Very romantic of you, Alex. I quite enjoyed it."

"You are missing the point. What I said, I said in private. You announced our private business to the world."

"Oh, I get it. It's perfectly fine that you hurt my feelings on my quote-unquote *special day*. I did the unforgivable not by saying the exact same thing as you said but in front of other people."

"They were my parents," Alex said grimly.

"And your parents don't know that this isn't a real marriage?"

"That's immaterial. And anyway, do you have to turn everything into a fight, Jessica?"

Jessica's jaw went slack. "Um...I believe you were the one who started the fight, Alex."

"I had a right to be angry."

"And so did I. Look, I'm tired, and we're really getting nowhere fast. Can we just get along?"

Her eyes met his with such desperate pleading that he had to smile and agree.

"Shall we shake on it, Jess?"

"Excellent."

Just like that the situation was defused as both of them deflated, moving back to the reception and letting go of their little spat.

The party eventually slowed down, and they were able to make their escape. Jessica gathered Jacob while Alex grabbed their bags, and they ran through the throng of people to the waiting limo.

Birdseed flew, cameras flashed, and they were both more than grateful to be inside the safe confines of the limo. They didn't have a very far drive, thanks to the generosity of his parents.

Though this wasn't what he'd wanted, and he'd certainly thought his life would go a different direction, family was important to him. He was closer to his two brothers than any other man of his age, and he truly respected and loved his parents.

His marriage would work out because it needed to. Jessica and he would learn to respect and care for each other. Because they were now a family, there was no other option that was acceptable.

*****

Jessica was more exhausted and more nervous than ever. She was finally alone with her husband. Was he going to expect her to sleep with him, or would she be allowed her own room? Did she even want her own room? The thought of sharing a house with the virile, masculine Alex and not sleeping with him seemed worse than keeping her independence.

She'd have to have to wait and see what happened.

They arrived at the gated entrance within a few minutes. Jessica rolled her window down to peer out. The endless driveway was well lit and flanked by huge pine trees, offering privacy to the house, which was still hidden from view. Upon rounding another corner, she saw that the narrow road opened to a spacious circular turnaround done in multicolored brick. In the center was a magnificent water fountain with angels dancing in the center and splashing each another.

Jessica was left speechless. The home was a smaller version of the Anderson mansion. Balconies on three stories wrapped around the entire house, while five huge columns adorned the front, giving the home the look of a southern plantation. Fresh flowers hung from the eaves, and even in the night, the white walls sparkled.

Her parents had an impressive home, but this made theirs seem like nothing more than a shack. It was the type of place she'd dreamed of one day owning, where she could envision long summer evenings with a glass of lemonade while watching a sunset, and cold winter nights in a hot tub with a glass of wine. She was afraid to step through the front doors, because the minute she did, she knew she'd be even more in love and would never want to leave. She'd be devastated if she and Alex split up and she had to start over.

The driver opened her door, and she reached in for Jacob, but Alex had him already. "I can take him," she said, irritated with her new husband for taking control. He never seemed to stop.

"I've got him. Go ahead and look at the house. I'll come back for the bags in a few minutes."

She wanted to argue with his high-handedness but decided it wasn't worth the hassle. He would get his way once again, but she was exhausted — too tired to fight. The door opened, surprising her, as she didn't expect anyone to be there.

"Hello, Mr. and Mrs. Anderson. I have light refreshments for you in the kitchen, and your room has been prepared. Would you like for me to lay Jacob down so you can look about your new home?"

Alex handed Jacob to the woman, and Jessica immediately wanted to protest. She wasn't going to let him hand her child over to a stranger.

"Jessica, this is Tina, our cook. She's worked for my family for more than twenty years and is one hundred percent trustworthy," he said, noticing her concern. Jessica was still apprehensive, but she took a deep breath and slowly let it out.

"I'll walk with you to the nursery so I know where Jacob is going to sleep. Are baby monitors set up so I'll be able to hear him throughout the home?" Jessica asked.

"Yes, and you can carry around portable listening and video devices, too. It doesn't do to worry about a baby's safety in a house this big," Tina said as they climbed the grand staircase.

Upon reaching the second story, they continued down a well-lit hallway. "The master bedroom is here to the right, and the baby's room is directly across the hall. Mr. Anderson said you'd want the baby close by." Tina pointed out a few more doorways and then led Jessica into a lovely nursery. The walls were identical to what she'd done in her old place. Alex must have taken pictures and had someone reproduce her artwork. All her nursery items were there, along with many new items. She noticed the security camera angled in the corner and nodded with approval.

Tina laid Jacob in his crib, and Jessica bent down to kiss his soft cheek and cover him up. If she could, she'd stand there all day and night watching her son sleep.

"Here's the monitor, Mrs. Anderson," Tina said, handing over a small device. Jessica looked at it. Not only were their voices coming through, but her sleeping son appeared on the small screen.

"Thank you, Tina," Jessica said with real gratitude.

Jessica turned to find Alex right behind her.

"I tried to match Jacob's old room as much as possible," he said, in explanation of the decorations. "My father bought this home a while ago, in hopes that one day one of his boys would choose to settle down."

That explained how he'd been able to have the nursery prepared.

"It's lovely. Thank you. It has a lot more space than Jacob's old bedroom."

"This door over here leads to the nanny's room… Now, before you protest, we'll hire one together, and I know you would never neglect our son. It's simply a good idea to have a nanny here to help you. That way you can have some free time to do whatever it is you want, or need, to do."

"I in no way need a nanny." How dare think he could make such a big decision without consulting her? This was her child and her decision. She'd been doing fine taking care of her son on her own.

"I know you can't run off to foreign lands to help people out. Still, your father told me you had a passion for writing but hadn't been able to do any the last few months because you were either too exhausted or taking care of our son. I just want to give you a chance to be able to do what you want to do. You can still be with him full time. The nanny can be more of a helper for when you need her," he said.

"Is this your way of saying you don't want to help with his care?" Jessica knew the statement was unfair when she saw him flinch, but what else was she supposed to think?

They'd been married only a few hours and she was in a new home with strangers, her son's life was being altered, and now Alex was talking of hiring a nanny. She really needed rest.

"I want to be active in Jacob's life. I will be there for him every single day. It's just that I'll be working regularly, and I don't want you to ever neglect your own needs for our child. It seems you've been doing that since you became pregnant. It's something we can discuss more before a final decision is made."

After a pause, Jessica realized she was simply looking for a reason to fight with him. Exhaustion, frustration, and a lack of control were making her cranky. She could compromise slightly.

"I'll think about it" was all she said. The thought of writing again was tempting, but she worried that she would feel like a bad parent, or a selfish one, if she passed her child off to a stranger. But she probably wasn't thinking it all through clearly; she'd at least consider Alex's suggestion.

He was her tour guide for the rest of the home. Everything was decorated in accordance with the taste she showed in the furnishings of her apartment, so again, Alex hadn't been completely inconsiderate and autocratic. Jessica wasn't sure she liked admitting that after some of his stunts, but she had to be fair.

They completed the tour in the kitchen, where two other staff members were waiting for them.

"This is Edward, our gardener. He's married to Tina, and they live in the cottage on the back of the property. And this is Maria, our housekeeper. They've all been with my family as long as Tina, which is why I wanted them here."

"It's really great to meet all of you," Jessica said and shook their hands. The staff left them to eat the beautifully prepared food, and then an uncomfortable silence fell. Tina had shown her the master bedroom, and it scared her. She still wasn't ready to share a room with her husband every night. She needed more time to protect herself — to keep her heart out of this.

She would keep her things in that room but sleep in the nanny's space for now. That should take any strain away, at least for the short term, she told herself. When the silence seemed to stretch on forever, Jacob's cry came over the baby monitor. Jessica jumped up to take care of her son, relieved to have a good reason to get away from the awkwardness.

She changed Jacob, and then fed him. As she was laying him down, Alex walked into the room. "Hold on. I want to kiss him goodnight," he said, then gently touched his lips to Jacob's head. She had a very difficult time staying angry with Alex when he treated their son with such love. They stood over the crib for a few moments, both of them content to watch Jacob sleep peacefully.

"Let me show you to your room."

Jessica breathed a sigh of relief, although she felt a tiny twinge of disappointment at the same time. This is what she wanted, she had to remind herself. She didn't want to share his bed, yet she was pained that he didn't seem to want her to share his. She was a little curvier since she'd had the baby. Maybe he was turned off by her new body, though he'd claimed that he liked the way she looked after pregnancy.

Alex led her into the master bedroom and she stopped in her tracks. There was enough space for an entire apartment to fit into the huge room. The master closet alone was the size of her old bedroom. With the antique rug covering the gleaming oaken floor, and the walls graced by exquisite original works of art, it was truly a room fit for the master of the house. Maybe Alex was playing the good guy and letting her have the room. She was hardly about to complain.

When she went into the bathroom, she immediately fell in love. Without another word to Alex, she shut the bathroom door and began filling up the huge jetted tub, thankful for the bottles of toiletries arranged nicely in a basket on the counter. She'd need to thank Katherine for such thoughtfulness.

Not only had she and Joseph given them a home to settle in, but they had also gone the extra mile to stock it with the items that made it more comfortable.

Chuckling at the size of the tub, Jessica tested the temperature before adding just a bit more soap for extra bubbles. Then, she put her hair in a bun and stepped into the warm water. As she sank down to her chin and the suds surrounded her, a sigh of ecstasy escaped her lips.

She finally relaxed as the light scents took her stress away. The wedding was over, her son was peacefully sleeping, and Alex was giving her a bit of room to breathe. That last part, well, she wasn't so sure she was pleased about it, but since it was what she should want, she decided to be happy.

Jessica stayed in the tub for more than an hour, and then finally managed to pull herself from the cooled-off water. She wrapped herself in one of the luxurious oversized towels and walked through the doorway, wanting nothing more than to crawl into the huge four-poster bed and fall headlong into a deep sleep.

She began to pull the towel away, and then noticed Alex sitting on the bed in nothing but a pair of pajama pants. The sight of the raw power rolling off of him had her heart rate rising and her breath hitching. He had to be the sexiest guy she'd ever seen. With clothes on, he was enough to make her heart go from zero to sixty in three seconds — OK, sixty to a hundred. With clothes off, he could cause cardiac arrest.

"Wh…what are you doing here?" she stuttered. She was praying he wouldn't come toward her,

. because if he took her into his arms, she would be forced to surrender to her needs. Proof that she couldn't seem to say *no* to him was in the next room.

"I've been waiting for you. I hope you enjoyed your bath. I know it's been a long day," he said casually.

Jessica braced her shoulders. She knew she had to get all of her words out quickly or she'd lose her courage to do so. "Alex, I know we're married, but I'm not sharing a room with you. I can use the one next to our son's if this is where you are planning to sleep," she finished weakly.

Alex's eyes went from casual to smoldering in one second flat. He slowly stood and walked toward her. He was like a panther, stalking his prey, and she was so tense, her stomach was crawling up into her throat.

It wouldn't take much to fall head over heels in love with him, and that, she kept lecturing herself, would be disastrous. She took an involuntary step backward and then another as he closed the gap between them.

He slowly looked at her, from her head to her toes and back up again without saying a word. When his gaze finally reached her eyes, he and she were both breathing heavily. He placed one hand behind her neck and the other at the small of her back before jerking her body against his.

"Alex, this isn't a good idea..." she tried to tell him, but he swallowed her words as his lips took possession of hers. He kissed her with anger, rising passion, and need. She tried not to respond but, after a few seconds, she was giving just as good as she got.

Her hands wrapped around the back of his neck to pull him even closer. He was pressing her stomach into his obvious arousal and knowing that he wanted her was like throwing a lit match into a puddle of gasoline.

His hand slid past the bottom of the towel and began caressing the bare skin at the top of her thighs. She pressed even closer, and a moan escaped her lips. Just when she was ready to move to the bed with him, he pulled back and turned away from her.

What?!

Confusion filled her as he muttered beneath his breath. Maybe she was repulsive to him now. This was good, right? She needed to gain perspective, and if he didn't want to be with her, then she wouldn't have to fight him. Obviously, she was hopeless at pushing him away.

*****

They both stood in silence while trying to catch their breath. Alex cursed himself. He hadn't meant for the kiss to go that far, but she had a way of blocking out every thought in his head except for his desire to take her.

When he finally gained control over his raging body and turned to face her again, he barely managed to keep his hands to himself. Her breasts were still heaving, and he could see that she was trying to gain control, but she wasn't doing a very good job of it.

He almost lost his will to turn away from her at the look of desire shining in her eyes. He had to prove a point, though. He knew that later, when the ice-cold water from the shower cascaded down his body to bring him relief, that he'd have to try very hard to remember what that point was.

"You're my wife. You *will* be sharing my bed, and you *will* be my wife in every way that matters. I won't disgrace my son, or my family, by having affairs, and in case you haven't noticed, I'm a man with a man's needs. This marriage is for better or *worse*, and we'll make the best of the situation." He said all this in a smooth, calm voice, but he saw that it was making her temper rise.

Alex was enjoying the light of annoyance entering her passionate eyes. She was so easy to read, and he could see she was ready to explode. The desire in him was growing. It was going to take all he had to walk from the room. He wouldn't take her in anger, though.

Jessica walked up to him and slapped him hard across the face. He stood there, too stunned to move for a moment. When she saw the anger light his features, she backed up quickly, realizing she'd most likely made a huge mistake.

He caught her arm and whipped her back around to face him. "If you slap me again, you will feel my wrath," he snarled.

"Feel your wrath? What does that mean?" she snapped. Maybe she should be scared, but there was no fear. The only fear was of her reaction to him.

Alex looked at her as if he didn't know what to say. It would seem that he'd never had to explain himself before after making such an asinine statement. She almost smiled, before anger got the better of her again.

"You will *not* tell me what to do or how to be a wife. Our marriage doesn't give you power over me. It doesn't mean I will be sharing your bed. I make my own choices and decisions. *No* one makes them for me," she said.

Alex smiled at her with his confidence back in place after her questions. "You want me just as badly as I want you. I won't *make* you have sex with me. You'll be begging me for it." He then kissed her quickly before walking to the door. "I'll give you tonight alone…so you can miss me. Tomorrow, and every night after, we'll sleep in the same bed. The sex will be entirely up to you."

With those words, he walked out the door, leaving Jessica standing there, angry and confused because she feared he was right. He'd barely left, and she wanted to call him back to her. She sighed, knowing it was going to be a long night alone in the empty room, and even worse, empty bed.

Chapter Fifteen

Jessica walked down the stairs with Jacob in her arms. She was cranky and exhausted. Sleep had been elusive, and it showed. After the parting kiss from Alex, she'd stirred in bed, thinking about him...with her body on fire. When she'd finally started to drift into a restless sleep, Jacob woke up and, after he ate, decided he wanted to stay up and play.

By the second hour of walking the floors with Jacob, she was thinking her decision that Alex leave the bedroom had been too hasty. She certainly could have used a bit of help.

So she knew she had circles under her eyes after that long night. She hadn't even bothered with makeup and was wearing old sweats and a baggy T-shirt. She didn't care if she looked like something the cat would have been ashamed to drag in. She just wanted caffeine and about twelve hours of uninterrupted sleep. Blushing bride? Hah!

"Good morning, Mrs. Anderson. Would you like me to take Jacob so you can eat your breakfast?" asked Tina, while she placed a cup of hot coffee on the table.

Jessica almost replied *no*, but the aromas coming from the kitchen changed her mind. "That would be wonderful, if you don't mind."

"My husband, Edward, and I weren't blessed with children of our own. I'm really going to enjoy having a baby in the house. I'm looking forward to spoiling him rotten," Tina said with a wink and a smile. She took Jacob in her arms and when he smiled at her, she laughed with real joy, making him smile even more.

Jessica relaxed.

"I'll have Maria bring your breakfast out. Enjoy your meal," Tina said, and then she walked into the kitchen with Jacob in her arms.

Jessica ate in silence and felt her eyes begin to droop. She couldn't believe how tired she was all the time. She would really like to sleep for eight full hours, a luxury, she supposed, for every new mother. Would it ever happen again?

"Good morning. I hope you slept well," said Alex, sounding far too happy.

Jessica snapped fully awake. He didn't look as if *he'd* lost any sleep, she thought accusingly. In fact, he looked as if he'd never lost a night of sleep in his life. How she'd love to wipe that satisfied grin from his face.

"I slept incredibly," she said. She refused to look up and make eye contact. He'd easily be able to see from the black circles that had become permanent accessories beneath her eyes that she was just this side of lying through her teeth.

Alex sat down across from her, and Maria placed his coffee and food in front of him.

"Thank you, Maria," he said. The conversation halted while he dug into his breakfast.

Jessica tried to get through the meal in one piece. She didn't like the way her world stopped turning whenever Alex was around. She'd bet objects just naturally fell from the sky and landed at his feet if he commanded them to do so.

"I have some work to do here in my home office. If you need anything, you can come and get me," he finally spoke after several moments.

Jessica simply nodded her head. She rose from the table and headed toward the kitchen. There was a bassinet set up in the corner, and her son was sleeping soundly. She smiled down at her sweet baby.

"Mrs. Anderson, if you'd care to lie down for a while, I would be more than happy to keep an eye on Jacob. There are still several bottles already pumped and ready in the fridge if he wakes up hungry," Tina offered.

Jessica's initial reaction, again, was to refuse. But she wouldn't be any good to him if she didn't get some rest. There was a houseful of people more than willing to help.

"Thank you, Tina. I'll take you up on your offer. Please wake me if you need anything." Jessica placed a kiss on her son's head and then headed up the stairs. She climbed into bed and quickly fell into an exhausted sleep from which she didn't stir for four hours.

When she woke, she felt disoriented. She wasn't used to taking long naps, and she panicked for a moment when she noticed the time. She quickly relaxed, though, knowing that if there'd been any problems, someone would have woken her up. She and Jacob weren't on their own any longer. And when she climbed into the shower and washed the sleep away, she thought again of what a rare blessing it was for a new mother.

She found Jacob in the living room with Alex. Her son was wide awake, making little grumbling noises at his father, and Alex seemed to be transfixed. She watched them for a few minutes without them noticing. The unguarded way her husband interacted with his son was something special to witness.

When she chuckled, Alex looked up to see her standing in the doorway. He quickly shielded his expression, and she felt let down. Their relationship wasn't going to get easier any time soon, and though she knew she wasn't helping it get any better, neither was he.

"You have great timing," Alex began, "our son was just telling me that he wanted food." He smiled, as his eyes once again went to Jacob. Jessica walked closer and, when Jacob saw her, his noises escalated, and his legs kicked out. He knew food was nearby, and he was letting his mom know he wanted it.

Jessica bent down to pick up Jacob, and her hand brushed against Alex's lap. Their eyes locking for a moment, Alex quickly inhaled, and his expression darkened with desire, stirring her own neglected body.

Jessica hurriedly gathered up the baby and sat down on the far end of the couch. Her fingertips were tingling where they'd touched her husband, and she had no idea how she'd be able to hold out against the desire she had for this one man. She hadn't been with anyone since her night with him in the elevator, and her body was aching to be taken.

"I'm going to feed him here," she finally said. He usually left her in privacy to feed their son, but not this time.

"Go ahead. I'm going to catch the end of the game," he replied.

There were no blankets nearby, and Jacob was getting ready to throw a full-blown fit any minute as he started rooting around on the outside of her blouse. Jessica turned slightly away from Alex, trying to give herself some semblance of privacy, and quickly led her son's mouth to her breast. He started eating greedily, and Jessica relaxed and watched the game with Alex in silence.

*****

Alex sat on the couch a few short feet from Jessica. He knew he should give her the privacy she wanted, but he liked having them in the same room with him. He'd been giving her space, but enough was enough. It was time they began their life as a family — together.

He got up and sat down right beside Jessica so their legs, hips and shoulders were touching. He then flung his arm over the back of the couch so her side was pressed against his chest. He felt her tense at his nearness, but she didn't protest. He just continued watching the game, although there was no way he could have told anyone what the score was, or even who was playing.

She finished feeding their son and quickly covered up. Then she transferred him to her shoulder and began burping him. Jacob looked up at his father sleepily, and Alex couldn't resist rubbing his nearly bald head.

"Did you get enough to eat, son?"

Jacob answered his father's words with coos. Alex chuckled and stayed sitting there, enjoying having Jessica pressed against him and their son in her arms. He could definitely get used to this marriage thing. And, hey, he didn't think he'd mind having a few more kids running around. The thought was sobering. He'd never pictured himself as a settling-down kind of guy, but this gig had its moments.

*****

They sat together for a while, Jessica finally allowing herself to enjoy the two men in her life. She was trying to keep an emotional distance, but it was becoming harder with each passing moment. Alex's scent was enveloping her, and, gosh, he smelled so good. But even though she'd just slept for four hours, before she knew it, she felt her eyes beginning to drift shut. *Oh well*, she thought. She'd close them for just a few moments.

Chapter Sixteen

Jessica woke to find herself wrapped tightly against Alex's chest. His arms were locked around her, and they were lying down on the oversized couch with a cover placed across them. "Where's Jacob?" she asked in a panic.

"Tina took him a while ago," Alex replied sleepily.

Their faces were inches apart. Without another word, he closed the gap between them and kissed her with all of his pent-up need. She responded without thought. He turned their bodies and was suddenly on top of her, pressing her into the couch. His hands roamed over her, while his mouth worked magic. He broke contact with her lips and ran his tongue down the outside of Jessica's throat. She couldn't hold back her moan.

When his hand ran from her hip upward to cup her breast, she throbbed with pleasure. Jessica wanted him badly, and her body was responding to each movement he made. Alex began unbuttoning her blouse and trailing kisses down her neck, toward her barely covered breasts. Jessica grabbed his head and pulled him back to her lips. She needed to feel his mouth pressed against hers.

She pushed her hips into his arousal, making him groan with pleasure. He fastened his lips back on hers and was close to taking her right there in the living room.

"Alex, someone could walk in," she said, panting.

She could see that he wanted to ignore her words and continue with his expert seduction, but there were too many people in the house. She doubted, though, that he could hold out much longer before they consummated their marriage. Disturbingly, the thought excited her further.

Alex sat up, and she quickly jumped to her feet. He stood, walked over to the bar, and poured himself a shot of bourbon, downing it in one gulp. Obviously, it wasn't enough, because he poured another glass.

The alcohol seemed to do its job, because when he turned to look at her again, the flame in his eyes, though still there, was tamped down. The promise shining from the depths of those beautiful blue eyes left her aching.

"Would you like a glass of wine?" he asked.

"Yes, please, but only half a glass," Jessica replied. She normally didn't even have that much, but her nerves were frayed and a half glass wouldn't hurt her son.

He poured her some white wine, and walked to the fireplace to stoke the fire. Jessica knew he was giving them both needed time to breathe.

"I have a few phone calls to return. I'll meet with you for dinner." With that, Alex walked from the room, and Jessica let out the breath she hadn't realized she was holding.

When Alex was with Jacob, she knew she'd made the right decision to marry him, but when it was just the two of them, she was filled with doubt. She needed to speak to her mother.

Walking into her bedroom, she grabbed the phone and dialed the familiar number.

"Hi, Sam. Can I talk to mother?"

Her call was quickly transferred. "Darling. I wasn't expecting to hear from you today. Is everything OK?" Just the sound of her mom's voice calmed her nerves as Jessica lay back and thought about how much information she wanted to give.

"I just wanted to check in, Mom."

"I can hear the strain, Jessica. Tell me what is wrong."

"I don't really know. It's hard to explain. Everything is fine, but at the same time it isn't. I just…I don't know, Mom. I'm just confused."

"That's not a great beginning to a new marriage. Did you have…difficulties last night?"

Jessica was horrified at the question and certainly didn't want to admit how easily her husband had walked from their room — even if that was what she'd wanted.

"No. It's just that you and I both know this is a marriage of convenience, Mom. We married for the sake of Jacob, not because we're in love…"

"Ah, I see. I think you will realize that love and passion can go hand in hand. And don't always fight him on everything, but don't cower to him, either. Give a little of yourself, and you may be happy with the results. I know how stubborn you can be, and I also know that Alex is certainly a…determined young man. If both of you quit drawing battle lines, you may find that you have more in common than you think."

"I don't know, Mom…" So many conflicting emotions were rushing through her.

"Just give it some time, baby, and I think you will find something there. Don't dismiss what you don't know."

Jessica chatted with her mother for a few more minutes, then wandered downstairs. Their dinner started out with too much silence, but it was still early in the day, and Jessica was dreading when it came time for bed. Or was she really?

"I scheduled a nanny to come in and speak with us today," Alex said toward the end of the meal.

Jessica was glad he'd waited to give the news, because she suddenly lost all appetite.

"I never agreed to this, Alex."

"I understand, and if you hate her, that will be the end of it. But she was highly recommended, so I wanted to schedule the interview before someone else snatches her up. I promise that if you say no, that will be that, and I won't bother with having another one come in until you give me the OK."

She looked at him suspiciously, but he seemed sincere, so she supposed it wouldn't hurt to speak to the woman. Jessica doubted she'd take to the applicant anyway, and the problem would be solved. No intruder, and no guilt over having help with raising her child.

"Fine," she replied after a few tense moments, then left the dinner table to check on her son. He was fine, of course, so she decided to spend an hour by the pool, enjoying the cool evening air as the sun dipped lower in the sky.

An hour passed before Tina came outside. "Mrs. Anderson, you have a guest in the living room."

"Thank you, Tina. I'll be right in."

Jessica dragged herself back inside the house and found Alex sitting in the living room with a pleasant-looking woman. She appeared to be in her fifties, with eyes that sparkled and laugh lines accentuating them. *What an uncooperative person*, Jessica told herself with an inner chuckle. *She isn't allowing me to dislike her on sight.*

"You must be Mrs. Anderson. I'm Julia Scott. I'm hoping to help you take care of your son." The woman stood up and shook Jessica's hand.

"It's nice to meet you, Julia. I'm sure Alex told you I still haven't decided whether I want to hire a nanny." She felt obliged to be honest.

"I understand it's frightening to leave your child in the care of a stranger. Why don't we just get to know each other and go from there?" the woman replied.

The three of them spoke for a while, and then Jacob woke up from his nap. Jessica fed him before handing him to Julia. Julia had worked for the same family for twenty years, but now that all the children were grown up, she was looking for a new family. Jessica could find nothing wrong with her. Added to that, the more time she spent with Julia, the more the thought of someone helping with the baby was beginning to look appealing.

"Your son is very beautiful," Julia said after a little while. Jacob was resting in her arms, kicking his legs as he made cooing sounds at her.

"We sure think so," Alex said.

"I think all children are a gift and precious, of course, but Jacob is very mild-mannered. Is this unusual, or is he a happy baby, for the most part?" Julia asked.

"He's an exceptionally good baby. I've heard horror stories of newborns staying up all night and having colic, crying for hours on end. I've had none of those problems so far with Jacob. He wakes every few hours, which is normal, but the only time he fusses is when he's hungry," Jessica said.

"It wouldn't matter to me either way," Julia said. "If a baby is crying, there's a reason for it. He's hungry, needs changing, needs some extra love, or is hurting and trying to tell you about it. One of my previous charges was very colicky. We would walk the floors for hours on end. It was an excuse for me to get to cuddle with him just a little bit longer," she remembered fondly.

Jessica felt truth in the woman's words. Julia seemed to have unending patience, and she actually adored children. In short, the perfect child-care provider. Dang! Jessica actually liked her.

"As much as I hate to leave this sweet little one, I'll get going and let you both get back to your evening," Julia said and handed Jacob back to Jessica.

"We'll discuss everything tonight and get back to you within the next couple of days. I have all your information. We really appreciate your coming by on such short notice and spending so much time with us tonight," Alex said as he led Julia from the room.

"Thank you both. You have a beautiful family, and I'd love to be a part of it," Julia replied before leaving.

Jessica took a moment to think as she waited for Alex to return to the den. Was this something she could handle? Would it be so bad if she began to do a bit of work?

"What do you think?" Alex asked as he returned to the room.

"I think she seemed pretty impressive. I guess the idea of a nanny wouldn't be *all* bad. It was nice to be able to take a nap today," Jessica conceded. Her face turned a shade of red as she pictured the way she'd woken up from her second nap that afternoon.

Alex's eyes darkened, apparently from the same mental image.

"I've already run the background check and verified her references. Her last family couldn't say enough positive things about her. The kids all remain in contact with her and consider her an honorary aunt. They adore her, and the family begged her to stay on with them, even after the kids had grown, but she told them she wanted to continue to be a nanny."

"I guess there wouldn't be anything wrong with giving her a try," Jessica said. "Just make sure to tell her we don't know if it will be a permanent situation," she added, not sure whether she wanted to commit to a nanny for the long term.

"I'll give her a call. She already told me she could begin tomorrow." He left the room, and Jessica was a little nervous about the speed with which things were progressing.

The rest of the evening flew by. Alex spent most of his time in his home office, and Jacob decided to belie his mother's words by being unusually fussy. She was grateful to have gotten the nap in because she had a feeling it would be a very long night. Jacob had a slight fever and was letting everyone know about it.

When he got done with his work, Alex took turns walking Jacob around the house. She was trying to keep her guard up, completely ignoring her mother's advice, but Alex made it very difficult when he was being so kind and caring with Jacob. Not once during the baby's continuous fussiness did Alex lose his patience.

Around ten that evening Jacob's fever broke, and the boy finally fell asleep. Both Alex and Jessica breathed sighs of relief as they stared down at their sleeping child.

"He's cutting his first tooth, and it's hard on him. But I think the worst of it's over now," she told her husband.

"I wish there were more I could do," Alex replied.

"I know, but the best thing to do is cuddle him and walk. He enjoys the motion, and I think getting to look around is a good distraction from the pain."

"Let's go to bed. I'm exhausted," Alex said, turning toward their bedroom.

Jessica hesitated. Alex had said he wouldn't push her into anything, but she knew he didn't really have to push.

"Jessica, we aren't going to do anything you don't want to. Let's just go to bed," he repeated. She could see the irritation in his eyes and hear it in his voice.

"Fine, Alex. I agreed to this marriage, so I'll share the bed. I'm sorry if I misled you on the couch today, but I don't want sex." She finished talking and moved ahead of him into the room. She grabbed her favorite nightie and went to the bathroom to change.

"You can try to run, but you want this just as much as I do," she just barely heard Alex whisper.

Their interlude earlier proved that he desired her. She hoped, at least, that it was *her*, and that he wouldn't have pursued any female who happened to be around. If only she didn't need him so much.

Yet why was she fighting her desires? They were married, consenting adults, so what was so wrong with making love?

She knew the answer to her question before it was fully formed in her head.

Each stroke of his hands, each kiss from his lips, every little thing he did to her would make her fall more hopelessly in love with him, while to him, she was just a convenient body — a way to fulfill his needs.

Jessica finally emerged from the bathroom, knowing she'd taken as much time as she possibly could get away with.

Taking a deep breath at the sight of Alex lying on the bed, wearing nothing but a pair of boxer shorts, Jessica braced her shoulders as she approached. The sight of him lying on his back with his hands underneath his head was enough to make her knees wobble. And with the covers pulled up only to his waist, barely hiding anything from her view, she was lucky not to drop to the floor.

She couldn't seem to tear her gaze away from his rippling muscles, his hard and defined stomach, and the trail of hair on his lower stomach — oh, that was beautiful, especially the way it disappeared beneath the blanket. Her mouth went dry as she imagined running her fingers across his skin, finding all the places that made him tense. As worn out as she felt, she knew she'd be lucky to get any sleep lying next to him.

He said nothing as she reluctantly approached the bed, but his eyes never left her trembling body. She hurried beneath the covers, turning away from him and hugging the edge of the mattress as if it were a lifeboat. She pulled the comforter up to her chin and started counting dancing chickens. He clicked off the bedside lamp and — surprise, surprise — before she knew it, exhaustion took her into blissful nothingness.

Chapter Seventeen

Alex lay there, hard and aching. He knew that if he reached out and pulled her close, she'd easily succumb to him. But he didn't want to coerce her; he wanted her to come willingly. If that meant he needed a few cold showers while he waited, so be it.

Earning her trust was the only way they'd make it through this situation. They were man and wife now, and as much as he ached, they were building a future together. That was more important that solving his immediate problem.

Never had he planned on having a marriage like his parents'; it was a rare thing to find —statistically almost impossible, he was sure. It wasn't that he was jaded to the world, or that some woman had destroyed his heart; he was just…somewhat selfish? He loved his family, respected the lives his parents had built. He just didn't think he was capable of loving someone the way his father loved his mother. He could admit that.

But, since he and Jessica had a child together, he had to make their marriage last. The only way he could do that was by making sure they had a mutual respect for one another. If they began thinking they were falling in love, it would lead to disaster. When romantic passion burned out, as it always did these days, it left emptiness and loathing.

As he gazed at the back of her neck in the slight glow coming through the curtains, he cursed his resolve. He lifted his hand and let the silk tendrils of her hair slide through his fingers, groaning as her scent of vanilla and spice drifted to him.

He must really be a masochist, he thought, to be tormenting himself this way.

With his hand still outstretched, he finally managed to drift into a restless sleep, hoping she didn't wait too long before admitting she needed him...

Alex woke up with Jessica pressed tightly against him. He was lying on his back, and she was facing him with one of her legs wrapped over both of his, and an arm around his stomach. Her head was resting on his shoulder, her mouth mere inches from his.

He looked over and saw that it was midnight. They'd been in bed only a couple of hours and she must have snuggled up to him in her sleep. He was too tired, and far too turned on, to play the gentleman.

She started to stir, squirming against him, causing his body to jerk in the air. He could feel himself harden, his erection pulsing. He wanted to bury himself deep inside her and damn the consequences.

He turned so they were facing each other, and his hands began roaming over her body. She pushed into him, letting out a moan of pleasure, as she began waking. Her leg was still wrapped over him when he turned, and his erection was now right at her core. Only a wisp of fabric separated the two of them.

Alex ran his tongue over her bottom lip, and her eyes opened slightly. Another moan escaped her lips. Giving up the will to fight, he gripped the back of her head and kissed her deeply. Jessica woke up fully and returned the kiss with urgency.

His hands continued exploring her curves, and he stopped the kiss long enough only to pull her nightgown over her head. He pulled her so tightly against him that not even air came between them. Jessica's hips were moving against his erection, and Alex was afraid their lovemaking would end far too soon for either of them.

Flipping her onto her back, he moved his mouth down to her full breasts and ran his tongue over her budded nipples. As he licked and caressed the fullness of her breasts, she jerked upward, seeking more. He wanted to give them far more attention, but he was conscious of her nursing. So instead, Alex ran his tongue down the center of them and nibbled his way across her smooth stomach.

"Alex…I need…"

"What? What do you need, Jessica?" he groaned, praying she'd ask him to take her.

"I…please…"

He was close to surging inside her, relieving the terrible ache tearing through him, but he wanted to make sure this time was great for her. Their only other time together had left something to be desired.

He ripped away her panties, the last barrier between them, and he kissed her in the most intimate way possible. She jerked her hips in the air as pleasure washed through her. "Alex, now," she demanded. He swiped his tongue along her heat, prolonging the torture for both of them.

When he couldn't take any more, he quickly shed his shorts and poised himself over her. "You're so beautiful," he gasped as he looked into her flushed face. "I want this to last all night, but I can't. It's been so long…"

He drove his tongue into her mouth and buried his manhood deep within her. She pushed her hips upward, urging him deeper yet, and he gladly obliged.

No longer able to hold anything back, he pushed into her fast, and she matched him thrust for thrust. She was gasping, and then she cried out. He felt her pulsing heat around him, and he lost all control. He drove into her and spilled his seed deep inside her.

Neither of them said anything, but after their breathing returned to normal, he felt her trying to pull away. But Alex refused to let her pull away from him again. No steps backward. He tightened his arms around her and said, "Go back to sleep, Jessica."

She gave up the fight and soon drifted off. He quickly followed her.

Chapter Eighteen

Jessica woke up and turned over, realizing she was alone in the very large bed. Her hands flew to her face as she replayed the previous night in her mind. She and Alex had made love not only once, but twice — the first time when she'd woken up plastered against him, the second time after she'd fed Jacob and had gone back to bed.

There'd been no hesitation on her part. Alex had reached for her, and she'd fallen instantly into his arms. How was she supposed to keep her distance when, the instant he touched her, she melted?

Though she'd known this was inevitable, she'd been trying to give herself a little more time. As she felt the delicious ache in her body, however, she couldn't regret what had happened. Alex had taken her to the highest peak of pleasure and beyond.

After a moment of stretching her arms, she rose from bed and checked on Jacob. Fortunately, the child was still sleeping, so she had time to shower and work out the kinks in her stiff muscles. She hadn't done anything that physical since before Jacob was born.

She finally dressed, gathered Jacob into her arms, and headed down the stairs.

"Good morning, Mrs. Anderson. I hope you slept well," Tina said.

"I did. Thank you."

"Mr. Anderson asked me to tell you he had to run in to the office today and would be gone all afternoon. He said the new nanny would arrive by eight," she said before placing Jessica's breakfast before her.

"Thank you."

Jessica fed Jacob his meal while eating her own. Then she settled down in the den to wait for the new nanny.

Julia arrived early and got her room organized in no time. Since it was the woman's first day, Jessica wanted to show her Jacob's routines and to see how the woman interacted with her son. So, Jessica, Julia and Jacob spent much of the morning together around the house. Finding no faults with Julia, Jessica eventually went out to relax in one of the gardens.

As Jessica sat among the variety of flowers and began planting her new calla lilies, she tried to figure out how she really felt about her husband. They did enjoy each other's company on occasion, she was definitely attracted to him, and they shared a child together.

She'd once had a huge crush on him, but that was just a teenage fantasy that meant nothing now, right? That he was unlike any man she'd ever known didn't mean she couldn't keep her head on her shoulders. She needed to look at this as primarily a...collaboration.

Jessica didn't know how long she sat in the garden, daydreaming, but soon Julia was walking toward her with a fussy Jacob in her arms. "Your son's ready for his lunch," Julia said with a smile.

"I'm sorry. I lost track of time sitting out here," Jessica said, immediately getting up and heading toward them.

"You deserve time to yourself. Don't feel guilty for enjoying a few moments of peace in an otherwise hectic day," Julia said gently. "Your son can wait long enough for you to clean up."

Jessica looked down at her hands and noticed they were covered with dirt. She looked up and smiled sheepishly. "I guess I should wash my hands before taking him," she replied. She bent down and kissed Jacob's soft head before they headed inside together.

"Tell me more about your last family," Jessica asked once her son was settled down and eating.

"They're a wonderful family. I worked for them for twenty years, as you know, and I was there for the births of the youngest two children. The oldest child, Justin, was only a year old when I came. Their mom was a lot like you. She wanted to do everything on her own, but found having a little help gave her the extra energy to be a great mother," Julia replied.

"I have to admit it's nice to have you around. I've always thought doing everything on my own was the only way to do something, but my mother has told me many times that it's OK to ask for help."

"I couldn't imagine my life any other way," Julia said.

The two women continued to chat while Jacob ate, and then Jessica excused herself and took him to bed. Surprised to be still so tired, Jessica decided to lie down for a few minutes herself, and fell asleep quickly.

*****

"Good morning, Dad. What are you doing here?"

"Me? What are *you* doing here? Aren't you supposed to be on your honeymoon?" Joseph asked as he sat down and put his feet up on Alex's desk.

"We have a house honeymoon, remember?"

"I know that, but there's a lot of honeymooning that can be going on at home. You certainly can't do anything from our offices."

Alex laughed at his father's antics. He was now married and the old man was still trying to meddle in his life. Typical. Nothing was quite good enough for Joseph Anderson.

"There was an emergency in Greece. I had to come in and sign papers and make a few phone calls."

"Ah, boy, learn how to delegate. You don't want to leave that pretty bride of yours all alone at home. She'll be thinking you don't want to be with her."

"Jessica is just fine, Dad. Tell me about this merger Lucas was speaking about last week. Will I need to travel to Italy next month?"

Joseph narrowed his eyes for a moment, and Alex was worried he'd keep harping on about a husband's duties to his wife, but finally his father sighed. "Yes, it looks as if it's all a go. If you want to leave the baby with your mother and me, you can take Jessica with you and turn it into a working vacation."

"Jacob is far too young for us to leave. Jessica would never be OK with that. Don't worry, though, Father; I'll take her away on a honeymoon when he gets just a little older," Alex said with a laugh. His old man just wouldn't let up.

"Alex, your brother Mark is on his way up."

"Thanks," Alex replied into his speaker.

"I wonder what brought Mark in from the ranch." Joseph commented.

"Maybe there was a horse or cattle emergency. I don't know."

His door swung open and Mark walked in, wearing a pair of his favorite worn Wranglers and a dusty shirt. People who didn't know who he was might have thought he rolled around in the dirt just for fun. Alex knew how hard Mark worked and he had complete respect for what his brother did for a living. Heck, he and Lucas loved heading to the ranch once in a while and helping out. He wouldn't admit it, but he was always sore as hell the next day.

"Glad I caught you, Alex. I need a huge favor," Mark said.

"You know that I'm technically not back to work yet, right?" Alex said.

"Come on. Don't be ridiculous. I wouldn't ask if it weren't important."

Alex nearly groaned. They both knew he was going to help out, so why fight it? "Fine. What is it?"

"There's a function I can't attend tonight. Can you go in my place, please? Missy's having a hard time with her delivery and I don't want to leave her."

"Don't you have a full-time vet to look after your horses?"

"Of course I do, but Missy needs me there," Mark said as if Alex were an idiot.

"I really don't want to leave Jessica all evening." That sounded reasonable — he *was* a newlywed, after all.

"You can take her with you. Here's the address. Don't be late, and wear black tie."

Before Alex had the chance to protest, Mark went rushing back out of the room.

"It looks as if you'll need a babysitter for the night," Joseph said, reminding Alex that he was still there, though he didn't know how anyone could forget his father was in a room.

"We have a nanny now, Dad."

"Nonsense! I want…I mean, your mother wants to see her grandson," Joseph insisted.

Alex had to hide the smile. The world thought Joseph was tough, but his sons knew what an old softie he was. Of course he could babysit Jacob. Alex just hoped Jessica was willing to come with him to this event, wherever it was.

Chapter Nineteen

"Mr. Anderson!"

Alex turned with a cringe at the high-pitched voice as he walked inside the ballroom at the downtown Seattle hotel. He was going to kill his brother. There was no doubt about it.

"What is this, Alex?" Jessica asked with a confused look as she gazed at the decorated room and its large stage.

"Revenge," Alex said with a sigh.

"What do you mean?"

"Last year, I auctioned Mark off at the fundraiser where you and I…danced. This is my payback," Alex said through clenched teeth.

Jessica's eyes widened and then her lips twitched. "I swear, if you laugh, Jessica, I won't be responsible for my actions," Alex growled.

That did it. She burst into laughter, and instead of anger, Alex felt his own lips twitch, too. It was a bit humorous if he really thought about it. Plus, it was exactly what he'd do to one of his brothers if given the chance.

"Mr. Anderson!" The voice was more insistent from the judges' table. With a sigh, Alex turned from Jessica and made his way to the group of women waiting for him.

"Hello, Mrs. Stanley. It's nice to see you again," he said as he leaned down and kissed her cheek.

"Oh, the pleasure is all mine, darling. Did you see my sweet little Patricia? She looks just like an angel, doesn't she?"

"And don't miss my darling Connie. She's been practicing all week!"

"Yes, my Amanda has a dance routine you are going to be stunned by."

Mothers of girls in the pageant kept joining the group surrounding him. There was nothing worse than trying to judge a young girls' beauty pageant. Yes, the girls were adorable in their little dresses and tiaras; it was the mothers who were nightmares. For the next few hours, he was going to have them in his face, yelling at him if he turned his head for a single second, and furious with him if their child didn't win.

Mark was a dead man.

What Alex had done at the auction was amusing. This was downright cruel and unusual punishment. One other time he'd been stupid enough to judge a young misses' beauty pageant — only one other time.

"I'm sure glad you got here, Alex. They are going to give me some peace now," one of the other judges said with a chuckle. Alex wondered whether any of them had volunteered or if they had all been fooled into being there.

"It's a pleasure," Alex gritted out.

"Alex, the show's starting!" a mother yelled.

"I'll just sit back here, darling," Jessica said with a satisfied smirk. Oh, she could enjoy herself all she wanted as she sat back and watched the show. She knew he was sweating beneath his expensive suit, and there wasn't a thing he could do about it.

Two hours later, Alex's head was pounding, and he was on the verge of calling his brother and... Hell, there was nothing he could do about it. When Mark's text came in asking whether he was having a good time, he gripped the phone so hard, he nearly broke the screen.

Payback's a bitch, Alex texted back, to which he just received a smiley face. Alex was man enough to realize when he'd been beaten, but he wouldn't be down for long. Besides, Mark's horse probably wasn't even birthing tonight. He was sure his little brother was sitting back on his couch, drinking a cold beer and laughing so much, his sides were aching.

"Alex, you're missing Mary's spin! That's the best part of her routine!"

Alex gritted his teeth again and focused on the stage. He needed a break, a nice long break that included a triple shot of whiskey. But he took notes and prayed the night would end. He didn't care who won; he just wanted to get the heck out of that room.

When the event finally ended, he turned in his judging forms and made a beeline for the bar, where he found Jessica sitting on a stool, laughing at something Mark was saying.

"I knew your horse wasn't giving birth!" Alex thundered, causing several heads to turn his way. He was past caring.

"Aren't you supposed to be at the judges' table?" Mark asked innocently.

"I swear, Mark…" He couldn't complete his sentence.

"Now, now, brother. There's no need to get upset. Missy gave birth and is healthy as can be. Thanks for asking, by the way. I just came down to see if I could help with anything."

"I have to get back there for the announcement. Be prepared to run like hell, Jessica, because there will be one happy mother, and twenty-four really pissed-off ones," he said before turning away from them. He said nothing else to his worthless, conniving, treacherous brother.

Their laughter followed him back to the crowded ballroom. He knew he was giving his little brother exactly what he wanted, but he couldn't help it. These women were terrifying.

When the winner was announced, he could practically feel the knives being thrust into his back. He vowed to never, *ever* attend another beauty pageant for as long as he lived. Not even for a swimsuit competition.

It took another hour before he managed to reach his wife, and by then, he couldn't say how many times outraged parents had whispered his name with a curse word attached to it. He wasn't the only judge, but he seemed to have a target placed right on his back. Probably it was because his father sponsored this particular pageant, but Joseph never got the death threats that he, Mark and Lucas seemed to get. Well, he would think of something equally vile to thrust upon his brother when the time was right.

"Did you have a good time, darling?" Jessica asked, her eyes wide and shining.

Her innocent act wasn't fooling him.

"It was just peachy. Now I'd really like to leave before the mothers decide to start in on round two," Alex said as he grabbed her arm and began moving toward one of the hotel's side doors. He certainly wouldn't attempt to leave by the front.

"They were telling me there's a dinner being served now. I'm starving."

"I'll take you anywhere but here," he answered, refusing to slow his step. If she tripped, he'd simply catch her, throw her over his shoulder and continue straight out of the room.

"Don't you want to wait for Mark?"

"Not even if the room were on fire."

He'd get hold of his big brother pronto so the two of them could tag-team Mark. It would be quite pleasing to make their little brother dance for them. That thought finally brought a smile to Alex's face as he reached his car and made his escape.

Chapter Twenty

The next couple of months flew by in a blur. With Julia there to help, Jessica was able to focus on her writing, and she thought she was accomplishing something. She still spent most of her time at home, but when she ran errands or worked on new material, she didn't feel that Jacob was being neglected.

Her nights were regularly filled with passion. She and Alex didn't spend much time together during the days, because he was at work. But when he came home, they laughed, played games, watched movies together, and sometimes would talk for hours on end. Then, each time that they climbed into bed together, it was as if they were there for the first time. It was magical, and she knew that if it were to end suddenly, her world would be destroyed. She was getting too dependent on Alex, and the attention he gave her.

With Jacob becoming more able to play on his own, and entertain himself, Jessica began feeling restless around the big house. There didn't seem to be a lot for her to do. When she received a call from an old college friend, informing her of a part-time job at the local newspaper for a reporter, she jumped at the chance. She'd already been weaning Jacob, and it would be great to get out of the house.

She was so afraid of losing her sense of self, and she could work part time without guilt. Her child was in more than capable hands, and the staff ran the house. It would be good to do something simply about her for a change.

She hoped that Alex wouldn't mind — but even if he did, she was going to give it a shot.

*****

"Now, Jessica. I want to remind you that this isn't exciting news. It will mainly be covering city meetings and school events, but it's still an important part of the paper."

"I understand, Marcia. I'm not out to change the world. It'll be nice to be writing and to get out of the house," Jessica reassured her new boss.

"Good. I'm glad we're on the same page. Your first assignment is at city hall. They have a meeting this afternoon at two. Do a short piece on the topics of discussion and any issues that arise."

"I'll be there. Thank you for this opportunity, Marcia. I appreciate it."

"I have to admit, I was a little surprised you wanted to work a job like this. You have a very impressive résumé and could work for any major publication you wanted," Marcia said.

"I'm a full-time mother now and the kind of careers I'm qualified for require sixty-plus hours a week. I'm not willing to be away from my son that much. I plan on eventually getting back to my research writing on third world countries and their customs, but would like to stay out in the workforce part time for now."

Many people assumed that because Jessica had access to money beyond what most people ever dreamed of, she'd behave like a spoiled heiress. It never took her long to prove herself, though, and she knew she would gain the respect of her co-workers at the paper.

"Well, then, we're happy to have you join our team. The story is due by noon tomorrow. I'll see you then." Marcia went back to work, and Jessica headed outside to her car. She had about an hour to kill before the city hall meeting, so she went to the mall for a smoothie and some light shopping.

It would be so much more pleasant to shop with a friend. She realized she was lonely. It was really why she wanted to get out there in the workforce, and why she was hoping to find someone she could talk with. She watched as two women walked past her, laughing together, and her heart ached a bit.

When she'd become pregnant with Jacob, her so-called friends had backed away. In her world, it was such a shame to be an unwed mother, especially since she refused to tell anyone who the father was. Since her marriage to Alex, some had tried to come back into the picture, but with friends like that, she'd rather they just stayed out of her life. Still, she would have loved to have someone to be close with, a female someone.

She was in no way miserable at home; Alex was treating her well. But she needed more. Shaking off her uneasiness, she left the mall and headed to city hall.

The meeting was a bore, as she knew it would be. It was difficult, but she managed to place an interesting spin on the events, and her editor was more than happy with her work. She found it amusing that she was taking so much pride in her small job, but she felt useful and good about herself. It was the first time in a while she felt appreciated and needed by anyone other than her baby.

She drove home, still feeling upbeat. When she went through the doors, she could smell the stomach-teasing aroma of dinner cooking, and she heard Jacob giggling. She followed the sound.

She walked into the den and found Alex on his back, with Jacob balanced on his father's knees as if he were flying through the air. She watched as the baby let out another giggle, and she enjoyed the special moment between father and son. When Jacob spotted his mother, he immediately started twisting in Alex's arms.

Alex looked up to see what had caught his son's attention, and then gave Jessica one of his killer smiles. Alex set Jacob on the floor, and the baby crawled to his mother as fast as his chubby legs would allow.

Jessica scooped him up into her arms. "How's my handsome young man?" she asked as she nuzzled his neck, causing more giggles.

"He's doing great. How was your first day at work?" Alex seemed genuinely interested, which surprised Jessica.

"It was actually great. I know it's not a big-time paper, and my name isn't going up in lights or anything, but I like the people at the office, and it's nice to be working again," Jessica said, a bit defensively.

"Hey, I'm not judging you," Alex said, while holding his hands out. "Seriously, I really want to know how your day went and what you did."

Jessica eyed him suspiciously for a few moments, and then told him about her news story and the people she'd met.

"I need to go in tomorrow for a couple of hours, and then I thought I'd go to the salon. I haven't had my hair or nails done since our wedding, and it would feel heavenly," she said with a little guilt for planning to leave her son while she primped and prettified herself.

"You deserve to take time for yourself, and there's nothing to feel guilty over. Jacob is fine. He knows you love him, and he won't be scarred for life because his mother got her nails done. Stop being so hard on yourself," he stated, as if he could read her mind.

"I know you're right, but I promised myself I wouldn't be one of those mothers who left her child in someone else's care while she ran all over the place. It feels wrong, especially with him still being a baby." She headed over to the bar and poured herself half a glass of wine.

Jacob had received his needed attention from his mom, so he crawled over to play with some of his toys on the floor. Jessica and Alex sat on the couch and watched him entertain himself.

"You're a great mother. If you take care of your own needs as well as you do his, you'll always be a great mother. Women who sacrifice everything for their husbands or children end up resentful. You don't want that to happen, do you?"

Jessica looked at Alex, slightly puzzled. It was nice to come home and voice her concerns with the man she loved.

It took a few moments for that thought to sink in. When it did, she froze.

Her world stalled as she realized it wasn't a random and ridiculous feeling, an idle fantasy without substance. From deep in her unconscious mind, the truth had somehow emerged. She loved Alex. She'd tried to avoid it, and there had been times when she would have happily throttled him, but she loved her time with him. She loved the way he was with their son, and she loved what he stood for — honesty, family, and faithfulness.

Afraid her face would somehow show her newfound feelings, she stood up under the pretense of checking a toy Jacob was playing with. She waited until she'd composed her features before turning back to Alex.

"Thanks, Alex. I needed to hear that. I love being a mother, but I love feeling feminine, as well. I'll take a little 'me' time and not beat myself up about it. I'm going to wash up and change for dinner." She didn't give him time to answer her. She slipped from the room and headed to her shower, where she prayed she could wash her worries away.

As the water pulsed down on her, Jessica felt a few tears slip from her eyes. She didn't know how to make any of this better. Alex was good to her, but what if she wanted more than that? What if she needed more? Could she be selfish and demand to be loved? What if he couldn't give her that? Was it worth ripping her family apart?

By the time Jessica came back downstairs, dinner was ready, and Jacob was seated in his high chair. He was happily stuffing creamed vegetables into his mouth. More food was on him than in him, but he was having a grand old time.

"I hope you had a good first day at work," Julia said.

"It was very nice. How did the day go with Jacob?"

"He was his usual happy self. He took only a short nap this afternoon, though, so I think he'll be ready for bed early tonight. He's almost finished with his supper, so I'll take him up for a bath while you finish eating."

"Thank you, Julia. I know I don't say it enough, but I'm grateful you're a part of our family. I could never have spent the afternoon away from my son if I weren't one hundred percent sure he was in capable hands." Jessica got up and gave Julia a hug.

"The honor's all mine," Julia said before looking at her quizzically.

"What is it, Julia?"

"Is everything all right, Jessica? You seem upset."

Jessica hesitated as Alex looked her way. She wasn't getting into this right now. "I'm fine. It's just been a long day. I appreciate your concern though." Julia looked at her, and Jessica knew she didn't believe her, but thankfully, she let it go as she cuddled Jacob close and walked from the room.

"I'll be going to my brother's ranch tomorrow," Alex said.

"That's good. You haven't taken a day off in a while."

"He has a roundup that he needs help with, and then we're all going to meet for a barbecue afterward," he continued. "I know you'll have a great time out there. I can't believe I haven't taken you sooner. It's been this project I've been working on. It makes me lose my head a bit," he added with a laugh.

Jessica was nervous. She hadn't been around his family since the wedding. There was the one night at the pageant with Mark; Joseph and Katherine came over regularly to play with Jacob; and Alex had taken the baby over to his siblings a couple of times. But there hadn't been any family gatherings. She was nervous to face them all as a group.

It was especially nerve-racking to be around Lucas and Amy. They were so obviously in love with each other, and she herself felt like a fraud.

"I'm not sure if I'll be able to attend, but if you want to have your parents stop by and grab Jacob, that would be fine," she tried to say nonchalantly.

Alex stared at her for a few moments before responding. "Look, Jessica. I understand my family can be overwhelming, and you're still trying to get used to everything, but they'd be hurt if you didn't come. Your parents will also be there, actually. Can you please just forget about everything else going on for one day and come enjoy yourself?" he asked, while maintaining eye contact.

Jessica tried not to resent the fact that Alex seemed to always get his way, but he hadn't handled this well — as usual. He'd sprung the outing on her at the last minute, as if her wishes didn't matter, and he used guilt to pressure her into going. He carefully waited to mention that her parents would be there, just to add to the pressure and guilt. She might have fallen in love with this fellow, but he wasn't making it easy.

So what could she do? She could protest and refuse to go, but then she'd look as cowardly as she was feeling. Her parents would drag her there, anyway, if they saw that she didn't show up. She could try to fake an illness, but her mother knew her better than anyone else. She would take one look at her, and it would be over.

"I just had to work on a news piece I was writing, but I'll do it the next day," she finally conceded, hoping he'd buy her story. She didn't need him to see how insecure she felt.

Alex continued to look at her for a moment longer before nodding. Thankfully he was man enough to not call her on her lies. That didn't mean, however, that she approved of his behavior. So right now it was best to walk away.

"I'm going to head up to bed and read for a while," Jessica finally said, having lost her appetite.

"I have some work to finish up. I'll try not to take too long," Alex replied before getting up and leaving the room.

Jessica walked slowly up the stairs and tried to shake off her melancholy mood. She was finally in the workforce again, even if it was a part-time job. She had a beautiful baby boy, a decent husband, and a loving family. She had so much more than others, so she needed to quit wanting the world. Though he was occasionally unreasonable and a bit self-absorbed, Alex was good to her. She didn't need to have him falling at her feet. She smiled, thinking it would be nice, though. She just couldn't picture him as the falling-over-himself kind of guy. She loved how strong he was — how capable.

She opened the door to their room and curled up under the covers. She knew she wouldn't be able to sleep until Alex joined her. She'd gotten used to him by her side — the way her body fit perfectly against his, the smell of his body wash mixed with his own unique scent. She grabbed her book, but gave up after reading the same page for the third time.

An hour later, when the door finally opened, signaling Alex's arrival, Jessica's stomach tightened. She wanted him, as she always did. She watched him quietly walk to the bathroom, and she waited. She knew he'd pull her into his arms the minute he lay down, and her body was ready.

Chapter Twenty-One

"Surprised you could climb out of the newlywed bed again long enough to join us," Mark said as he punched his brother's arm. "Heck, we didn't see Lucas for at least six months," he continued.

"You're lucky you're seeing me now," said Lucas, looking down at his phone for the hundredth time. "It's so hard waiting like this."

"Trust me, your ringer is working just fine. If anything happens with Amy, you *will* be the first one who knows about it," Mark said, laughing.

"I know. I know. I worry so much about her being this far along in her pregnancy. I know she's with Mom and Dad but…man, it's hard to be away from her right now." Lucas smiled sheepishly.

"Thank the Lord I'm still single. You two are just a little too mushy for my taste," Mark said before jumping the fence.

Lucas and Alex were right behind him.

"You'll be next, you know," Alex said. "We both thought we would hold out, and look at us. Not only are we married, but we're fathers, too. Your day is coming." Alex grinned at his younger brother.

"No way, man. Unlike you two, I really am a confirmed bachelor, and that's how it'll stay. I have my hands full with all these animals. I don't have any time for human babies in my life."

Lucas and Alex just looked at each other and smiled. They knew their younger brother would fall, and it would be their pleasure to watch it happen. "I thought you said there was some work to be done," Alex goaded him.

"You'll be begging me to stop by the end of the day. I bet you keel over and embarrass yourself in front of your new bride," he said with a hopeful wink.

"Bring it on, little brother," Alex replied.

In their worn Stetson hats, boots, and painted-on jeans, Lucas, Alex and Mark could fell any woman with a heartbeat from two thousand yards away. And it didn't hurt that they handled their horses with the mastery of rodeo champions.

Any outsider looking at the trio would have thought they all belonged on a ranch. No one would be able to tell Lucas and Alex both worked behind desks and jetted around the world. Only Mark was a full-time rancher; early on in his life he'd decided that office work wasn't what he wanted to do, and Joseph had fully supported his son's decision.

All three had been spending time on this ranch since they were little. It had belonged to their grandfather before Mark took over the operation. Though Joseph loved the land, he had no desire to live outside the city, and neither did Lucas or Alex. It was Mark's baby, through and through.

"Have you heard anything from Trenton or the others? I can't remember the last time I was able to get one of them on the phone, let alone visit with them."

"Same here, Lucas. I tried calling Max and he hasn't returned my calls. I know that after their mom died, they were all having a hard time, but I thought by now they'd want to come over here, get away from the memories, anything other than be by themselves. Last I heard from dad, Uncle George took off on some world cruise, and none of our cousins were talking to each other," Mark answered.

"Maybe we need to make a trip out there and see if there's anything we can do," Alex added.

"I don't know if it would be a welcome visit. I know if Dad or Mom died, I'd be a wreck, too," Lucas said.

"So would I, Brother, but I certainly wouldn't push my family away. I'd need you guys more than ever if that were to happen."

"That's good to hear, Mark, 'cause the worst thing I can imagine is losing any of you," Lucas said.

"OK, you're both sounding like freaking girls. Are we going to work, or what?" Alex said, but even he had a slight frog in his throat. The subject dropped as they moved along the fence.

The brothers spent the afternoon bringing the cattle in and branding them. In midafternoon, they stopped by the lake for lunch and basked in the summer heat. The best part of branding was taking a swim in the middle of the day, when you didn't think you could stand the sun beating down on your head for another second.

"Any time you boys are ready to trade in your suits and run the ranch with me, you know you're welcome," Mark said with a cheeky grin.

"You know I love the land, and helping you out here is a little slice of heaven, but it wouldn't take long before foreign travel and a nice clean suit would be calling my name," Alex said.

"You know Dad would lasso you up for trying to take me away from the office. He's retired and doesn't want to come back," Lucas added.

"I'm just saying…" Mark left the sentence unfinished.

Lucas and Alex both sighed in unison.

"OK. Last one in has to do the grilling," Mark said while stripping down to his boxers in record time and diving into the lake.

"Aw, crap," Alex yelled while trying to yank his boots off. He glanced over and saw Lucas had the lead. Lucas dived in about two seconds before he did.

"I think you guys cheated again," Alex laughed. "You know you just want me grilling because I'm the best one at it. You two always burn that beautiful Angus meat," he added.

"Hey, when you're right, you're right," Mark said before sending a slew of water right into Alex's face.

"Now the war's on," Alex said, and a massive water fight erupted.

"OK, OK. I call a truce," Lucas finally said, dragging himself from the water. Mark and Alex followed. The three of them settled down on the soft grass and enjoyed the sounds of nature surrounding them.

"So, how are things with your wife and son?" Lucas asked Alex.

"Things are great. Jacob is growing like a weed. I can't believe how important he is to me. I can even imagine having about ten more of him running around," Alex said.

"And what about Jessica?" Mark asked.

Alex hesitated for a moment. He didn't really know how to describe his relationship with his wife. He knew if he told his brothers it was none of their business, they'd back off, but it would feel good to talk about his conflicting emotions.

"Honestly, it's really complicated. We married because, basically, I didn't give her any choice. She had my son — whom she kept from me," he said with an edge to his voice. He was still unhappy she hadn't told him about the pregnancy. "But you know that part. Somewhere along the line, though, in the last few months, I've found I'm excited to see her every day. I look forward to coming home, knowing she'll be there." He didn't add anything else. He didn't want to even think about the *love* word.

Neither brother spoke for a few moments. They seemed to understand that Alex was trying to figure it all out in his own head.

"You know things didn't start out well for Amy and me, either," Lucas finally said. "I fought hard against my attraction to her. I in no way wanted to be in a relationship. On the other hand, I'd never wanted a woman like I wanted her. She would walk into the room and I was on instant alert. I tried to tell myself it was just some weird hormonal imbalance, but even though I was fighting it, I knew it was a losing battle."

"Everyone can see that you and Amy were meant to be together. Things may have started out rocky, but you're disgustingly in love now. There isn't a woman out there who could love you like she does. It's the only reason she puts up with your ugly hide," Alex said and punched Lucas in the arm. "Of course, technically, it's not a reason…"

"It sounds to me as if the *both* of you are just lovesick and whipped. It'll never happen to me," Mark added with a cocky smile. He crossed his fingers behind his back.

Lucas and Alex looked at each other and smiled. They knew their brother would go down kicking and screaming, but he *would* go down. It would be immensely pleasurable for them both to watch.

"I may not be in love like Lucas, but it's nice to have something to come home to," Alex said. He felt a twinge of pain as he said the words. He figured he was lying to himself, saying he wasn't *in love,* but it was better than the alternative. Being in love, needing someone that desperately scared him, and Alex Anderson would never admit to such a fear.

"Yeah, I think you're fooling yourself, little bro. I've seen the way you look at Jessica. It's more than just lust. You look at her the way I look at Amy. The sooner you accept that fact and enjoy being married, the sooner you can stop hurting all the time. Man, when I finally just let myself open up, my whole world changed. Seriously, if something were to ever happen to Amy, I couldn't survive it." Lucas pulled his phone out for the millionth time plus one to see whether he'd missed her urgent call.

"Give it a break, Bro. Your wife will call you if she goes into labor. Your phone will not miraculously miss a call, and if both of those things does happen, someone will come running to find you and rush you to the hospital," Mark said.

"I know, I know, but wait until you're in my position. There's nothing greater than your wife giving birth. It's amazing and beautiful and, at the same time, terrifying. I'd gladly take her every pain if I could. It kills me to just stand by, only holding her hand while she…you know. But then there's this beautiful child resting in her arms, and she's smiling with this radiant joy on her face. There's nothing like it in the world," Lucas finished.

Alex sat there quietly, listening to Lucas talk. He was jealous of his brother, which was very unusual. He wished so much he could have been there for the birth of his son, and he was still angry Jessica had taken that from him. He should have heard his son's first cry. He should have been there so he could protect them both if they needed it.

He knew he had to take some of the responsibility, but the thought that she could have become pregnant after their night in the elevator had never once crossed his mind. It shamed him to admit that. They were both fools for the time wasted.

"That sounds like heartache that I don't want to deal with," Mark laughed. The joke brought Alex back to the present. He laughed, but it was forced. Thankfully, his brothers let it go.

"Well, we'd better get back to work. Everyone should be here in a couple of hours. We don't want them to realize we play out here more than we work," Lucas said.

The three men quickly dressed and headed over to the cattle. When they'd finished up there, they made their way to the barn to brush their horses down.

"It's about time you boys quit playing around and got back here," came the booming voice of their father.

"Hey, Dad," all three boys said in unison as they approached and then gave their father a hug.

"You have a house full of people all waiting on you three."

"Well, that's because they all know I'm doing the grilling," Alex smiled.

"I think it's because they know your mama and your beautiful brides have been busy making everything else," Joseph answered back.

"Mmm...I hope Mom made her famous chicken salad," Lucas said.

"Well, you should know your mom still spoils you boys rotten. I try and tell her you're all grown up and don't need her spoiling, but she won't listen to me," Joseph said. The three boys looked at each other and rolled their eyes.

"Sure, Dad. Mom's the only one who spoils us," Mark said, smacking his father on the back. "Let's head on in so we can get some of Mom's salad, and Alex can get those steaks on the grill," he continued. His mouth was starting to water just thinking about it.

"Did you lose again?" Joseph turned his attention toward Alex.

"Aw, Dad, you know they cheated because I'm the only one who can cook worth a lick," Alex said in his own defense.

*****

They had a laugh and walked companionably up to the house. They could hear people laughing and talking, even from the barn.

"So, Mark. When are you going to settle down like your brothers and give your poor mama grandbabies? You know she's not getting any younger, and she cries at night from the heartbreak of a son intent on living alone," Joseph said.

Mark sighed before he spoke. "You know none of that's true, Dad. You're the one who wants all those grandbabies running around. I think Lucas and Alex are doing just fine at giving you a bunch of little Andersons," he said. "And if Mom heard you say she was old, you'd be in for a world of hurt," he added with a wicked grin.

"Now don't talk back, boy. Of course it's your mother who's worried about you. And if you dare tell your mom what I said, you'll be the one in a world of hurt," Joseph said.

"OK, Dad, you can let her know I'm staying a bachelor. There are too many hearts that would be broken if I decided to tie the knot. I don't want to be responsible for all that heartbreak," he said with a chuckle. "I'm a major humanitarian."

"You know he'll collapse like an empty sack, just like we did," Lucas said.

"You stay out of this, Lucas," Mark said. "Your two cents aren't worth one." He knew he was a lucky man; there was no need for a woman in his life, he thought. OK, so he felt a little alone at times. Who didn't? He pushed that thought — and the slight pang it caused in his gut — right from his mind.

"Don't worry about it, Bro. Married life isn't all that bad, and it's way cool to be a father. Speaking of fatherhood, where's my boy?" Alex asked his dad.

"He was playing with his cousin when I headed down here," Joseph said and smiled fondly.

Alex and Lucas both picked up their pace so they could see their kids. Mark shook his head, thinking his brothers had it bad. At least he liked their wives, and those kids *were* pretty dang adorable.

Chapter Twenty-Two

Jessica stopped short at the sight of Alex walking around the corner of the house. The man was a hunk and a half all the time, but in skintight Wranglers, boots and an old Stetson, he was the sexiest thing she'd every laid eyes on.

As if Alex felt her gaze, he looked up, and they stared across the yard at each other. Without conscious thought, she began moving in his direction, and when she met him halfway, forgot everything around them. He smelled like a hardworking man, and she found herself practically drooling.

She was in a trance as she lifted her hand to his dusty cheek and wiped away a piece of grass clinging to the slight stubble dotting his skin, making him look rugged and tough. Her knees shook as heat flooded her and she fought the urge to jump into his arms and ravish him right then and there.

Without saying a word, he pulled her into his arms and crushed her lips to his. Her arms wrapped around his neck to pull him even closer. Her heart was racing, and fireworks were shooting off all through her body. *Let freedom ring!* His hands began roaming up and down her back, and she was ready to take off his clothes.

"Ahem…Alex, those steaks should get started," Mark said.

Jessica jumped back as if lightning had just struck them both. She'd been so focused on Alex, she'd forgotten where they were. She could feel her face turning many dark shades of red as she looked around in embarrassment. Thankfully, no one was paying the least bit of attention to the two of them.

Alex looked at Mark and growled. Jessica did a double take. She couldn't believe her husband had actually growled, and her mouth gaped open in shock.

Mark laughed and pulled Alex away. "Come on, Bro. You have all night to be with your bride," he said. Mark turned and gave Jessica a wink, making her blush even more.

"Whoa, girl. That was so much steam, I'm surprised my water didn't burst right then and there." Amy was laughing as she walked up to Jessica.

Jessica's furious blush miraculously grew even deeper. "I'm a bit mortified right now," she managed to say.

"A bit?" Amy chortled. "But really, Jessica, don't ever be embarrassed for desiring your husband. He's a sexy, vibrant man, and you guys are newlyweds. I can't wait for this beautiful baby to make his entrance into the world so I can rub up against my husband again. Right now he has to try to make his way around my whale-like body." Amy smiled sheepishly.

"You're the most beautiful pregnant woman I've ever been around," Jessica said. "I'm serious."

"Thank you, but I feel as if I swallowed not just one watermelon, but about ten of them." She said the words while she rubbed her stomach. There was real pride in her eyes and voice.

"I know I did a lot of moaning and groaning in the last month of my pregnancy, but all the bloating and aching were well worth it when I held my baby boy in my arms," Jessica said. "I don't get to hold him much when this family is around, though. He's definitely a celebrity here," she finished with a smile.

"It's the same way with Jasmine. They adore her. I love how much this family values each of their own. I also love how much they love the adopted family members, like you and me. Once you're a part of this family, it's for life," Amy added with a smile.

"I'm so nervous around everyone, though," Jessica admitted. "You and Lucas obviously love each other with such a deep passion. Alex was forced to marry me because of Jacob," she added with a sad quiver at those last words. "I've known this family since I was a child, but I was so shy that I remained in the background. I remember watching Alex, wishing I had the courage to go up to him, wishing I were one of those girls who could catch his eye. I guess I finally did catch his eye, but not exactly the way I wanted to." Pain ripped through her at the reminder of who she was. When would she have the self-confidence that her sister-in-law did?

Amy immediately wrapped an arm around Jessica. "I love Lucas, heart and soul, but trust me when I say that it didn't start out strong. We seemed

to have an instant dislike for each other. I wasn't
willing to marry him. I was ticked with how he dared
to try and dominate me. To tell you the truth, he was a
horse's ass when we were first together. I knew he
was out of my league, and I felt the way you do. I felt
as if I were trapping him. I'd wanted a baby so badly
for so long, and I'd wanted to belong to a real family,
and I felt as if I'd somehow made the pregnancy
happen. We were both fighting our attraction like
crazy, but luckily he pulled his head out and he's an
amazing husband. I can't, of course, admit that I
needed to change anything," she said with tears in her
eyes and a watery smile at her attempted joke.

"How did it all work out so beautifully?" Jessica
asked, not able to imagine that the two of them had
ever had a terrible time together. Their love was so
obvious.

"I was so *very* wrong," Amy replied. "I want to
really emphasize that point to you. We fought our
attraction, which was stupid because I see that now as
wasted time. We love each other, and it only grows
stronger. Plus, this family loves my daughter and me
beyond anything I could have ever imagined when I
was a lonely little girl. They love you too, and so do I.
You will one day wake up and wonder what took you
so long to see how much you're meant to be with
Alex forever," Amy finished.

"It's so amazing that two people can have so
much in common, even coming from such different
backgrounds. I remember the other girls in my school,
how confident they were. They were handed
everything, just like I was, but many of them were
horrid creatures. Yet, those were always the girls the

boys went for. I don't know if it was their confidence, or their looks, or both, but I hated them so much. I tried making friends, and even managed to have a few companions on occasion, but we were from two different worlds. The only thing connecting us was our large bank accounts. I am so sorry for what you went through, Amy. I can't imagine how frightened you must have been all the time. It makes me feel guilty for ever complaining, when I was raised by two amazing parents and lived my life more than comfortable."

"Don't downplay your own trials and tribulations, Jessica. Yes, I went through hard times, but it's nobody's right to judge who had it worse. Just because you didn't have to worry about where your next meal was coming from doesn't lessen the pain you went through. To feel unloved, to feel all alone in the world, hurts no matter who you are, or what possessions you have. I know the two of us are going to be best friends. We may have grown up in two different places, but we share the same insecurities. Lucas is healing me, a little more each new day. If you let him, Alex will do the same for you."

Jessica was amazed by how much her sister-in-law knew. Maybe they truly were kindred spirits. She would love to open up and let Alex in, but how was she supposed to do that?

The two women finished by giving each other a hug, even though it was a little bit difficult with Amy's belly a hard lump between them. Amy giggled. "See, I told you this thing is always in the way."

"Well, I repeat, you're absolutely gorgeous," Jessica said.

"There's my pregnant wife. How are you feeling? Shouldn't you be sitting down? Can I get you anything?" Lucas walked up, fired off a bunch of questions at Amy, and then put his arm around her as if he were planning to pick her up and carry her off to bed.

Amy laughed at her worried husband and reached up to place her hand on his face. It was such an intimate moment, Jessica felt like an intruder.

"I'm fine, honey. You need to quit worrying so much. I told you that if there was anything at all wrong, you'd be the first to know," Amy assured him.

Lucas then bent down and kissed Amy with such a tender passion, it brought tears to Jessica's eyes. If only…

They finally broke apart, and now Amy's face was the one that was flushed. "Now go and help your brother cook while I waddle over to that comfy lounge chair and continue chatting with my favorite sister-in-law. No, wait. Scratch that…just *my favorite sister*," she finished, smiling fondly at Jessica.

The words choked Jessica up even more. She was grateful she'd decided to put her worries aside and join the family gathering. Her son was getting all kinds of love, and she knew she and Amy were going to be true friends. And Jessica definitely needed one.

"I'd listen to her, Lucas. Pregnant women tend to change moods faster than a speeding bullet." Both girls giggled. Then Amy took Jessica's arm, and they walked toward the lounge chairs sitting next to a warm fire as the sun began setting and the air quickly cooled.

"But Alex lost fair and square, which means I can hang with you," Lucas said, sounding like a little boy. Amy gave him a look, and he conceded defeat.

*****

Lucas walked up to his brother, offering his help. "Ha! Looks like you were annoying your wife as much as you were annoying us today with all your worrying," Alex goaded him.

"I wasn't annoying her. She was just having girl talk with your wife about you," Lucas said with a wicked smile.

Alex's head whipped around as his confident smirk fell. "What were they saying?"

"You know, it's girl talk. No boys allowed in that conversation," Lucas said, enjoying having the upper hand again. His smirk faded, though, as his eyes involuntarily sought out his wife.

Alex knew his brother was wishing he could take Amy home and keep her safe.

"Yeah, kinda sucks being over here, huh?" Alex mocked him good-naturedly. Lucas was gazing like a puppy at Amy.

"I love her so much, Alex. I really can't remember life without her," he said. "I know you love Jessica, and I know you're confused right now, and I know things aren't perfect, but they didn't start perfect for us, either. I promise you it will get better. You have to let all the bad go and just focus on what's in front of you. She's a good woman and the two of you have a beautiful little boy. You can have so much more if you just allow yourself to."

"It's all good. Why don't you quit talking like a girl again and help me grill?" Alex said.

"OK, I don't want you running to Amy and telling her you did all the work. I'll get in trouble," he said as he grabbed some tongs and started flipping the steaks. The smell reminded Lucas he hadn't eaten in hours. "Let's get this done before I die of hunger. Man, Mark worked our butts off today."

"No kidding. I think he was trying to kill us," Alex said, and laughed.

"Did I just hear you tough boys whining?" Mark suddenly popped through the doorway.

"Not whining, Mark, just discussing how sore I'm going to be tomorrow," Alex said with a chuckle. "I guess I should try to get out here a little more often. I'm getting a little too used to that desk."

"Hey, speak for yourself. I chase around a kid on the verge of the terrible twos every day. Let me tell you, it's a workout that rivals rustling up cows." Lucas immediately looked around until he spotted his daughter. Her grandfather, of course, was pampering the child.

"Notice how Dad's always telling us we need to give Mom grandkids, but he's the one who's hogging them all the time," Lucas said.

"I know. Dad's all bark and no bite. We all know he wants those grandkids for himself, but, man, have you noticed how good he looks? Having those two babies has given him a whole new youthfulness," Alex said.

"I've made billion-dollar mergers, traveled across the globe, and spoken with dignitaries, but nothing gives me more joy than sitting in my living room with Amy cuddled up against my side and Jasmine asleep in my arms. Note that I said *asleep*," he joked. "Having Jasmine around doesn't always give *me* youthfulness! But I love it."

"Yeah, Jacob is about the greatest kid in the world. I didn't think I wanted to be a father, but now that I have him, my life would be empty if he wasn't there. It's odd how much can change in your life in a single day." After he realized how serious the conversation had become, he added, "Of course, I have to say that. Women love guys with a sensitive streak."

*****

Mark stood beside his brothers, feeling a bit left out. He hadn't felt that way since they were all young kids and Lucas and Alex would sometimes run off ahead of him. He'd been too young to keep up, but they'd always come back for him eventually.

"Well, I think I'll just enjoy being a favorite uncle," he finally spoke up.

As if Jasmine had heard him, she looked up from where she was with her grandpa and spotted her dad and uncles. She started toddling over towards them as fast as her chubby little legs would carry her. "Unca Mar! Unca Mar!" she demanded as she held out her arms to him. Her words were getting so much better, but Mark wished she would keep the sweet baby talk forever.

"How's my beautiful princess?" he asked, swinging her up into his arms and blowing raspberries on her tummy.

"Hungy," she said and pointed to the steaks.

"That's my good girl. Let's get you some dinner. You can be my hot date. I will most definitely have the prettiest one here," he said in a very father-like voice.

"Yeah," Jasmine said and clapped her hands together. Then she grabbed Mark's face and gave him a sloppy kiss.

"Looks as if these are ready," Alex said. He motioned for the staff to gather up the food, and he went down with his brothers to be with the rest of their family.

During dinner, it was hard to get two words in with all the laughter and stories being passed up and down the large picnic tables set up on the lawn.

*****

Jessica finally allowed herself to relax and found that she was having a great time. She loved to watch Alex interact with his brothers. They all behaved like little boys, always trying to best each other and telling many embarrassing stories about one another.

"...Seriously, you should have seen him standing there with his pants around his ankles..." Jessica heard Mark saying as she tuned back toward the conversation. She'd have to ask Alex about that later. She'd clearly missed out on a great story.

"OK, everyone, ignore my brother. I think he's had one too many, if you know what I mean," Alex said, motioning in the air as if he were glugging away from an upturned bottle.

"You're just upset because you're usually the one who ends up at the losing end of all these childhood stories," Mark said as he lightly punched his brother in the arm.

Alex shrugged at the good-natured teasing. He turned to Jessica and gave her a smile.

"I enjoy the stories," she said somewhat shyly.

Alex couldn't help himself. He leaned down, brushing his lips against hers in a soft kiss. It brought tears to her eyes, and she quickly looked away and forced a bite of food down.

"Are you OK?" he asked her quietly.

"Yes, of course."

He continued to look at her for a moment, making her want to squirm in her chair. Then someone else asked him a question, which gave her time to compose herself. She was praying no one had noticed.

Jacob gave a little giggle from his high chair which was placed right next to his grandpa, who happened to have a knowing look on his face. It wasn't easy to keep anything from Joseph, and he was well aware of the struggles going on between his middle son and wife.

"They are pretty silly, aren't they?" Joseph said to his grandson, and everyone laughed.

Suddenly there was a commotion at the other end of the table. Lucas was jumping up, looking around in all directions, as if danger was approaching and he was going to take on an entire army.

"What are you flying all around for?" Joseph asked.

Lucas looked at his father with panic in his eyes. "It's time, Dad. Amy's water just broke," he said as if he were a lost little boy.

"Well, why didn't you say so?" Joseph said, He, too, wasn't immune to panic.

"Boys, would you please calm down? Childbirth is natural, and nothing to go nuts about," Katherine said to her husband and son. "How far apart are your contractions?" she asked Amy.

"About two minutes," Amy said, a little bit short of breath.

"Well, then, we'd better get you to the hospital."

"Let's go," Lucas almost shouted.

"I'll drive her, Lucas. You're too stressed to be driving anybody," Katherine told him.

"OK, Mom." He never argued with his mother.

"Thank you to everyone who came out and spent this evening with us. You're all so special to us," Katherine said to the large group of family and friends. "We'll keep you all updated on this beautiful new addition to our family, and please keep Amy, Lucas and Jasmine in your prayers as they bring this new baby into the world."

Everyone applauded, then got up to leave. It wasn't a time for guests.

"Mark, you ride to the hospital with Alex and Jessica. The babies are getting tired, and Julia can take them both back to Alex's house, if that's OK with you," Joseph said. Everyone nodded.

"Well, good. That's settled," Joseph said. "Let's get going and wait for the dramatic appearance of the newest member of our family."

Chapter Twenty-Three

"It's a boy!" Lucas came bursting through the hospital doors, and his family immediately engulfed him in hugs and congratulations.

"Mom, Dad, Amy wants you both," he said through the tears of joy rolling down his cheeks. Neither of them had to be told twice. They were immediately through the doors and off to see Amy and their newest grandson.

Jessica watched the rejoicing all around her with a mixture of happiness for her newfound sister and regret that her life was not so blessed. The idea of having another child, one who was planned with a husband who loved her, was something she was almost afraid even to think of, but she wanted it so badly.

"The rest of the family can come see Amy and the baby now," a nurse said from the doorway.

"Last one in is a monkey's uncle," Mark said with a sly grin at Alex. "Scratch that; last one in is a monkey." Mark was the first one out of the waiting room. Though he insisted he didn't want a family of his own, he was certainly excited when a new baby showed up in their lives.

The rest of the family followed him. "He's so beautiful, Amy," Jessica said.

"You may get a chance to hold him if his grandpa ever lets him go," she teased.

"I have to make sure the little tyke is doing OK," Joseph said, not bothering to look up from his new grandson.

"What are you going to name him?" Alex asked.

"We decided on Isaiah Allen, after Dad's father," Lucas said.

"That's a real fine name, son," Joseph said, with some tears of his own. He then quickly turned away.

"Ah, Dad, we all know you too well. You don't have to pretend to be some tough old guy," Alex said.

"Now, boy, you're not too old for me to take you out behind the woodshed," Joseph said, but with no oomph behind his words.

"Hey, now, there's no bickering in my recovery room," Amy said with an indulgent tone. Men were all big babies.

The littlest baby started to fuss, and Joseph handed him to his mother with reluctance.

"Amy needs to feed him now. Why don't you all go home and get some rest and then come over tomorrow for Isaiah's homecoming?" Lucas asked.

They all said their goodbyes and headed out. Jessica was even more convinced that she didn't want her son to grow up without siblings. Maybe Alex wouldn't mind having another child. Even if their marriage wasn't one of love, they planned to stay together for Jacob's sake, so why not have a sibling for him? But how on earth did she approach her husband with such a subject?

The two of them were always civil, but they didn't discuss feelings, emotions, anything that might upset the delicate balance of their truce together. Well, it was past time they got over that. She needed him to understand that growing up an only child was an incredibly lonely thing — she needed him to know she had feelings, period.

Alex took her hand as they walked to their vehicle. "He sure was cute. I wish so much I had been there for Jacob when he was born."

Not again. Jessica automatically tensed, thinking they were going to have another fight. But she was too tired for it. "I'm really sorry about that. I know we haven't talked much about it since the day you found out about him, but I can admit I was wrong not to tell you. I should have given you the benefit of the doubt."

"I know. I messed up, too, and I'm sorry, as well," he said.

She was so surprised, she didn't know what else to say. He didn't sound angry or even hurt. He just sounded a little bit down.

"I hadn't exactly led a life that would have made you believe I would be ready, or willing, to settle down," he continued. "I understand everything now that I know you better. You thought you were doing the right thing in not telling me. I hope you realize I would have been there for you the moment you found out. I don't shirk my responsibilities."

Jessica wanted to cry. Alex probably thought he was reassuring her, but what he'd said was making her heart break in two. He thought of her as just another one of his responsibilities — not his wife. He was doing the right thing, nothing more, and only because he'd been taught to do so. She wanted him to be with her because he loved her, not because he'd screwed up and now had to pay the price.

"I know you would have done the right thing from the beginning," she said in what she hoped was a normal tone of voice.

Jessica pulled her hand from his as they approached their vehicle. She couldn't maintain the contact any longer; it was slowly killing her. But without warning he pushed her up against the car and kissed her. His tongue traced the edges of her lips before opening her mouth and slowly sliding inside, melting her in a second. All heartbreak healed as he rubbed his hands down her sides, and then reached up to hold her head as he deepened the kiss.

Disappointment filled her when he broke away, but it was quickly replaced by hope.

"Let's go on vacation," Alex said. "We didn't get a honeymoon, and I have to take a trip over to the Virgin Islands this week. Come with me. Jacob will be fine for a few days. I'll hurry and get you home; I promise."

He was looking deep into her eyes, and Jessica found she couldn't say no. She couldn't even find her voice. She finally nodded her head.

Alex lifted her up into his arms, gave her another quick kiss, and then helped her into the car. "We'll have a great time. I have meetings in the mornings, but then we'll have all day to play in the water and all night to dance." He sounded like an excited teenager getting ready for summer.

"I'd love to go," she finally managed to say, and instantly blushed at her use of the *L*-word.

Jessica was nervous. She'd never liked large crowds and prayed his idea of dancing wasn't in the middle of a crowded club. But, wherever it was, it would be worth it. He wanted to spend time alone with her. This could be the chance she'd been waiting for. She could talk to him about extending their family — possibly even tell him of her feelings for him. Could things really go on as they had been?

"Pack up tomorrow. We'll be leaving in two days. We can let Julia know tonight, and you can get all your time in with Jacob so you won't feel guilty."

She looked ahead at the road. She hated that he knew her so well. She did feel guilty about leaving their son at home, but at the same time, if she ever hoped to make her marriage a real one, this was the time to do it. They were going to be in a romantic hotel on an exotic island, and completely alone. She had a few days to let her defenses down, show him her love and see whether it made a difference.

"It sounds great. I know Jacob will be fine, but I'm glad I'll have tomorrow," she said.

They rode in a comfortable silence the rest of the way home. She was planning what needed to get done before they left and how she was going to talk to him. He was just happy to take Jessica with him, though he wasn't putting too much thought into why he felt that way.

*****

"We have to leave, Jessica," Alex said for the tenth time.

"I know, I know. It's just so hard," Jessica said as she kissed Jacob for about the hundredth time. "I love you, sweetie. Mama will be home in a few days. Julia is going to take really good care of you — I promise."

They headed to the limo, and Jessica smiled as she climbed inside. He had champagne chilling, a vase with two dozen roses, chocolates, and a small wrapped package waiting for her.

"What is this?" she asked.

"I didn't give you a honeymoon, so even though this is a business trip, I plan on doing minimal business and giving you a romantic honeymoon the rest of the time. I wanted to start the trip out right," he said with a little shrug.

Jessica was so choked up at his thoughtfulness, she couldn't speak for several moments. "Thank you," she finally managed to get out.

"Here, open your gift," he said with a sparkle in his eyes.

She took the package from him, slowly taking the wrapping off of the gift. When she opened the jewelry box, she couldn't take her eyes off the exquisite ruby necklace inside.

"It's so beautiful."

"Turn around, and I'll put it on for you. I thought it would match your favorite dress, so I knew I had to get it for you," he said. His fingers trailed down her neck when he was finished fastening the necklace, and she shivered with need.

Alex slowly turned her around and kissed her with such tenderness, she felt as if her whole body would melt. She loved the undiminished passion they shared, but this tenderness threatened her complete undoing.

"You look beautiful, necklace or not," he whispered as he trailed his lips down the side of her neck. Her body shivered again and she reached for him, desperate to have his lips on hers.

Jessica hadn't realized how much time had passed when a voice came over the intercom, saying, "We will be arriving at the airport in five minutes."

Jessica jumped back as if she'd been caught necking in the locker room. But wait! This was her husband and they weren't doing anything wrong. Why was her face suddenly flaming?

"You are stunning when you get embarrassed," Alex told her as his finger rubbed down her cheek.

"I don't know why I blush so easily. I hate that about myself," she admitted.

"Never give up your innocence. It's one of the things I admire most about you. So many people in our world are jaded and cold, but no one could ever accuse you of being either."

Jessica melted all over again at his loving words. She was growing confident in her plans of telling him how she felt. Maybe he cared for her more than she imagined he did. Her heart swelled at just the thought.

"I'm glad you decided to come on the trip," Alex said as he helped her from the car.

"So am I," she said.

"I promise not to work too much."

"I will hold you to that promise." Jessica looked forward to a few days of really getting to know the man she'd married.

They boarded the company jet, which was luxurious even for her, with her privileged upbringing. After they ate a meal served by a bubbly flight attendant, Jessica's exhaustion took over, and she slept the rest of the flight curled against Alex's side on the couch. The last thing she felt before drifting off was his hand gently caressing her back. If this were all a dream, she had no desire to wake.

*****

"Wake up. We're here." Alex's voice stirred Jessica from her sleep.

"Already?" she grumbled. She was warm and comfortable and didn't want to open her eyes.

"You slept the whole flight," he said with a slight laugh. "I'm glad because now you will have a lot of energy for our night out."

They emerged from the jet, and she breathed in the beauty of the island. It was so warm, with a pleasant breeze gently ruffling their hair. Before she got the chance to enjoy the balmy weather, they climbed into the waiting car.

"I have some business to take care of right away. Why don't you get settled in the room and then relax on the beach for a while? Be ready by six tonight for dinner and dancing. And wear a sexy dress," he added.

"Are you suggesting that I don't look sexy no matter what I have on, dear?" she asked, archly.

"You got me there! I have to brush up on the husband's manual for trick questions and dangerous remarks. And, just in case you ever ask, no, nothing you own makes you look fat, darling."

"Thank you, Alex. You'll learn. The beach idea sounds perfect, by the way. I haven't lain on the beach in forever. Seattle isn't exactly known for lounging weather," she said with a smile.

"No. I think that's one of the reasons I love my job so much. I get to travel to places like this all the time and it makes the months and months of continuous rain in Seattle just a little more bearable. I don't know if I'd be able to stay there without frequent breaks. The cloud cover alone would get to be too depressing."

"I sort of know what you mean. But I've definitely had mixed feelings about Seattle. When I was in Africa, it was such a change from Seattle that it took me a couple of months to get used to it. With my personal Pandora's box of fears, especially of the dark, I would lie in bed shaking most nights. After a while, though, I got more used to the weather, and I started appreciating the beauty around me. The area where I stayed was so remote, so untouched by the rest of the world, that it was a true joy to be a part of it. Now, I would much rather live in Seattle, where they don't have spiders the size of cars, but it is fun to travel," she said with a laugh.

"The size of cars?" he asked with a raise of his brow.

"OK, maybe that was a slight exaggeration, but seriously, there are some huge insects over there!"

"All girls are afraid of the poor defenseless spiders," he teased.

"Defenseless, my butt. Those things have fangs the size of giant needles and you can see the determination in their eyes to get you. It still gives me nightmares to think about."

When Alex openly laughed, Jessica turned to him with an impish smile. "There were monkeys, too. All kinds of monkeys — everywhere. They would come into camp and do whatever it was they wanted. While you were sleeping, they'd…"

"Fine. I call a truce," he said, holding up his hands and laughing.

At the hotel, Alex escorted her to their room, decorated in soft pastels and with the curtains rippling in the breeze from the ocean. It had the feel of a cabana and wasn't incredibly fancy; Jessica was instantly in love. She quickly changed clothes and headed to the semiprivate beach. Several people from the hotel were there, but they were mostly couples, and everyone seemed to be enjoying the beauty around them.

Jessica jumped into the warm ocean and swam around until she was tired. Then she found a covered lounge area and pulled out her favorite romance book. She was reading about the hero and heroine, and thinking her life was so much better than that of the fictional characters, when she drifted off.

When Jessica woke, she glanced quickly at her watch and gave a little squeak as she realized it was four-thirty. She gathered her items quickly and headed back to the room to get ready for her date.

There was a message waiting, asking her to meet Alex in the bar, as he was running a little late. She jumped into the shower and then took her time making sure she looked perfect. Their trip here had gone beautifully, and she wanted their easy banter and opening up to continue over the next few days.

She'd purchased a dress she normally never would have worn, but she wanted to let loose on vacation. The neckline was her lowest by far, and it showed a generous amount of cleavage. The back of the dress dipped down to the small of her back, and the hem reached midthigh. It hugged her hips tightly, and the skirt flared out in a flirty style. She had to be quite proud of her after-baby body. Her curves were slightly more pronounced, but after some hard work, she'd managed to get her stomach back into pre-pregnancy condition, and her legs were toned.

She'd even purchased sexy new undergarments for the outfit, including a lace garter belt. No panty hose this time! She wanted to excite passion in her husband, and, with the outfit she was wearing, she was hoping he had an uncomfortable evening. A woman had to do what a woman had to do.

As Jessica looked at her image in the full-length mirror, she was a little shocked by her own boldness. Yet she was forced to smile as she turned to look at herself from all angles. She almost didn't recognize the woman staring back at her. Since she'd become a mother, she'd taken too little time with herself. She wore sweats too often and hardly ever applied makeup. Alex hadn't seemed to mind, but Jessica liked feeling like a woman and vowed to take more time to make herself beautiful from then on.

Who said you couldn't be both a great mother and a woman? Slipping on her heels, she walked with confidence to the door, though anticipation was stirring up butterflies in her stomach.

She made her way to the hotel lobby and stepped into the bar, where she spotted Alex right away. When he turned toward her and his eyes slid by and then whipped back to her, Jessica smiled with triumph. So far, so good.

Chapter Twenty-Four

Alex almost slipped out of his seat when he spotted his wife. She was always beautiful, but he'd never seen her in anything like the dress she was wearing. His pants became uncomfortably tight. But, unconcerned with any onlookers' surprised, and impressed, stares, he got up and walked to her, almost in a trance.

"You're the most ravishing woman I've ever met," he said before pulling her into his arms and taking her lips with his. Damn. He could take her right there in the middle of the bar. Reluctantly, he released her, vowing to have her soon.

"Thank you. You're looking quite dashing yourself," she answered breathlessly.

"I'm going to have to fight off every man in this place," he said. He shot a swift but deadly glare at a guy who was practically drooling.

Alex wrapped his arm possessively around her and led her to the restaurant outside.

"How was your day?" Alex asked as they were served their wine.

"It was incredible, though perhaps not the stuff of lengthy sagas. I went to the beach and read for a while before falling asleep beneath the warm sun. I can't remember the last time I've been so relaxed," she answered as she took a sip of the wine.

"I'm glad to hear that. I missed you today."

Her heart stalled at his words. He'd never said such a thing to her. And her heart started again and then soared. Maybe he was ready to discuss what their future held.

"I missed you, too," she responded shyly. Why did she have to be so embarrassed to say such a thing to the man she was married to? "What business are you here for? I can't believe I didn't ask you earlier."

"My father is helping to build a community center and I'm checking in on the progress and dealing with a few red flags that have been thrown our way."

"Is it anything serious?"

"No. It will all be worked out quickly. Whenever we build, some issues always come up. But the people are anxious to see the project completed. It will offer a safe place for teenagers to hang out together, and also offer educational services," he said proudly.

"That's wonderful, Alex. I had no idea you were doing such projects."

"It's nothing," he replied, a little too quickly, and changed the subject.

After a dinner filled with laughter and excellent food zipped past, he hailed a cab and took her to a different part of town.

Their destination shocked her. How did Alex know about such places? She could hear the music from the street, and the neighborhood looked almost threatening at night.

"Are you sure this is a safe area?"

Alex threw back his head and laughed. "Don't worry, my love. I'll protect you from any dangers," he said, leading her through the open doorway.

Jessica caught her breath at his words. Did he know how badly she wanted to be his love? But all her thoughts fled once they went inside.

The club was so dimly lit that it was hard to see anything. A steamy song was playing loudly, and people were mashed together all throughout the club. *Great*, she thought, *a crowded club*. But she forgot her fears when she took in the sights around her. Most of the couples looked as if they weren't dancing, but having sex. They slid seductively against one another, bumping and grinding.

Her eyes were drawn to the couple in front of them. Her stomach tightened, and she told herself she should look away. The moment seemed so intimate between the two people, she felt like a Peeping Tom.

The woman's head was thrown back, and her lips were open in what Jessica was sure was a moan escaping. The man had her plastered against him, with his hands running up and down her back and thighs, while his mouth was moving over her neck and breasts. Jessica finally managed to turn away and felt like running from the club.

"Let's dance," Alex whispered in her ear. His voice sounded deep and husky, causing her stomach to tighten even further. She nodded; she couldn't speak right then.

Alex pulled her into his arms, reminding her of their first dance together. He'd been so flirty and cocky, and though she'd tried to escape him, it had been what she'd dreamed about as a teenager. Now, she could dance with him every single day if she liked — that was, if he'd take the time. Dancing in his arms at that moment, Jessica couldn't understand why she'd ever felt the need to fight him in any way.

"I want you so badly. You look so amazing in this dress, I could take you right here," he whispered, causing a shiver to pass all the way down her spine. Heat surged straight to her core, and she melted where she wanted his touch so badly.

Words still couldn't escape Jessica's tightened throat. Alex kissed her with passion, making her forget the room around them. His lips moved from her lips to her neck and down the plunging neckline of her dress. She was now dancing like all the others in the club, not caring that anyone could see, only wanting his mouth caressing her skin.

His hands stroked up and down her back, getting lower and lower with each pass he made. They were barely moving to the music as he slowly began walking her backward until she felt the hardness of a wall behind her.

His hands were now running along the side of her body, touching the sides of her aching breasts and tender stomach. He began moving his fingers down her hips until he finally found the hem of her dress.

They ran up underneath and cupped her bottom, left bare by her lacy thong. She let out a moan of pleasure as he caressed her skin.

He pulled her roughly into his arousal, and his lips once again connected with hers. It was pure seduction, and she didn't care where they were. She just wanted him to end the torture and plunge deep inside her swollen folds.

She lifted her hands up to begin unbuttoning his shirt when he suddenly stopped and pulled back.

"We have to get out of here now," he said through clenched teeth. Without saying any more, he grabbed her hand and led her from the club. He pulled her quickly down the walk and hailed them a cab.

Jessica was beginning to think she'd done something wrong because he was sitting several feet away from her in the cab, not uttering a word. They reached the hotel, and he helped her from the car. He then pulled her around the building, and they walked out onto the beach and took a secluded path.

She was just working up the courage to ask him what was wrong when he drew her back into his arms and kissed her again with all the force he'd shown her at the club. She forgot all about her worries as her arms came around his neck, and she gave him full access to her mouth and body.

Alex threw his jacket on the ground and lowered her gently to the grass-covered mound in the middle of a deserted trail. The silver moon cast a soft glow, providing only enough light to see the need in his face, leaving everything around him in shadows. He stripped her dress off in one movement, leaving her exposed and vulnerable.

He was awed by the sight she made, wearing only a piece of black lace barely hiding her from him, plus the garter belt and red heels. She was bathed in moonlight, giving her a surreal look. He wanted nothing more than to bury himself deep inside her without ado, but he wasn't a selfish lover.

He quickly stripped away his clothes and then brought their bodies back into intimate contact. He took her lips in his again, making her cry out her pleasure, as his hands explored every inch of her skin. His lips caressed her neck and the tops of her breasts.

Jessica could barely breathe, the pressure was so great. She wanted to cry out her love for him but held back — barely. When his lips finally took her hardened peak into his mouth and he sucked her aching nipple, her whole back arched off the ground. When he gently nipped the sensitized skin, she almost came undone.

"Please," she begged. She didn't know whether she was begging him to continue what he was doing or to cut to the chase and join them together.

Alex kissed his way down her smooth stomach, causing it to tighten even more. His tongue dipped into her belly button, and Jessica moaned at the intense sensations he was bringing her. He finally moved to kiss and caress her thighs, making them open to his administering. When his mouth finally touched her burning heat, she thought she would explode.

Her body wouldn't stay still. He deepened the intimate kiss, and she could feel her body begging for release. When he dipped his fingers inside her, she couldn't hold back any longer. She cried out and finally let go, waves of pleasure washing over her.

Alex slowly kissed his way back up her body, starting to stir her heat once again. She didn't understand how he could make her want him so much. This was more than anyone should have, and it was exquisite.

He brought his lips back to hers, and the taste of their passion on his tongue fully brought the fire back to her body. "Please," she begged again. She wanted him deep inside her.

"Please what?" he asked, knowing the answer.

"Please love me," she gasped, and she meant those words fully.

He said nothing more, but just slipped inside her heat in one sure thrust. He threw back his head and moaned out loud. He didn't move, as if to calm himself. She jerked her hips up, needing him to move inside her.

That little movement was all it took. He grabbed her backside and thrust hard in and out of her. His lips latched back onto hers, and he loved her with a passion that should have set the grass around them on fire.

Jessica felt the heat building up inside her again, even stronger than before, and suddenly her body jerked with a pleasure so intense, it bordered on pain. Her tightening heat around him sent Alex over the edge and, with a final thrust deep inside her, he let go and cried out in his own pleasure.

His body was covered in a fine sheen of sweat, glistening in the moonlight. He collapsed on top of her, but quickly shifted them both, bringing her on top. They were still connected together, and it felt so right.

He was rubbing her naked back, and she was so content, her guard was down. She finally whispered the words she'd wanted to say for so long. "I love you, Alex."

She felt him stiffen, which told her more than words ever could have. He didn't want her love. He wanted the passion, and he even wanted companionship, but he didn't want love.

She was close to tears as he pulled their bodies apart and started to get dressed. "We'd better get out of here before some unsuspecting tourist happens to walk by," he said in an almost cold tone.

Jessica's heart was breaking into a million pieces. What had started as the perfect day was ending with devastation. The hurt was unlike anything she'd ever experienced before. She loved him so much; why couldn't he feel the same way about her? She thought she felt love when he held her in his arms. Maybe to him sex and love were two completely different things.

She quickly dressed and then walked slowly back to the hotel with her husband. It was like walking with a stranger, he was so distant.

"I know I told you I wouldn't be working much, but something came up, and I'll be busy all day tomorrow," he said as they entered the suite.

"I understand," Jessica replied.

"I need to finish some work tonight," he said and headed to the office in their hotel suite.

She didn't even reply. She went to take a shower and then go to bed, where she could cry herself to sleep.

Chapter Twenty-Five

For the next two days and nights of her honeymoon, Alex was gone all day, returning too late for them to go out. She spent her time on the beach and going shopping. All alone. Although they made love in the evenings, it was different — it wasn't *making love*. She could feel he was holding something back, and when it was over, he turned away from her, seeming to fall asleep quickly.

"A honeymoon for the ages," Jessica said to herself, and rolled her eyes grimly. She was relieved when, on the third day, he said his business in the Virgin Islands was finished up and they could head back home.

She could hardly be optimistic about what to expect. Once again, she would rarely see him, and her love for him would be locked up inside her, yearning to breathe free. She had a decision to make, and sooner, rather than later.

Their marriage had never been one built on love, but she had fallen in love with him anyway. Now, she didn't know if she could stay with him when she was the only one who felt that way. But how could she take her son away when father and son so obviously adored each other?

Her cheeks stained with hopeless tears, she finally fell asleep alone in the large bed.

*****

"I was a complete ass," Alex said to Lucas. "I knew she was falling in love with me, but, selfishly, I wanted her to keep it to herself and not bring it out in the open. I don't have the time or energy for that kind of relationship. But I've really shut her out and don't know how to make things go back to the way they were."

Lucas shook his head back and forth. Had he heard wrong? "But…but…what's so wrong with your wife loving you, and you her?"

"There's nothing wrong with it when you have a relationship like you and Amy do. Jessica and I have an understanding. We have Jacob to think about, and if we get all of these emotions mixed up into it, then we're jeopardizing the whole thing."

Alex knew, even as he said it, how wrong it sounded. They had a child together, so how could love mess that up? Well, apart from his parents and now Lucas and Amy, Alex hadn't seen a lot of good marriages. They all ended in ugly divorces, with bitter custody battles. A combination of statistics, his field of expertise, and logic, another favorite, suggested an answer. Alex figured that, if he kept love out of the equation, he'd never have to worry about splitting up. The thought of Jessica and Jacob not being there with him every day tore his heart to pieces.

"I think you're in a buttload of denial, Alex. You have an amazing wife, who obviously loves you, and you know what? I think it's pretty obvious you love her, too. Why not quit fighting it, and just enjoy being with your family?" Lucas asked.

"I can't explain it, Lucas."

"Well, then why not try? Because right now I think you are just making a complete and utter fool out of yourself."

Alex glared at Lucas; his brother was being a little harsh, he thought. But when Lucas didn't back down, he sighed. "I had no choice but to marry Jessica — "

"I'm going to stop you right there. That's a load of crap and we both know it. A heck of a lot of people in this world don't get married just because of a pregnancy. Now I know we were raised better than that, but I honestly think there's more to you and Jessica than just Jacob," Lucas interrupted.

"Yes, there is. I care about her. I won't deny that. It's just that I don't know what the hell love is. I see it in Mom and Dad, and you and Amy, but I've never been in love before. I don't know what to do or how to act around her."

"You aren't making any sense. Why don't you just talk to her? She's probably frightened right now."

"I'm making perfect sense. You just don't get it!"

"You're right. I don't. Listen to me. I screwed up horrendously with Amy. It's one of my deepest regrets. I'm simply trying to save you from the same pain that I went through, and worse, that I put *her* through," Lucas said.

"I don't know why I came here. This isn't helping."

"If you'd bloody well listen to me, then maybe it *would* help," Lucas said with a roll of his eyes.

"Yeah, whatever. I have to get going. I'll be gone all week, and I'm sure everything will be normal when I return home," Alex said. One could hope.

"Good luck," Lucas said before Alex departed.

Alex heard the disbelief in his brother's tone, but how could he explain himself to Lucas when, despite his protestations, he didn't understand what he was feeling, himself? A week out of the country, on his own, would help him get his head on straight again. Then, things could go back to normal — to the way they'd been for the last six months with Jessica.

Change was bad. They didn't need to alter anything in their lives; the way it had been before she'd spoken those three little stupid words had been just fine with him. There. He'd figured it all out and he hadn't even set foot on the jet yet. He knew he felt a lot better as he boarded the jet and got ready to fly from the city.

But the nausea wouldn't let up.

*****

"How are you doing? You look as if you don't feel well," Amy said.

She and Jessica had met for a girls' day out. Jessica had almost refused, but she sitting at home in misery wasn't helping her in the least, so she was now at the salon having her nails done.

"I had that nasty flu that's been going around, but I'm fine now. Just a few leftover symptoms," Jessica replied.

"If you need to rest up, we can reschedule our day out," Amy offered.

"No, I'm grateful you got me out of the house. I know I was reluctant, but this is exactly what I needed to do. Alex has been gone for a few days, and even before he left, I hardly saw him. I need some good old-fashioned girl talk. So enough talk about me. How have you been since Isaiah was born?" Jessica asked. Darn that queasiness.

"I'm doing so much better. Can you believe Isaiah is already two weeks old? He's such a great baby, too. He actually lets me get four hours of sleep in a row. I'm really glad I hired the nanny, though. She's been such a tremendous help. Jasmine absolutely adores her, and I've been able to get plenty of naps in. Plus, I feel safe stepping out for the afternoon with you," she said with enthusiasm.

"I know how quickly time flies. I can't believe Jacob is already nine months old. I want to go back to the beginning, though the full night's rest part is pretty nice."

"I think I would be happy having about ten more kids. Don't look at me with that horrified expression on your face. I love being a mother, and Lucas is about the best husband in the world. Plus, I think Joseph would think he'd died and gone to heaven if he had that many grandkids surrounding him. I love this family so much, and I can already picture sitting around a Christmas tree with a dozen kids and two dozen grandkids," she gushed.

Jessica sat for a few moments without saying anything. She wanted more children so badly, but if things didn't change with her husband, she couldn't see that happening. He seemed content having just Jacob. And if she told him she wanted another baby, she didn't want to think about his reaction. He'd probably shut her out even more.

"I've always wanted to have a large family. I adore my parents, but it was lonely growing up as an only child. I've never wanted that for Jacob," Jessica finally admitted.

"Are you guys planning on another little one any time soon?" Amy asked with a wink. "The trying part is so much fun," she added with a giggle.

"We haven't talked about it" was all Jessica said. She was having a hard time fighting off the tears. She wasn't normally so emotional, but her loneliness of late was most likely contributing to her mood swings.

"Alex adores Jacob so much that I'm sure he'd like to have a few more running around. Talk to him about it. You know Grandpa is going to be expecting another one soon," Amy said.

"Joseph is about the greatest man there is. I can't believe how lucky Jacob is to have such an amazing grandfather. Plus, Katherine is a dream grandmother. I love the quilt she made for Jacob. And she comes over and visits all the time. I really regret that they didn't have those first three months with their grandson," Jessica said.

"They completely understand, though. You were unsure about the relationship and thought what you did was for the best. What matters most is that you're all together now. I know things can be really tough sometimes, but hang in there," Amy encouraged.

Jessica didn't want to talk about the tension between her and Alex, so she pulled a conversational switcheroo. "I've been dying to try the new Thai place a few blocks away. Do you want to go there for lunch?" she asked.

Amy took the hint, and they discussed lunch and the kids and just about everything else except husbands. Jessica felt herself relaxing, and she enjoyed the rest of the day. By the time she got back to the house, she was more relaxed than she'd been since before her impromptu honeymoon.

How could she walk away from any of this? She'd be giving up not only Alex, but also her best friend, and an extended family that had become so very dear to her. And she didn't want to leave Alex; she just wanted him to love her. If only she had some idea how that could happen.

Chapter Twenty-Six

After the mournful honeymoon, the months dragged by in a slow progression of hours. Yet Alex was finally staying home much more often, and he and Jessica were back to making love regularly. An outsider might have thought they were a perfectly happy little family.

Jessica hadn't repeated her vow of love to her husband, and he'd started to relax. She didn't want to break the truce they'd established.

Jacob was turning a year old that afternoon, and they had a party planned with both of their families invited. She loved it when everyone got together and couldn't believe there was ever a time she'd feared the Anderson family. They were such humble and kind people, and they wanted only the best for her and her son.

Jessica stole Isaiah away every chance she could get, but when Joseph was around, fat chance of that.

He would hold all three of his grandkids on his knees and was like a Papa Bear when someone tried to take one away.

The kids adored their grandfather just as much as he adored them. The second he walked in the door, Jasmine and Jacob would run — or crawl — to him with their arms out, and the baby would coo at him. Joseph was in baby heaven.

Jessica finished getting ready for the party, knowing Julia was dressing Jacob at the same time. She was grateful for the sweet bond between Julia and Jacob. Everyone was happy except…

"Mama, someone is looking for you," Alex's voice came around the corner about a second before he stepped through the doorway.

Jessica drank in her handsome husband and son. Jacob babbled happily and reached out to her from his father's arms.

"Of course, my sweet boy. I can't believe you're a year old today. Is it your birthday?" she asked him before tickling his belly.

"Burble," he said in his sweet baby voice.

"Yes, it is your day, and you have both sets of your grandpas and grandmas and also your aunts and uncles coming to see you."

"Gampa," he said and started looking around.

"He's not here yet," she said with a smile. Her son was close to both his grandfathers.

"Gampa," he demanded with a little scowl between his brows, and he reminded her so much of her husband.

"I like how he knows what he wants and isn't afraid to demand it," Alex stated proudly. "Come on,

Jacob. I think I hear Grandpa in the hall," he said as Jacob eagerly leapt back into his father's arms.

Alex laughed and bent down, kissing her quickly before leaving the room. Jessica slowly followed her two favorite men.

"About time you brought my grandson down here. I've been waiting about five minutes now," came Joseph's booming voice.

Alex chuckled as Jacob practically flew into his grandpa's arms.

Jacob patted Joseph's face to get his attention, "Burble, Gampa," he said with a cheeky smile.

"Did you say it's your birthday, Jacob? Yes, it is! Let's go sneak some candy," he whispered, although everyone in the room could hear him.

"Dad, don't give him a bunch of junk food, or he'll get cranky," Alex said, although he knew his words were falling on deaf ears.

Jessica had to laugh. When Joseph wanted to spoil his grandkids, there was nothing anyone could do to stop him.

"I forgot to tell you how beautiful you look today," Alex said to her, and then he took her into his arms and kissed her softly. Jessica immediately melted as he deepened the kiss.

"You guys want to go upstairs for a while? I'll cover for you," said Mark's laughing voice.

Jessica jumped out of Alex's arms and could feel her face getting hot. Even after almost a year with Alex, she wasn't blushing any less than at first. And it seemed to be Mark's mission to catch them every time they decided to share an intimate moment outside the bedroom.

Alex glared at his brother. "You could have gone out back with the rest of the family and not interrupted us so rudely," he said with too much edge, in Jessica's opinion. But Alex was even sexier when he was mad.

"Oh, quit being a stick in the mud. You have all night to continue 'kissing.'" Mark formed his fingers into quotation marks. "Now, be a good brother and get me a beer," he said and practically dragged Alex from the room.

Jessica took a few moments to compose herself before heading in the direction of the party. She stared at the large group of family and friends on her back deck and smiled. Whenever she began to think she couldn't stay another day in the house with a man who didn't love her, she would be at a family gathering, and her resolve to stay would deepen.

It wasn't as if Alex were cruel to her in any way. He was simply honest, saying he couldn't love her, maybe not with so many words, but with every action he took. He obviously wanted her, and their passion burned nightly. But was he capable of being in love?

Jessica snapped back to reality and looked around the crowded yard once again. Her smile was genuine as she spotted her beautiful child and her niece and nephew.

Jasmine and Jacob were on the swings, with Grandpa pushing them both. "Higher, Gampa," Jasmine yelled and then squealed with delight when he did her bidding.

"How are you doing, dear?" Katherine asked as she approached Jessica.

"I'm great. Thanks, Mom," she replied. Katherine was such a quiet person that sometimes she got swallowed up in the shadow of her larger-than-life husband and confident sons. All the kids knew Grandma was the real source of magic in the family, however. Though she was quiet, when she put her foot down, what she said might as well be law.

She had an amazing heart and more love to give than any other person Jessica knew. Jessica was glad her family meshed so well with the Anderson family. It was like a good marriage, she thought a little wistfully — two units had become one.

"I can't believe Jacob is a year old already. The time simply goes by too quickly, in my opinion," Katherine said.

"I agree. It seems like just yesterday I was bringing him home from the hospital. He will be off to college before I have a chance to blink," Jessica said. The sudden realization affected her with something like panic.

"It doesn't happen quite that quickly, but it sure seems like it. I'm grateful my boys decided to live close to home. When Mark graduated high school and moved out, a piece of my heart broke. Letting go of any of your children is hard, but the youngest one is the final piece, and it feels as if a part of you leaves with them. I'm also grateful they're finally marrying and giving me grandkids. It helps ease the heartache a little," she added.

Jessica looked guiltily down at her feet for a moment. She knew her father and Alex's parents were hoping to have many more grandkids, but she refused to broach the subject with Alex. If he said no, as was too likely, she'd finally have to accept that they couldn't stay together.

"Three grandchildren in just under three years is pretty good," Jessica said.

"Yes, they really are a blessing. Joseph has been mumbling now about Mark settling down. I've told him time and again to leave the boy alone. He'll have kids when he's ready for it, but you know Joseph. He's stubborn. He thinks he fools me, but I've been married to the man for so many years that he doesn't get away with much," she said with a wink.

"He's definitely stubborn. And his sons and grandsons have inherited that trait," Jessica said with a fond smile.

"I'm going to steal that new grandson of mine before Joseph gets his hands on him," Katherine said. She kissed Jessica's cheek and then headed over to Amy, who had just rounded the corner.

When Amy walked up to Jessica, her arms were empty. "I barely get to see my kids when we are around this group," Amy complained, but the twinkle in her eyes took away any bite to the words.

"I know how you feel," Jessica agreed.

"I really couldn't imagine being a part of one of those families who never speak to one another. It breaks my heart now to think about that," Amy said.

Jessica knew that Amy spoke feelingly. Lucas's wife had grown up with a drug-addicted mother before she went into the foster-care system. But despite her grim beginnings, she'd worked her way through college and met Lucas while working for the Anderson Corporation.

Having a close family was something Jessica had always taken for granted, whereas Amy had never known such a loving group of people. Jessica reached over and gave Amy a big hug. "I'm so glad you're my sister, Amy, and that you were able to find the family you were meant to have," Jessica said.

Amy had to wipe away a few tears. "Now look what you made me do," she said with a sniffle. "I'm so glad to have you, too."

"What's wrong, Amy?" Lucas came running up, as if he had radar built in. He gathered Amy in his arms while scoping out the yard to make sure his children and the rest of the family were all OK. When he didn't find any danger, his brow furrowed in confusion.

"Everything is just perfect. That's why I'm crying," Amy said with a sniffle.

Lucas looked at her as if she'd lost her mind, and that set both women off in a round of giggles. "Lucas, you have to understand that we cry when we are happy *and* sad. It's just one of those mysterious things about women," Jessica said between giggles.

"Is everything OK?" Alex asked as he approached, looking from his brother to the two laughing women.

Lucas gave him a look that seemed to say, "You figure them out," which sent the girls off on another round of laughter. They were both holding their stomachs, and tears were streaming down their faces, they were laughing so hard.

"You've got to stop talking, or I'm going to get a major cramp," Amy finally managed to get out.

"Agreed," Jessica said.

Both guys threw up their hands and, by mutual consent, edged away from the girls.

"I'd better go finish the grilling," Lucas said.

"Yeah, I'll help you," Alex said, eagerly taking the cue, and they fled.

After a few minutes, Jessica and Amy were able to quit laughing. "I love doing that to him," Amy said mischievously.

"That *was* quite fun," Jessica agreed.

"Let's go get something to drink. All this laughter is great but, man, my stomach hurts now," Amy said. "Plus, I've got to get off these feet. I swear, they're still swollen and acting as if I'm pregnant."

"I could use a lemonade. I've been fighting the flu again and am having a hard time keeping things down, so don't bring the baby too close to me. I'd never forgive myself if I got my nephew sick," Jessica said.

The girls joined the rest of the party, stealing two very comfortable chairs for themselves. The food was excellent, and Jessica felt relaxed and calm.

"It's time to sing 'Happy Birthday,'" Alex shouted above the voices as he came out of the house carrying a large chocolate cake with a single candle burning in the center.

Jacob blew out his candle with the help of his father and then clapped his hands with everyone else. Everybody roared with laughter when Jacob stuck his little hand into the cake and smeared it all over himself, saying something that sounded like *yummy* over and over again.

Jessica's eyes filled with tears as she watched Alex stick his face into the cake with their son.

"Da-da. Yummmmmy," Jacob squealed, or words to that effect, and then giggled.

"Grandpa yummy, too," Joseph said and took a big handful for himself.

"I think I'll pass on this cake and wait for the other one to be brought out," Jessica said with affection, staring at her chocolate-covered men.

"I'll second that," Amy added.

"You don't know what you're missing," Alex said. Before she could stop him, Alex took a chocolate-smeared finger and rubbed it down her nose. She stood in shock for a moment and then, fast as lightning, scooped up a small piece of the cake and chucked it at her husband.

She saw the light of mischief enter his eyes and decided it was a great time to retreat. She took off running, but Alex caught her in no time. He gently tackled her to the ground and rubbed his chocolate-covered face against hers.

Jessica was laughing so hard she could barely speak. "OK, OK. I call a truce," she finally managed to get out.

"There are no truces in a food war," he said and rubbed against her some more. Suddenly he seemed to realize he was stretched out on top of her. He had her hands pinned above her head, and she was completely at his mercy.

Alex forgot their yard was filled with people. No one else seemed visible to him but his beautiful, chocolate-covered wife. He bent his head down and, instead of smearing her with more chocolate, his lips met hers, and he kissed her with an intensity that wiped away all laughter.

Alex released her hands, and they immediately wrapped around his neck so she could pull him tighter to her body. All her earlier confusion was wiped clear from her mind for a moment as he kissed her the way a woman should be kissed, his tongue tracing the edges of her mouth before slipping inside and sending heat to her core.

Jessica pushed her hips against his, elated at feeling the hard evidence of his arousal. Whether she was unsure of his love or not, she never felt unsure of his desire, and that was something a lot of people didn't have.

"Um, guys…I hate to interrupt you twice in one evening, but this is a G-rated party," came the laughing voice of Mark.

Alex pulled apart from Jessica reluctantly and snarled at his brother. Jessica looked at her husband, then around her in embarrassment, extremely grateful no one else was paying the least bit of attention to them. At least that's what she thought.

Alex finally got up and pulled Jessica to her feet. "This party can end any time now," he said, with a promise of completion to come. "As a matter of fact, probably no one would even notice if we disappeared for a little while," he offered hopefully.

She was getting ready to agree with him and sneak off upstairs when Joseph approached.

"Now that Jacob is a year old, when are you planning on giving him a sibling?" Joseph asked Alex. "You know a boy needs to have younger siblings to harass," he added and looked pointedly over at Mark.

Jessica was the only one who noticed the shutter lock tightly into place on her husband's face. Her heart broke a little bit more. He'd gone from passionate lover to marble statue in about two seconds.

"Dad, you already have three grandkids. Quit being so greedy," Alex finally managed to say in a stilted voice.

"Now, son, you're not getting any younger. You'd better get working on things," Joseph continued, seeming to not notice the sudden tension in his son. He winked at Alex and Jessica both, which made her blush again.

"Yeah, yeah. Just enjoy the cake," Alex said and then quickly changed the subject. Jessica had the answer to the question she hadn't wanted to ask. Her husband definitely didn't plan to have more children with her. How could a night so full of promise just a moment ago have suddenly gone so dark?

The party went on well after Jacob finally succumbed to his exhaustion and went to bed. Jessica usually loved to watch the brothers laugh together and act like teenagers. She was putting on a mask the rest of the night, however, because all she really wanted to do was crawl into bed and have herself a really good cry. She and Amy sat back and visited while the rest of the guests slowly started to depart.

Somehow, she managed to keep from falling apart the rest of the night. She could go curl up in bed and think about what she was going to do about her future soon enough. She knew she couldn't stay in the marriage if Alex didn't want to be a real family, but she didn't want to think about it just then.

"We need to have another girl day. How about Friday?" Amy asked.

"That sounds great," Jessica said before hugging her goodbye. She was almost sad to see the rest of the guests go, but she needed to be alone.

"I have some work to finish up. I'll be up later," Alex said before quickly turning and heading to his office.

Jessica climbed the stairs to their room and curled up in bed. The longer she lay there, the more angry she became. How dare he think everything he said was the only way it would be? They were going to have this out. Before he entered their room, exhaustion overtook her and she fell asleep.

The showdown would happen — and it would happen soon.

Chapter Twenty-Seven

Another month, another thirty-one days of heartache. Alex was home more often than not, but if Jacob wasn't there as a buffer between them, he locked himself up in his office.

They engaged in a lot of family activities together, but Alex seemed to make sure they were never alone otherwise. They still made love in the dark of night, but even that had changed. It was still intense, but only while it lasted. Afterward, he no longer held her tightly afterwards.

She knew she was going to have to confront him, but she also knew how the conversation would go.

"I thought we could go out on the lake this weekend, if you'd care to go," Alex said at dinner one evening.

"That sounds great," Jessica said.

"I think Jacob will like the boat. There's nothing like the wind blowing through your hair as you navigate the water."

"Well, your son doesn't have much hair," she said, smiling at Alex.

"That's very true. The sun will be good for all of us. It's supposed to be a really nice weekend, and those are few and far between," he said with a genuine smile.

Jessica hated the way she responded to him so quickly when he gave her the least bit of himself. It made her feel weak, and she wasn't a weak woman. All these unanswered questions between the two of them were turning her into somebody she wasn't. And what if her son could already see the sort of role models his parents were providing? Neither Jacob's mother nor his father would come off perfectly, to say the least. Surely matters couldn't go on this way forever.

The weekend came, and Jacob had a cold, so they went out on the boat alone. She was afraid Alex would cancel, but he was in a good mood, and they left the house early in the morning.

"I thought we'd do some crabbing while we're out," he said.

"I'd love to do that. Amy said she and Lucas did that a couple weeks ago and had a good time."

"Yeah, I got the idea from Lucas."

"Amy said the critters smelled terrible, but the taste when they were cooked was so worth it," Jessica said with a wrinkle of her nose.

"I haven't heard you mention the paper in a while. Is there anything new you're working on?"

It was pathetic how she glowed instantly at his interest in her work. She'd always known love wasn't rational, but this was taking things a bit far.

"As a matter of fact, I did a story last week on the robberies that have been taking place downtown. It was very interesting to interview the witnesses."

"What? I hope you weren't alone," he said, turning to look at her with concern.

"Keep your eyes on the road! I was perfectly fine. It was daytime, and I was just speaking to the shop owners. Apparently the person is very good at what he's doing. Well, they actually think it's an organized group. They seem to be coming into the stores in teams. They have a couple of suspicious-looking people who distract the shop workers, while the respectably dressed patrons are the ones robbing them blind. They are also very aware of the cameras, and there hasn't been a good image of them caught yet."

"It sounds dangerous that you are down there when this is going on," Alex insisted.

"I promise you that I was in no danger. Certainly in no more danger than riding along with you now, or than going to a seedy club in the Virgin Islands."

"Now, really…"

"Yes, really. But I would be overjoyed if one of the robberies were to take place while I was on the spot. I'd have some real firsthand knowledge to write about," she said excitedly.

"Are you finished with the story now?"

"Sadly, yes, for now, at least. If there are any breaks on the case, I will be back in a second to do a follow up."

"Well, if that happens, I want to be there with you. I don't like the idea of you in harm's way," he insisted.

"Be careful, Alex. I might just think you care about me," she said as a joke, but the pain inside didn't go away just because she added a laugh at the end of her statement.

"I do care about you, Jessica. You are the mother of my son, and I don't ever want you to suffer harm."

"Those words are music to my ears," she said with a hint of sarcasm.

The rest of the drive went by in silence as they both sat there brooding. It had to get easier one of these days. If she just gave it a real chance, the two of them would be fine, wouldn't they? Or was it worth it? She didn't know anymore; confusion seemed to be her main emotion. But she knew that her son deserved happier parents.

When they arrived at the marina and boarded the boat, the warm sun streamed down and the cool breeze caressed her heated skin. To her surprise, she found herself having fun. Once the temperature warmed up enough to allow her to strip down to her bikini, she lay out on the deck. Her worries seemed to float away on the gentle breeze.

*****

It was taking every bit of Alex's willpower not to find a secluded cove to park the boat and pounce on his wife. She had no idea what power she had. He was like a teenager, constantly aroused and in need of what only she could give him. He wanted her day and night, and he resented the hold she had over him.

When would all of this become easier? They had their son to think about, and of course, he himself wasn't going to be a monk; he needed to feel release in her arms. He just wanted the urgency to die down a little — the seemingly unstoppable need he had for her.

As he steered the boat farther out into the water, Alex's eyes were continually drawn back to Jessica, lying on the deck just a few short feet away from him.

Since the night she'd told him she loved him, he'd backed off dramatically — except at night. He knew he was hurting her, but he also knew she would be better off, in the long run, if he gave her some space. She needed to realize that she wasn't in love with him. He knew she was more in love with the idea of love and marriage than the actual reality of it. Women's emotions, and lives, were dominated by ridiculous fairy tales, and it perversely meant fewer, not more, happy endings.

His dad had freaked him out when he'd brought up having more children. And his own reaction scared the heck out of him. He could visualize a bunch of miniature Jessicas running through the house, and the further chipping away at his beloved freedom, and yet he rather liked the images in his brain. He couldn't figure out what he was doing or thinking anymore.

"It's so warm out here," Jessica said, turning toward him suddenly. "Can we stop somewhere so I can take a swim?"

"I can see a cove over here," he said and steered the boat toward the secluded beach. Damn. Too secluded. Everything in him was saying, *Head back to the docks! Don't give in to her again!*

What he really needed to do was talk to his brothers, find out why he was constantly fighting his desire for her, but then they'd know how messed up he was right now. What real man admitted to such a weakness? Jessica had him on his knees. His only power was in the fact that she didn't realize that.

"Oh, it's so perfect." She gasped at the slice of heaven that was the beach. As soon as he got the anchor down on the boat, Jessica dived into the water. Alex was impressed with her form — in more than one sense of the word. He was feeling much too hot himself, so he stripped down and jumped in after her.

They both swam around in a contented silence for a while; the exercise was making him feel less on edge, and helping him unclench his teeth. This had to be the ticket. Some guys thought about baseball to dampen their desire, but he could make big plans to upgrade that pathetic excuse for a home gym that he had. And he'd use it — boy, would he use it.

While Alex was lost in his happy trail of thoughts, Jessica cried out in fear and pain. In less than an instant, he swam to her and sucked in his breath as he noticed blood coming to the surface of the water.

"What happened? What's wrong?" he fired off at her. At the same time, he was holding her close.

"I don't know," she cried. "It's my leg. I think I cut it on something," she whimpered.

Alex couldn't see anything, so he towed her back to the boat, praying it was nothing too bad. He lifted her up into his arms and climbed aboard.

Quickly laying her down, he scrambled to retrieve the first aid kit. When he returned, he was shocked by the amount of blood coming from her leg.

"It looks worse than it is," she finally said. "I was checking it out, and it looks as if I cut it on a rock or something. It just seems to be bleeding a lot. If you clean it out and bandage it, I'll be fine."

"I'll start cleaning and assess for myself how bad it is," he said gruffly, while giving her a painkiller. His shoulders were taut with anxiety.

Jessica had to laugh. Men never listened. She knew it was only a surface wound, but he was so sure he knew better. Typical.

Chapter Twenty-Eight

Even though Jessica was hurting, and though she knew Alex was behaving like an idiot, she had to smile at the command in his voice. She loved it when he got all determined and acted as if the world should bow at his feet. He demanded great respect, and she was more than happy to give it to him; she just wanted him to earn it from her by treating her the way a man should treat a woman.

She was offering him everything; all he had to do was accept.

She flinched when he cleaned the wound, but the Advil kicked in and the pain subsided quickly. "I'm fine now," she assured him.

She'd been right, of course. It pained him to admit that, but yes, the wound was not much more than a big scratch. Had he been a suspicious sort, he told himself, he might have suspected her of having planned the whole thing. Maybe she wanted him to freak out at the idea of losing her to a shark's bite or something, and then the light bulb would go off in his head and he'd say to her, "Oh, honey, I've been such a fool. I see now how much I love you, and I hope that you'll forgive me for taking so long to see it." Wasn't gonna happen.

"We can head on home," he suggested.

"As I said, I'm fine. As a matter of fact, I'm feeling very hungry," she said. She didn't want to head back to the house right away, knowing he would disappear into his office as he always did. Their day had been more good than bad, and she didn't want to give up her time alone with him. She didn't know when the next chance would come that they could do something like this.

"Dinner sounds good. I'm pretty hungry myself. It will take us an hour to get back to the docks, so if you lie down and rest up, I'll take us somewhere nice to eat," he offered.

"I can't argue with that. All this sun and fresh air is tiring me out," she replied drowsily before lying down.

Alex covered her up with a blanket, and was looking down at her face, and her heart hammered. Slowly, he kneeled down and his hands rubbed beneath the blanket along her bare stomach, then lifted to slide over her barely covered breast.

"Alex?" she questioned.

"You take my breath away in your bikini," he said as he bent down and kissed her lips.

"Yes, Alex…" she practically purred as her arms lifted to hold him to her. These were the moments that kept her hanging on. Yes, he was obviously turned on, but his lips were soft and gentle, a caress against her mouth. He massaged her body, warming her from the inside out.

"I need to stop now, or we'll never get to our dinner," he moaned as he lifted his head.

"I'm not hungry anymore," she lied, not wanting him to quit.

"Then why did I just hear your stomach growl?"

His hands kneaded her breasts for a few more seconds, making her nipples ache as they extended toward him. With a final groan, he stood and walked to the front of the boat.

Jessica lay there aching as she curled up and thought. She had to get up her courage soon — very soon. But she kept telling herself that. Would it ever happen?

*****

"Jessica, wake up. We're back at the docks. I called Lucas, and he and Amy are going to meet us in half an hour at this great little seafood place I know about," Alex said while gently shaking Jessica awake.

"What?" she stuttered, struggling to rouse herself. "I wasn't planning on actually sleeping. I was going to keep you company. Sorry," she said when she finally came fully to. Great. Their time alone would instead be their time with another couple.

"Hey, no problem. I really enjoy the water and having the soothing silence," he responded before securing the boat.

Jessica felt a little bit as if she'd been slapped. She felt he was basically telling her he'd enjoyed his day much more because she wasn't there to talk his ear off. *Well, fine,* she thought, *if he wants silence, silence is what he will get.* She didn't always wake up in the best of moods, and with her body still keyed up from his teasing kiss earlier, she was grumpier than normal.

She quickly got dressed and limped behind him to their car. She kept silent the entire ride to the restaurant, and so did he. The day had started off with such promise, but now Jessica simply wished to get home so the wretched afternoon could end.

"Jessica, I'm so glad you guys called." Amy came walking up and put her arm through Jessica's while chattering away. "It's so nice to get out of the house for some adult conversation. Don't get me wrong, I adore my kids, but they do lack certain communication skills," she finished with a laugh.

"I don't know. I think Jasmine communicates very well, and, for that matter, Isaiah has no trouble at all letting everyone around him know when something isn't going his way," Jessica joked right back.

"You have that right," Lucas said.

"I guess I'm the only one with a perfect child," Alex said.

"Ha," they all said in unison, which brought on more good-natured laughter, and Jessica was snapped out of her disgruntled mood.

"OK, kids can be quite demanding when they want something, but even though I didn't know I'd love fatherhood so much, I seriously couldn't imagine my life without Jacob in it. He's just so amazing," Alex said in awe.

"Agreed, little bro," Lucas responded.

"This is a grown-up night. No more talk of our kids. I get one glass of wine and anything at all I want to eat. If it causes problems with Isaiah's tummy later…well, that's OK because it's Daddy's turn to get up with him tonight," Amy said with a wicked smile.

"You deserve whatever you want, babe," Lucas said.

"Now, *you* are a man after my heart," Amy said with a smile filled with love that had Jessica aching with envy. Would she and Alex ever have this easy repertoire of banter, this unquenchable love for each other?

As the evening progressed, Jessica relaxed. She absolutely loved Lucas and Amy, and it helped to mask the tension between her and Alex.

When it came time to say goodnight, she was sad to watch the other couple leave. She hugged Amy tightly and promised to have a girls' day out later that week. She then rode home in complete silence with her husband.

When they walked inside, they both went to Jacob's room to check on him. It was well past midnight, and Julia had long ago retired. Jessica had hoped to learn how Jacob's day had been.

"I think he's back to normal," Jessica whispered.

"He was pretty much better by the time we left. I just didn't want to expose him to the water so soon after his cold," Alex said.

"I agree."

"You're a great mother. Never doubt that," Alex said tenderly. "Don't feel guilty about taking a day out without him. It's good for you and him. My parents had many vacations by themselves, and my brothers and I are fine. They were with us more than away, and we always knew how much they loved us."

"It was the same at my house. I knew my parents always loved me. I would have traded a little bit of that to have a sibling, though. It got lonely at times," she said.

*****

Alex knew what she was implying — she wanted another child. But they didn't have that kind of marriage. The boat they were in was precarious already; another child would rock it right over.

As he looked from his son to his wife, an uncustomary fear seized him. He sure as heck didn't want her to leave him; where would he be then? But there were principles involved. It would be so easy, so tempting, to give her the words she so longed to hear. But it wouldn't be honest, and lying to her would go sorely against the grain. Both of them would have to suck it up; they'd ultimately be a lot happier, wouldn't they?

"I should get some work done," he said. No guts, no marital mess, he thought, and avoided the subject altogether. "I'm going to change," he added and went off to their bedroom.

When Alex emerged from their adjoining bathroom, planning to head straight out of the room, he took one look at his wife, and his plans changed. She was lying on the bed, completely naked, with a "take it or leave it, sucker" look. He walked to the bed like a puppet on a string. He stripped out of the clothes he'd just put on and climbed in the bed beside her without a single word.

Power.

There was the power she had over him that he'd been thinking of earlier. He desired her insanely, and that was his biggest weakness with her. The thing was, he wouldn't trade it for anything. She made him feel emotions and passion that were beyond anything he could imagine.

When Jessica wrapped her arms around him and their lips met, a fire ignited in his body, as it always did. When he rubbed her from her breasts to her hips and back up again, he could feel the fire spreading. The sounds of pleasure escaping her lips just made the inferno rage ever more fiercely, and he was consumed by the exploding flames. Her pleasure was his own.

Jessica took control from him before he was able to stop her. She pushed him over onto his back and climbed on top of him, continuing the passionate kiss melding them together. After she finally released his lips, she trailed hers down the side of his neck.

She continued kissing him down the column of his throat, over his smooth pecs and lower, to his shaking abs. She ran her tongue in swirls over the small trail of hair leading her to his eager manhood.

Alex tried to pull her face back up to his.

"No. It's my turn," she said, and he lay back down to let her pleasure him. It took his full willpower not to flip her over and plunge inside her trembling body.

"Jessica," he moaned out loud when she licked the top of his thigh. He really couldn't take much more. He was so close to exploding beneath her skilled mouth that he was shaking.

She took a second to look up at him seductively before she finally ran her tongue up and down his length. His entire body shook from the pleasure. They'd been married long enough that he'd have thought he wouldn't come so unglued, but she turned him on past the point of reason.

"Please," he begged.

Jessica didn't say a word, but just took him deep into her mouth, and his whole body arched off the bed. She moved her head up and down his shaft, gripping him tightly with her hand and mimicking the movement of her mouth.

She swirled her tongue around the head, and he jerked up. "Enough," he growled as he grabbed her in a lightning quick movement and flipped her beneath him. Her mouth was heaven, but, for this purpose, nothing compared with the hot, velvety folds of her tight body.

"I'll finish inside you, and make you suffer as much as you've been making me suffer," he said between clenched teeth.

Jessica jerked her hips upward toward him. He tormented them both by resting his pulsing arousal at her entrance, rubbing it outside of her heat, drawing out the moment.

Now she was the one to beg. "Please, Alex," she moaned.

Her pleas sent him to a whole new level of hunger. "Just a minute. I don't want this to end before it even begins." He groaned as she returned the favor and rubbed against him.

He took her hands and placed them over her head and then brought his lips to hers. He kissed her with all the desperation of a drowning man fighting for air. If this was the brink of death, then he didn't want to be brought back to life.

"Please, Alex," she begged him again.

He couldn't take any more, and, with one thrust, he buried himself deep inside her. They both moaned in pleasure as their bodies joined.

He started moving, and the waiting ended. He drove quickly in and out of her as their panting escalated.

"Alex!" she shouted as her body started convulsing around him.

He unleashed a final barrage of hard thrusts and groaned loudly at his own release.

They both lay there, almost motionless. Her hands stroked him from his shoulder blades to his lower back and then up again. As he rolled off her, she moaned her displeasure at the separation.

"Shh. I'm too heavy for you," he said. Alex saw the disappointment in her eyes. He knew she thought he was going to leave her, but he held her closer. After he covered them both, he caressed her back until sleep overtook her.

Alex lay there for a long time, still stroking her while thinking about their lovemaking and the way it was so much more than sex. He knew he should have walked away earlier and let them both think clearly, but he wasn't in control around her.

She was his wife, and he needed her to feel comfortable, needed her to be happy. If only the sex were enough. If only he could make that pain in her eyes go away.

But he could. He knew that. Why wouldn't he just give her what she wanted so desperately? What was truly holding him back?

He finally left their bed when he knew she was sound asleep. He heard Jessica moan and saw her reach for him, but she was still asleep. When she found only empty space, her brow furrowed, but she didn't wake up.

Alex headed to the bathroom and took a long shower. He let the spray try to wash away the tension that seemed to be ever present in his shoulders. But it didn't do any good.

So he wandered down to his office, turned on a bright lamp, and tried to analyze why he couldn't surrender to his wife.

He'd always been big on freedom. Though he'd had a grand time playing with his brothers, he was the one who sometimes sneaked off to the attic and read, or climbed up trees by himself and looked out over the landscape. He'd never needed other people to feel complete. But Jessica didn't cramp his style; not at all. He didn't resent her for being there. So it couldn't be anything abstract like freedom.

His mother was a hard act to follow, but he'd never been one of those sickos who would want to kill their dads and marry their moms. He guffawed at that one. And he'd never compared Jessica with his mother and found his wife lacking in any way.

Was it because the thrill of the chase was long over? Didn't all guys love the chase and lose interest afterward? But he'd given up his girl-chasing ways.

Maybe she was a little more exciting when she used to fight him, but he could hardly blame her for those tear-stained cheeks and woebegone eyes. Sometimes, though, they made him want to run.

No, that was unfair. They made him feel guilty, made him see all the areas he was so lacking in as a husband.

More pressure. Always pressure.

But he'd grown up with pressure, and it had never bothered him.

No, none of this made sense.

Alex finally gave up and decided to go back to bed. He would try to get some sleep and figure things out later.

Time.

He only needed a bit more time to figure this all out. When he did, they would be fine.

As soon as he climbed back into the bed, Jessica immediately snuggled up to him. Even in her sleep, she was drawn to him. Alex gave up trying to create distance, at least for the night, and held her, quickly falling into a deep sleep. An earthquake couldn't have roused him.

The next morning, he woke, quietly got ready for his day, and left for his office before Jessica opened her eyes. He avoided her the rest of the afternoon and, even though he noticed her sad expression whenever they passed each other in the evening, he knew it was better to keep his distance.

It wouldn't do him any good to speak to her until he had everything figured out. She would thank him for that later — he knew she would.

*****

Another week passed, and Alex wasn't any closer to figuring out how to fix his problems. He was hurting Jessica, and he hated that, but he couldn't seem to stop doing it.

He sat in his office and rubbed his pounding temples. He knew he'd been avoiding Jessica too much, and he wanted to just go back to the way things had been for a brief time in their marriage.

Everything that had happened over the past several months seemed to keep pulling them further and further apart. He was trying to keep distance between them, to prevent the very problems he seemed to have created.

That night at dinner, she'd barely touched her food, and her countenance seemed so downtrodden, so despondent. Alex knew he could fix it, though he didn't know how to make their problems fade away without giving her his heart.

Jessica was a reasonable person. If he explained they were doing what was best for their son, she'd understand a marriage didn't have to be filled with romance and love. It needed to be filled with an understanding that two people did the best they could in order to be great parents.

Nothing could go wrong if he took that approach.

Chapter Twenty-Nine

Jessica slowly mustered the courage to walk down the stairs to her husband's home office. She took another deep breath outside his door and then stepped in, her head held high. This was it. She wouldn't back down this time, no matter how much he tried to divert her attention.

He was either going to give her all of himself, or the marriage had to end. It would hurt her to part from him, but she was afraid it would kill her to stay without his love.

*****

"Is everything OK?" Alex asked as his wife approached. She never disturbed him in the office, except once — they'd ended up making love in front of the fireplace.

His eyes were automatically drawn to that spot, and he could feel his body's response. But he quickly squelched it when he turned back to Jessica.

As she stood before him, he couldn't help but think of taking her right there on top of his desk. Her eyes, however, held a determination within them that forced him to halt his unruly train of thought. Obviously, she needed to talk.

"I don't know if things are OK," she began.

Alex was getting really concerned. "Jacob…" he began. He started getting up, ready to charge up the stairs to his son.

"Jacob's fine. This has to do with us. I need to talk to you about our relationship."

"Our relationship is fine," he said firmly, and looked back down at his computer screen, as if the discussion were over and there were no need to interrupt his work any longer.

He'd known for a long time that this conversation was coming, but he was determined not to have it. He didn't want to hurt her, but he couldn't lose her, either. He was feeling more stress than he ever had in his life.

He still hadn't come up with any answers — which was absurd with his mathematical brain — and he wasn't ready to take this path with her.

"The thing is, our relationship isn't OK for *me* anymore," she said. "Alex, I love you. You know that. I've been in love with you for a long time now, and I can't live in this marriage loving you with all my heart while wondering when you're going to walk out the door." A tear slipped down Jessica's cheek.

Alex's heart warmed for a moment at her declaration of love. But no, he didn't want it. He refused to allow the warmth; he blocked out any emotion as too unstable, too liable to bring disaster to their marriage. He'd reason with her. He'd make things OK for them.

She was just confused, that was all.

"Don't be silly, Jessica. You know I would never leave you," he said. "What more can I say?" There, he'd reassured her. Maybe this conversation wouldn't be so bad after all.

*****

Jessica had hoped to get through the conversation without tears. She didn't want to appear weak, and she didn't want Alex feeling sorry for her. She wanted his love or nothing at all.

He looked at her with the same shuttered expression, although she'd thought for a moment that she saw a flicker of concern in his eyes. But she'd most likely imagined it simply because she wanted him to care.

"If there isn't love, you will eventually leave, Alex, or have an affair. This isn't the times of old when couples never divorced. Now, people divorce for the stupidest reasons and never look back; they just jump into another marriage. Our entire marriage is based on an unplanned pregnancy, and some people in our circumstances might be willing to settle for what we have; they might even think we're doing pretty darned well. But like a fool, I want more. I want love. I want more children. I want it all. And I can't accept less than that. I've waited, I think rather patiently, for you to love me, but I'm tired of waiting. You need either to give me what I want, or to let me go and let me get on with my life." It hurt her, but she had to put her foot down.

Alex sat back in his chair for a full two minutes before finally speaking. She'd waited this long, though, and she would continue to wait.

"Jessica, I care for you greatly. You are an incredible mother and a great wife. I'm comfortable with the way things are, and if you thought about this more rationally, you'd think the way I do."

Her eyes narrowed. "I'm *so* sorry that I'm such a weak, irrational female."

"Getting upset won't help now. Really, Jessica. I never wanted to marry, and it was because I haven't exactly seen a lot of shining examples of lasting love, other than my parents and my brother. I know you want me to say, 'I love you,' but I can't. It's just not who I am. I'm giving you everything I'm capable of. I think that's more than many people have. Why can't that be enough?"

His words were like knives, slashing and stabbing again and again. She didn't know how it was possible for her still to be standing. She pressed her hand against her heart, pressing against it, and thought it might explode from the intensity of the pain coursing through her.

"I understand, Alex, and I will be rational, but my reason leads me in a different direction from yours. Under these circumstances, I can no longer stay married to you. You're an amazing father, and I'd never keep Jacob from you again. We'll have to work out all the details, but I just can't do this. I'm so sorry." She turned and walked from the room.

She choked down the sobs that threatened to burst forth. Not this time. Though she was ripping apart inside, she also felt right for the first time in months. She'd stood up for herself. She was no longer accepting less than she deserved.

Jessica didn't know how she arrived in the bedroom she'd shared with Alex for almost a year. Their nights had seemed so special. That was the only time he'd completely let down his guard. No, he hadn't, she realized; it was wrong to kid herself. He hadn't been open with her since their so-called honeymoon, when she was stupid enough to express her love for him. But she'd barreled ahead for months, sometimes fooling herself that when she looked into his eyes, she saw love shining through their blue depths.

She turned away from their bed — she just couldn't look at it anymore — and walked across the hall to check in on Jacob. He was sound asleep in his crib and looked so peaceful. He was so beautiful, and he'd grown so much in his first year. And she loved the way he resembled his father so closely. She rubbed his sweet little head, but her baby didn't wake up. Jacob was content in his crib — safe. There was no point in disturbing him right then. She would pick him up the next day.

She knocked on Julia's door, and it quickly opened.

"Hi, Jessica. Is everything OK?" the nanny asked with concern.

Obviously, Jessica thought, *I'm not doing a very good job of hiding my emotions.*

"Everything is fine. I just wanted to let you know that I'll be gone this evening. You have the number of my cell phone if Jacob wakes and there are any problems."

"I'm sure things will be fine. Are you certain you're OK?" Julia asked again.

"Yes, but thanks. I'll see you in the morning." With that, Jessica turned and walked back into her bedroom. There was no way she could sleep there that night. She'd find a hotel room and then look for something more permanent the next day. Her son would be fine overnight, and she'd make sure she was back before he woke up. She packed an overnight bag and slipped from the house.

As she climbed into her car, she had to wait a few moments because she was crying so hard, she couldn't see to drive properly. When she finally pulled herself together and her vision cleared, Jessica turned away from the house. She watched it in her rearview mirror until the trees blocked her view.

The farther she got from the house, the more she regretted her decision to leave. She loved Alex so much, and leaving him was even more painful than staying with him, even without his love. She had to try again.

Then her tears dried as anger set in. Who did he think he was? No. She wasn't going to be this weepy girl. She was damned if she was going to allow him to treat her like crap for almost a year, then give her only moments of his love. He talked incessantly about reason and statistics, about the likelihood of marriages falling apart. Well, he was the one making it fall apart, and she was sick of allowing it. She knew they had something. She knew there was a heart buried deep down inside him.

She'd seen it on those few occasions he allowed himself to open up to her. She'd seen it when he was with his family members. She'd seen it in the way he looked at their son. He was acting like a monster, but he wasn't one, and she was determined to hash this out.

As she began to really think back over their year together, she realized he was so gentle and kind when he made love to her. They had passion, and fun, and laughter. He only pulled away when she said the words, but he showed his love in so many other ways.

Well, no more! She wouldn't let him hide behind his numbers, his excuses. She deserved more than that, and he would give it to her. She would go back in there and tell him he loved her, tell him they were going to change things, but she wouldn't run away. That was the coward's way out, and she was finished with being a coward.

She was making a U-turn to drive back to the house when her car was suddenly filled with bright lights. "What..." she began to say aloud, when there was the sickening sound of splintering glass and crunching metal, and she blacked out.

Chapter Thirty

Alex sat at his desk with his head in his hands. The things he'd said to Jessica were starting to make less and less sense. Had she demanded anything of him that he didn't have it within himself to give her?

All thoughts of work were gone. He was thinking back over all his time with Jessica. He was at peace only when he knew she was secure. And throughout his days at work, he would continually check the clock, counting down the hours until he could return home. He'd done more work from home recently than he'd ever done in the past. Anything that didn't require him to be in the office was done from home.

He also delegated more work than he'd ever before. He just wanted to spend time with his son and his wife. Work was no longer the top priority that it used to be.

Their nights were unlike anything else in creation. Jessica was always eager to fall into his arms, and she was the most beautiful creature he'd ever known. He could picture her pregnant with many more of his children. He couldn't picture his life without her.

His heart seemed to grow too full for his chest as the realization hit him. "I love her," he mumbled, just to hear how it sounded and to know how it felt to say the three simple words that possessed so much power. Then he repeated the words, louder and stronger. Alex felt his mouth lift up in a grin. He really did love Jessica. Shock radiated through him as he found himself wanting to run through the house yelling his love, going to a game and posting it on a billboard, something, anything that told the world what a fool he'd been.

He knew he'd sat there too long, but old habits die hard — he needed to get control over his own emotions. But he finally stood up and went to find Jessica. He hated the pain he'd caused her. He couldn't believe he'd just sat there as pain flashed in her eyes and she struggled to restrain her tears. Well, that would never happen again. He'd make up for that, and so much more.

He walked up to their bedroom and looked around eagerly, but there was no sign of her. He went searching throughout the rest of the house, but still to no avail. Worry began to set in. He walked back to his son's room and found Julia in there. "Do you know where Jessica is?" he asked breathlessly.

"I thought you had both gone out. She came in about an hour ago, saying she would be away for the night," she replied. Her eyes then narrowed slightly as she looked at him. "She looked as if something was really bothering her, although she was doing her best to cover it up," she finished accusingly.

Alex dashed over to his bedroom, planning to call Jessica's phone. His extension rang before he had a chance to make the call, and he picked up on the first ring.

"Hello."

"Is this Alex Anderson?" a stranger's voice asked.

"Yes, may I help you?"

"Sir, your wife has been in an auto accident, I'm afraid. She's at the Mercy West Hospital in surgery, and you are listed as her emergency contact."

Alex dropped the phone without another word and ran for the door. He shouted out for Tina, blurted out the terrible news and asked her to notify their families, and then raced to his car. He couldn't lose his wife. *Please, God,* he prayed, *don't take her from me.*

Alex made it to the hospital in record time. Hell, he couldn't even remember the drive. One moment he hopped into his car, and the next he was rushing through the emergency entrance. "I'm looking for my wife — Jessica Anderson!" He was practically shouting at the poor woman at the desk.

"One moment, sir." The nurse looked at her computer for what seemed like hours. "She arrived about an hour ago and is still in surgery. I need you to fill out these papers, please," she requested as she pulled out a packet of paperwork.

"To hell with the paperwork. I want to know what's happening with my wife!" he yelled.

"Sir, I understand you're upset right now, but the doctor will be out shortly to inform you of your wife's condition. We really do need to have these forms filled out," she tried once again.

Alex was about to grab the insufferable woman by her shirt lapels and demand to be taken to Jessica when a hand clasped his shoulder.

"Come on, son. Let's fill out this paperwork and wait to hear from the doctor." Alex's shoulders slumped in relief and defeat. His father was there, and he was right. He shouldn't take out his distress on hospital employees.

"OK, Dad," he conceded.

"I know you're worried, boy. We all are, but your family is here now, and we'll wait together. Jessica is strong, and I know she'll pull through this." Alex thanked God that he had his family there with him. He wouldn't have been able to sit in the waiting room and maintain his composure without them.

A few minutes later, his brothers, Lucas and Mark, were there with him, and then Jessica's mother and father came. No one did any talking. They were there to be a support system to one another, but no one could seem to form words.

Lucas's wife, Amy, came in with coffee and food for everyone and wrapped Alex in a hug. "It will all be OK. She's a fighter," she said, and then kissed his cheek before heading over to sit with her husband.

"Son, let's take a walk," Joseph said and led Alex from the room.

"What if the doctor comes in, Dad?" Alex asked in a panic.

"We won't go far. Trust me, if the doctor does come in, one of your brothers will get you right away," Joseph reassured him.

"OK," Alex said, realizing he really did need some air to clear his head.

"Is everything going OK for you and Jessica?" Joseph asked. He was never one to mince words, and he got right to the heart of the matter.

"I haven't been a great husband," Alex said, fighting hard to hold back a sob. "She told me she loved me, and I just freaked out. I told myself that love wasn't logical, that it always burned out and left…nothing. I told her, essentially, that I didn't want her love; I just wanted a nice, stable marriage."

"But you don't believe that's really what was going on?" Joseph asked.

"You have to understand, Dad. A lot of it was my passion for things that make sense. But I think there's more. It goes back forever. I fought her, I think, because she was a nicer, more serious person than I was. Heck, she even went into the freaking Peace Corps. How can you get more impressive than that? I give money to charity and do auctions or judge pageants. Sheesh. But anyway, I always knew she was just too good for me."

"So what are you saying, son?"

"I don't know. Maybe I was so afraid that if I admitted to her how much I cared about her, she would end up being disappointed in me and would walk away. It's really the only thing that makes sense, I suppose. Well, and this — I've been a fool," Alex finished.

"Well, admitting that is the first step," Joseph said with a small chuckle.

Alex didn't find humor in his father's words. "I do love her," he finally said.

"Have you told her that?" his dad asked.

"I was going to, but we kind of had a fight, and that's why she was out driving. This is all my fault, and if anything has happened to her, I'll never be able to forgive myself," Alex whispered.

"She'll be OK, Alex, and you'll have the rest of your life to reassure her about how much you love her. When two people are meant to be together, nothing can stop them except their own bullheadedness. I'm glad to see you waking up," Joseph lectured.

"Thanks, Dad. I wonder where that stubbornness came from," Alex countered.

"Ah, boy, your mother has had to kick me in the butt a few times, and I sure deserved it, but you know I'd walk on fire for that woman."

"I didn't think it was possible to have a love as great as yours and Mom's, but now I know how wrong I've been. Knowing that Jessica is hurt and not being able to do anything about it is killing me. I feel as if a piece of my soul has been ripped out of me. I need to make her better," Alex said.

"You've sure grown into a fine young man. You know I'm always here for you, and we'll get through this. Families always stick together. There's no way Jessica will leave her son behind, so have faith, say a lot of prayers, and know everything will work out."

"Thanks, Dad. I'll feel better once the doctor lets me see her," Alex said, glancing through the doors into the waiting room.

"Let's head back inside," Joseph said, and they walked back to the family.

Alex was pacing the room for what seemed like the hundredth time when a doctor walked through the doors. The man headed toward the large group. "Alex Anderson?" he asked.

"That's me," Alex answered quickly.

"Your wife is out of surgery. She's in stable condition, but unconscious right now. We're hoping that it's only from the general anesthetic. Her collarbone was broken, and she had a large cut on her left leg. We've fixed both of those problems successfully. Her head was hit pretty hard, and that's our main concern right now. We had to relieve the pressure buildup, and we'll have to keep an eye on her."

Alex stood, digesting the words the doctor was saying, feeling as if he were being slapped with each new injury that had been inflicted on his wife. "May I please see her?" It took all of Alex's control not to grab the doctor and demand to be taken to Jessica. He wasn't normally a man who would ask.

"She's being moved into her room right now. The nurse will take you up in a few minutes," the doctor replied and then left through the double doors.

"We'll wait here, son," Joseph said, patting Alex's arm.

A few minutes later, a nurse led Alex through some corridors into Jessica's room. Alex gasped in shock as he saw his wife lying in the small hospital bed. Her face was bruised and slightly swollen. He felt a tear slip down his cheek as he realized how close he'd come to losing her.

He pulled the chair up next to her bed and gently placed her hand in his. "Jessica, I'm so sorry for everything I've put you through. We'll be just fine. Please wake up so we can be a family. I love you so much and can't live without you," he said to her, willing her to open her eyes and look at him.

She didn't stir. He sat with her most of the rest of the night. The nurse had come in and told him visiting hours were over, but she gave up after a few minutes. Sometimes rules just cried out to be broken.

The next day, when he was waiting in the hall, a doctor walked out of Jessica's room with her charts. "Well, we have some great news, Mr. Anderson. She's healing nicely and we think she should wake up at any time. It also looks as if the baby wasn't affected by the accident, and her pregnancy is proceeding quite well," he finished.

Alex sat in shock. He had a mixture of emotions running through him. Did she know she was pregnant? Surely she would have told him. "How far along is she?" he finally choked out.

"I'm sorry. I assumed you already knew," the doctor said, stumbling over his words. He glanced back down at the chart. "About twelve weeks," he finally said.

Alex's face lit with joy. They were going to have another child. He loved his son so much, and now they were going to have a sibling for him. Even better, he himself would be there for the entire pregnancy. He would see this child come into the world, and he would be there every single day to enjoy every moment.

He rushed in and sat next to Jessica, thanking the heavens for the blessings in his life. His wife was going to be fine. He was going to have another child to love. Jacob was the most perfect child in the universe, so it seemed only proper to bring more children into the world. He smiled to himself, thinking he sounded a bit prejudiced, but that was all right.

Later that afternoon, both families came in to check on Jessica, bringing in more flowers and balloons. Her room looked as if a floral shop had exploded.

"We're going to have another baby," Alex said to everyone in the room. He knew he should wait until Jessica was awake, but he couldn't help himself.

There was a moment of silence before the room erupted in excited chatter.

"Congratulations, son," Joseph nearly shouted before grabbing Alex up in a huge bear hug.

"That's wonderful — just wonderful," John added with tears in his eyes.

His brothers each gave him a hard hug, and Amy kissed him on the cheek. They were as excited as he was.

"I don't know if Jessica even knows yet, but I couldn't wait to tell everyone," Alex said sheepishly. His mother gave him a tenderly outraged look.

"Hello."

Alex's head whipped around as he heard his wife's quiet whisper.

"Baby, it's so good to see you awake." He settled down into the chair next to his wife and took her hand into his.

"…Alex."

Jessica's eyes were cracked open in confusion, and she was looking right at him.

Chapter Thirty-One

"Wh…what happened?" Jessica finally managed to croak out. Her throat felt like sandpaper.

The rest of the room went completely silent.

"You were in a terrible car accident, but everything is fine now. You should be able to return home in a few days," he said.

"I don't remember. I was driving, and then everything went black," she said, sounding scared.

"You have nothing to worry about. The doctor said you're going to be fine," Alex reassured her.

"Jacob's OK, right?" she asked. Her heart monitor started beeping as she frantically looked around the room for her son.

"Jacob is fine. You need to relax. Your heart rate is getting too high," he said calmly and breathed a sigh of relief as the beeping slowed. "He's home with Julia. She'll be down here in about an hour with him," he said and kissed her gently.

Jessica drank in Alex's face. He looked as if he was the one who had been in an accident. His eyes had dark circles, and his face was unshaven. His clothes were in desperate need of changing. He'd never looked better to her.

"I'm sorry for the things I said, Jess."

"It's all right, Alex. Really," she said.

"No, it's not all right. I do love you more than you could ever imagine. I do. I was such an ass."

"Well, I might not fight you on that remark, Alex."

"And I understand fully. What I didn't understand is why I was acting the way I was. But I think I finally figured it out. I was just scared. You've held my heart for so long, and I was afraid if I told you how I felt, you'd somehow have control over me. I should have realized sooner that it didn't matter. When I thought I could lose you, I went out of my mind. Please forgive me for being such a fool," he pleaded.

Neither of them noticed their family members quietly slipping from the room, giving them much-needed privacy. They didn't notice the happy looks between Joseph and John, their two meddling fathers, either.

"Of course I forgive you, Alex. I love you so much. I wanted to come home the minute I left. I was already thinking I'd rather live with you, without love, than without you. I also knew you loved me, but that you were just too stubborn to admit it," she replied.

"If you had any sense, Jessica, you'd kick me out."

"Haven't you figured out that love doesn't make sense?" she said. "I know how much you admire logic and reason, but there's nothing logical about our truest and best feelings."

"I hate to break this to you," Alex countered, "but my love for you is eminently logical. You are such an amazing woman."

"And you're an amazing man. Most of the time…"

"So we're going to be all right?" he asked.

"We're going to be more than all right. I think we can finally be a real family," Jessica said.

"Speaking of families," he began, "how do you feel about giving Jacob a new brother or sister?"

Jessica beamed at him. "Nothing would make me feel better than having a houseful of children filling up the empty corners," she smiled at him. "As soon as I get out of here, we'll have to start working on that."

Alex gave her a blinding smile. "I don't mind practicing for baby number three, but number two is already on the way," he said.

Jessica looked at her husband in confusion for a number of heartbeats before she realized what he was saying. "Are we…" she began. He nodded his head. "We're really pregnant?" she asked eagerly.

Alex nodded his head. He was so overcome with emotion, he couldn't speak for a moment.

"I can't believe it," she gasped. "How do you know?"

"They ran all kinds of tests to make sure you were all right and found out you were twelve weeks along. The baby's fine. As a matter of fact, they're going to bring a monitor in this afternoon so we can have our first peek at the little one," he said.

"I can't believe I didn't know I was pregnant. I just thought I had a touch of the flu. I guess even the flu can't last that long," she said, blushing at her foolishness.

"I should have noticed something was up myself. We have to get you taken care of so you can properly take care of our baby," he said and gently rubbed her belly, which was already showing a slight bump.

Jessica looked at his hand on her stomach and gave a small laugh. "I thought I was just putting on weight," she said, turning a little pink.

"I would love you no matter what you looked like," he said, and his words were filled with truth.

Jessica was thrilled to be carrying another baby of Alex's. "I never thought my life could be this perfect. I do love you, Alex."

"I love you too, Jessica, and I'll spend the rest of my life showing you just how much," he said as he gently kissed her.

*****

Jessica shivered as the doctor applied the cold gel to her belly, but soon all her discomfort faded away as she got her first look at their baby.

"Is that her?" Alex asked in awe, as a perfect little head came into view on the monitor. He was grasping Jessica's hand in his as he got the first image of their child.

"How are you so sure our child is a girl?" Jessica asked with a proud smile. She, too, had a feeling the baby was a girl.

"Because this world won't be complete without a mirror image of you in it." He stated it as fact.

Jessica's eyes filled with tears once again. She couldn't believe just a couple of short days ago she'd been filled with such despair. She felt as if she would burst wide open from the joy she was feeling at this moment.

Her eyes returned to the monitor, and she took in every detail of the three-dimensional image of her child, who was safe within her womb, and becoming stronger each day.

"Thank you for being a wonderful husband and father," she said, barely able to get the words out of her tightened throat.

"No, Jessica. I'm the one who needs to thank you for having so much faith. I love you, Jacob and our growing family," he said.

Jessica knew, from that day forward, that her life would be a great adventure, and even though there would be trials now and then, things would work out for them. She looked from the monitor to her husband, and then she sent up a silent thank-you to God for blessing her life with so much.

Epilogue

Thanksgiving was Joseph's favorite holiday. It was a time of gathering with his family, sharing great food, and reflecting back on another wonderful year. His cup was truly running over this year, since the birth of another beautiful granddaughter made his trove of grandchildren now equal four.

He cuddled Katie close and breathed in her magical scent. She was only one week old, and he'd been overjoyed when she'd made her entrance into the world.

"You're such a great gift to our family," he whispered to her gently, while stroking her soft head.

Katie stared up at her grandfather, seeming to be mesmerized by his voice.

"Tell us another story, Gampa," Jasmine demanded.

"Of course," he replied to his eldest grandchild. "'Twas the night before Christmas, when all through the house…" he began, and all four grandkids gave him their full attention.

Just as Joseph was finishing the poem, Katie started to fuss, and Jessica walked into the warm den. "It sounds to me as if Katie is ready for her Thanksgiving dinner, Dad," she said to him before bending down and giving him a kiss on the cheek.

Joseph reluctantly handed Katie over to her mother.

Jessica chuckled. "Don't worry, Grandpa. You can have her back soon," she said.

"I'll take the kids out and let you have some privacy," he replied gruffly before departing.

*****

Jessica sat down in the comfortable rocker Joseph had bought for her and Amy. She fed her child and felt contentment unlike anything she'd ever known.

"There you are, Jess. Dinner is being served. After you've fed her, I can burp her while you go sit down. You need to keep your energy up," Alex said as he walked into the room.

"We're almost done," Jessica said quietly.

They sat in a companionable silence while Katie finished eating. Jessica then handed the child over to Alex and sat with them as he gently burped his daughter Katie.

"You can go in with the others," he said to his wife with an affectionate smile.

"I know, but I'd rather wait. I still can't get over how wonderful she looks in your arms. Your hands are bigger than her little body," Jessica replied.

Alex chuckled. She knew how afraid he'd been to hold his tiny daughter the first time. He worried that she was too little and he might break her. The moment Jessica placed Katie in his arms, though, he'd looked as if he could hold her twenty-four hours a day and it still wouldn't be enough.

Alex finished burping Katie and held on to her until she fell soundly asleep. He then placed her in her bassinet, and he and his wife walked hand in hand toward the laughter emerging from the dining room.

*****

Joseph was out on the balcony saying a prayer. He got a twinkle in his eyes as he thought about his youngest son. "Ah, Mark, I've found you the perfect match," he whispered into the night.

Joseph chuckled to himself as he imagined his youngest son fighting to keep his bachelorhood. The boy would put up a mighty struggle, but the fall would be ever so sweet.

"Joseph, everyone is waiting on you" came the gentle sound of his Katherine's voice.

"They can wait one more moment. Come here, my beautiful wife," he said, holding his arm out to her.

Joseph pulled her into his arms and kissed her with a deep love that went beyond mere passion. She was a part of his soul. He'd been through the good and the bad with his wife and prayed each night that they'd have many more years together.

"Ah, now, let's go have some dinner," he finally said. They joined their family in the dining room.

Joseph looked around the large table, filled with merriment and comfortable chaos.

Jacob was mashing his food all over his face and high chair. Jasmine was giggling over a joke her Uncle Mark had just told her, and Isaiah was asleep in his father's arms. Joseph looked toward the den and knew baby Katie was safe in her bassinet.

He was so filled with love that he had to sit there for a few moments longer before finally standing to make a toast. Everyone knew Thanksgiving dinner didn't officially begin until Joseph made his toast, and each year the blessings became greater and greater, making his speech so much longer.

"I'd like to propose a toast," Joseph began in his normal booming voice. "To the adult additions to our family, for whom we are all truly thankful. Amy and Jessica, you have brought such light and joy to my sons, and I'll be grateful every day you somehow manage to tame these hooligans."

Everyone at the table laughed while the happy couples moved just a little bit closer to each other.

"Of course, the biggest blessing of all is to finally have the pattering of little feet running about. To each of you beautiful babies, whom I dearly love" he continued as he looked at Jacob, Jasmine and Isaiah. "And what a blessing to have Katie born just one week before this most thankful of days," he said and then gave a slight cough.

They all pretended not to notice and gave him a moment to regain his composure.

"I know this next year will be filled with many more blessings," he said, and looked over at Mark, his youngest son, who started to squirm a bit in his seat.

"Ha! Little brother, I think Dad's prophesying that you're going to be the next to give him a grandkid," Lucas said to goad his youngest brother.

"You know that's not going to happen. I'm completely happy remaining a bachelor, and that's just what I'll do." Mark spoke with a laugh, but there also seemed to be longing in his eyes. Both Jessica and Amy spotted it, and they exchanged glances and smiled.

"Your brothers were, too, until they met the loves of their lives. Now they're far happier than they ever were before. We're meant to have someone by our side," Joseph said. He then took his beautiful wife's hand in his.

"I'm most grateful of all for every day I'm blessed enough to spend with you. To my light — my whole reason for being," he said. Everyone was silent as they witnessed a love that couldn't be surpassed.

"I love you too, Joseph," Katherine replied before discreetly wiping a tear from her face.

"Now, let's all eat this wonderful food," he said in a slightly unsteady voice.

"Hear, hear," everyone shouted.

The rest of the night was filled with spontaneous laughter and unqualified joy — especially since Mark had no idea how far along were the plans that were brewing in his father's head.

Continue with the Anderson family in the next book,

The Billionaire Falls,
Available now!!

ABOUT THE AUTHOR

Melody Anne is the author of the popular series, Billionaire Bachelors, and Baby for the Billionaire. She also has a Young Adult Series in high demand; Midnight Fire and Midnight Moon - Rise of the Dark Angel with a third book in the works called Midnight Storm.

As an aspiring author, she's written for years, then became published in 2011. Holding a Bachelors Degree in business, she loves to write about strong, powerful, businessmen and the corporate world.

When Melody isn't writing, she cultivates strong bonds with her family and relatives and enjoys time spent with them as well as her friends, and beloved pets. A country girl at heart, she loves the small town and strong community she lives in and is involved in many community projects.

See Melody's Website at: www.melodyanne.com. She makes it a point to respond to all her fans. You can also join her on facebook at: www.facebook.com/authormelodyanne, or at twitter: @authmelodyanne.

She looks forward to hearing from you and thanks you for your continued interest in her stories.

The Billionaire's Dance

CPSIA information can be obtained at www.ICGtesting.com
Printed in the USA
LVOW11s1511100715

445789LV00001B/31/P

9 781468 008869